Song of the Benjai

By Ramsey Keller

Published by Arkhos Atlantic

ISBN-13: 978-0692671993 (Arkhos Atlantic)
ISBN-10: 0692671994

Contents

CHAPTER 1 – Emergency Call

The bed was vibrating slightly. Now it was shaking. Zeidra slowly opened her eyes; *'Is this a dream?... Maybe an earthquake... nothing rattling... my god! .... Eyes... big black, "bug" eyes... no! NO!'* ...

"Don't touch me... NO! Don't touch me!!" Zeidra was screaming; it was inaudible ... where was her voice?

The room was dark – very dark... but they were there... in the shadows... barely visible... except for those gleaming black eyes. One was standing over the bed, staring at her, reaching out a claw-shaped hand toward her.

Then she realized there was another one at the foot of the bed, holding a strange metallic instrument. Some unseen force elevated her legs. Her gown was up around her neck.

'NOoooooooo!!!' She screamed silently.

Regaining her muscle control, she leaped from her bed, knocking the creature to one side as she literally flew across the room and out the opened door. Red-hot adrenaline was surging through her body.

'*Where are the guards? ... Not one to be seen!... what time is it? The lights? No lights!!... Good Lord! What about the generators!*' Her mind was racing.

Zeidra ran through the blackness like a scared rabbit unexpectedly flushed from its hiding place. She ran aimlessly, first one way and then the other. '*Where are the people?... maybe they're all dead!!*'

She burst into the guards' command building. In the darkness, she could see the faint outlines of bodies lying on the floor in various positions, scattered about as if they had been carelessly thrown there, cast like dice on a black velvet slab. It was as still as death. '*What's that pounding? A heartbeat... HER heartbeat!*'

'*They're coming... Oh NO!... Here they come... no one here to help! Their shadows... insect like shadows... moving across the courtyard... must be six – maybe seven... moving steadily... not quickly... just steadily. Oh god!.... This HAS to be a dream! A nightmare!!! They're coming this way... they instinctively know... can't hide... nowhere to run!*'

Zeidra hurriedly picked her way across the room in the dark, falling clumsily over the heaps of bodies strewn about the floor.

Upon reaching the door on the other side

of the room, she literally fell out and onto the walkway, on the opposite end of the building. Picking herself up off the ground, she raised her head; coming face to face with a grotesque gray entity.

Suddenly there was a sound like thunder, and instantly, a large human figure materialized behind the Alicupion; it appeared from virtually nowhere. He was just there – dressed in black from head to toe. Some sort of masking covered his face, and he was holding a strange silver box above the head of the creature standing between them.

Time seemed to be suspended.

The box began to vibrate. The Alicupion turned back to see what was there, and in a brilliant flash of light, the creature vanished.

Just as instantly as the stranger appeared, he disappeared. Zeidra stood there dazed, unable to comprehend what was happening.

Coming from the other side of the building, she heard another thunderous sound, and huge flashes of light illuminated the sky. Zeidra saw a large Alicupion craft rising into the air; without warning, it disintegrated overhead. Suddenly, all was mysteriously quiet.

Just then, she heard a hum and a lurch; the generators kicked on, and there was light.

The princess turned to look through the

glass door into the command building, and she saw, to her amazement, the guards; they began drunkenly staggering to their feet – one by one.

"Zeidra... Zeidra!" Someone from the other side of the structure was calling her.

She looked around dazedly, still unable to find her voice. Then she saw him. He was running toward her. It was Niporo, her trusted friend and cabinet minister.

She was relieved to see him. When he reached her, she collapsed into his arms like a rag doll.

"My god, Zeidra," he gasped hoarsely, "did they hurt you?"

"I .... I don't... I don't think so," she replied weakly.

Niporo looked at Zeidra's bare feet. They were stained with blood. He reached down and raised her gown slightly. The inner sides of her legs were also bloody. He didn't say a word. Niporo swiftly scooped her up into his massive arms and headed for the royal chambers. Zeidra lost consciousness.

"Get the physicians and send them to Princess Zeidra's suites!" He yelled, barking the orders at a guard running across the courtyard.

Niporo carried Zeidra's limp body into her chambers. He stopped short at the bed. It was saturated with blood.

Three of the temple physicians burst into the bedroom along with several assistants. Quickly they stripped the blood-soaked linen from the bed, replacing it with fresh sheets.

Niporo gently laid Zeidra onto the bed. No one spoke.

He left the room as the Temple doctors began the examination.

It was morning. The Ulonican cabinet had called an emergency session. They voted unanimously; the Galactic Council of Deis was contacted; a security force had already been deployed. A Deis fleet was in the vicinity, and the Galactic Council was changing the orders and the course to facilitate the Ulonican request for aid to the House of Benjion.

The incident last night had been a close call, but routed just in time. No permanent damage was done to Princess Zeidra, however, all were sure there would be other attempts.

"This is it, men," said Meno, the head navigational officer of the Deis fleet. "Notify the others. We'll dock here." Meno was thumping his finger on the highlighted area of the star map; it was displayed on a screen, which was built into the control panel in front of him. "What's your reading, Jason?"

"Looks like you hit the spot dead on, according to my coordinates," Jason answered, manipulating various dials on the command console spread out before him and punching the information into the computer. "..... Perfect reading, Meno. You couldn't have come any closer without an over-shoot!" Jason said, commending his friend.

"So... get them into formation and let's lock 'em up," Meno ordered, switching off the screen. He left the command room.

"What's with him?" the radio operator asked, looking toward Jason.

"He's not very happy about this assignment," Jason said, "he's tangled with Alicupions before, but those Drothuarians bring back bad memories for him. I understand he lost thirty ships out of thirty-five last time he was commissioned to stand against those devils. Blames himself, I guess."

"That's too bad." The officer shook his head. "But then, he didn't have us backing him up that time." He sounded confident.

"No... and he didn't have the Master Kyate fighting alongside him, then; this time he'll definitely have the advantage – and so will we!" Jason motioned for Tyrone to go ahead with the transmission.

The order to dock was given. Twenty-seven silver disks of various sizes silently drifted into position for the docking procedure; like graceful ballerinas moving in slow motion on a vast black stage, the ships glided into a circular formation. The cargo bays were opened and the telescoping duct-like device extended from three sides of each craft. Robotically controlled, the connection was completed; each craft was securely joined with the others; they now became one circular solar station, rotating in place, holding the position – waiting.

Hours passed. The command ship, located at the hub of the ring, was the center of activity. After the long flight from the star system Xanthia, in the far north regions of the galaxy NT4, most of the crew members on the other ships, in the outer ring, had welcomed a chance to relax. It had taken four months to reach this rendezvous point, and the scheduled arrival time for the Master Kyatc was still twelve hours away. The flight course had taken the ships through some hostile regions. The tension during the flight had taken its toll on the men. They had lost three craft to opposition forces, suffered numerous mechanical failures, and had trouble locating some of the unmanned supply modules. The wait was a necessary respite.

Suddenly all the alarms were going off. The microwave emulator was flashing red and orange points all over the screen.

The crew responded quickly, taking up their defensive positions throughout the modular station. Meno was back at his command post in an instant.

"Tyrone, have the others get the shields up!" Meno ordered, frantically assessing all the data now tracking across his screen; in endless rows of marching glyphs. "Good Lord!" Meno shouted, "There's a whole squadron of Drothuarian destroyers moving at warp, and into our southeast quadrant! Tell 'em to deploy a tactical nine maneuver! *NOW MAN*! Get on that horn!"

While Tyrone was issuing the orders to the other modules, Jason was busy throwing switches and feeding data back into the central processing unit. There was a frenzy of activity on each of the individual ships.

Although not yet in visual range, the Drothuarians were bearing down on the Deis position at an incredible speed. Meno was not yet sure whether the oncoming enemy vessels had detected his fleet.

In moments, the circular unit of connected Deis modules began spinning at an unbelievable rate. Turning onto its rim, it appeared to roll out across the void like a giant wheel detached from a vehicle while traveling at great speed. It turned and veered and rose, then plummeted. Just as the

Drothuarian fleet moved into view on the edge of the blackness, the electromagnetic shields were switched on; the Deis unit vanished from sight. Was it too late?

Besides bending the available waves of light around the craft, and creating the illusion of invisibility, the betatron motion would also refract microwaves around the hulk, impeding detection by radar.

Breaking formation, the Drothuarians fanned out into a semicircle as they closed in. It was at once obvious to Meno that they had detected *something* before the Deis shields were employed.

"Those devils know there's something out here," Meno said, checking his readout, and taking a visual survey. "... Looks like they've decided to sweep. Cut the thrust and let's just sit here... see what happens." He rotated the command dome to get a better look.

Tyrone issued the communication to the other modules while Jason was busy at the thrust controls.

"Get the antigravity vacuum weapons ready, just in case," Meno said. Then, pausing thoughtfully and wiping the droplets of perspiration from his brow, he continued, "Tell you what... let's see if those Drothuarians would go for a ghost. – Jason, set up a hologram of an Alicupion scout ship... maybe they'll feel better if they can shoot at something!" He laughed; it was a strained, nervous laugh.

Jason immediately pulled a lifelike image of the Alicupion craft up on his screen, and initiated the hologram systems that would project the illusion of that specific craft onto the ethers just beyond the sweeping Drothuarian gunners. The other officers took their stations and began arming the antigravity weapons. Tyrone continued relaying data to the other Deis ships. The hologram setup was complete.

"Begin count down!" Meno ordered.

Jason held his breath as he engaged the projection device. Aiming the device far beyond the Drothuarians and then bringing the hologram in from the north, the illusion darted into Drothuarian range, stopped, turned, and then sped off to the west.

".... Just a high-tech video game!" Jason shouted, as he controlled the apparition. "I sure hope those damned Drothuarians take the bait!"

"Get it out there further!" Meno yelled. "If they get much closer, they'll get a fix on it!"

"They're taking it by god!" Jason said sucking in his breath.

"Engage the thrusts, let's move it!" Meno called out his orders, hoping they could get back to their original position before the Drothuarians realized they'd been had.

"Jason, wait 'till we're about twenty degrees east, then if you see 'em fire on you, give 'em one hell of an explosion... make 'em think they got you... make it good... you better damned well make it good!"

The Drothuarians were seriously pursuing the image of the Alicupion scout vessel. There were fifteen destroyers darting through the empty space, closing in on the specter. Suddenly, one of the fifteen, veered off to the east in the direction of the invisible Deis wheel.

" What's he doing?!" Meno yelled, "Roll, dammit, roll!"

"I can't see him, sir!" the pilot screamed back.

"They're firing!" Jason shouted.

"Who's firing?!.... Get this thing into a roll! Where's that damned Drothuarian ship? ... ... Engage the pulsators!"

"They're firing at the hologram!" Jason yelled, desperately keying in the data that would cause the image to appear to explode.

Everything seemed to explode at once. The darkness exploded into a shower of brilliant flares, as Jason manipulated the demise of the Alicupion ghost ship; the Deis Wheel lurched to one side as the Drothuarian craft, careening out of control, disintegrated on impact when it hit the pulsator shields, which were set up around the invisible Deis orb.

The jolt was so violent, that the men were thrown to the floor, the systems were short-circuited, and the communications were disabled throughout the modular craft. The electromagnetic shields were about to break down.

Meno scrambled to his feet. Looking out over the darkness, he saw that the Drothuarian fleet was apparently satisfied with its *kill*, and was proceeding, once again in formation, toward the west. As the enemy faded into the darkness, the electromagnetic generators sputtered and died. The Deis ships immediately became visible.

Meno collapsed into his chair in relief. He exhaled a long deep sigh.

"Let's get on with the damage control, men."

Jason laid his head down into his arms on the console. "Too close," he whispered, over and over in a low shaking voice.

Everyone aboard looked at one another in disbelief as they picked themselves up from wherever they had landed when the Drothuarian craft collided with their own.

The Deis orb crippled back to the rendezvous point and settled into a stable slow rotation while the crews began damage assessments and repairs.

Efficiently organized, the technicians soon

had all systems up and on line. Once again, the members of the Deis fleet resumed an uneasy wait. The Master Kyate and the Deis Warrior Monks were due to arrive at any time, now.

Kyate, Master of the Deis Warriors, and spiritual teacher in his own right, had been deployed by the Galactic Council of Deis to command the Deis fleet and protect the Province of Ulonica, on the planet Earth, from the Alicupions and the Drothuarians; both groups battling for control of the planet.

The Sacred Tribe of Benjion ruled the Province of Ulonica, and the population was made up of highly advanced humans due to the education and spiritual traditions carried on by the Benjai. Of the original Benjai race, only one pure strain had survived over the millennia.

A distant ancestor of the Benjai, the Drothuarians had broken away from the Galactic Council of Deis to pursue their own power struggle with the Críonnachtian Order. Both groups, at one time, had worked together, co-creating the life on Earth and enhancing the physical and intellectual characteristics of the Earth-beings by using their own genetic material.

It had been an ongoing struggle between the Críonnachtian Order, the Drothuarians, and the humans, as to which race would rule upon Earth. With the withdrawal of the Críonnachtians, the power struggle had changed to a power conflict between master and servant... until the appearance of the Alicupions, that is.

CHAPTER 2 – The Master Kyate

"My Lord, behold your servant." The princess bowed low at the teacher's feet. Her purple robes lay in soft folds upon the marble floor of the ouckibid. She remained; her head bent in reverence; eyes cast down in respect. The golden ringlets of her long hair fell across her shoulders in cascades of curls; down to the floor and into a heap upon the purple silk. She was silent.

The Master Kyate stood quietly, staring down at the respectful sovereign kneeling beneath his gaze. There was an endless gap in the essence of time and reality as he pondered the magnitude of this moment.

Kyate's entourage was becoming noticeably restless as the minutes passed.

Finally, the master bent down, catching Zeidra's hand, raising her to her feet. Never in his life had he experienced this type of spiritual and physical intensity upon meeting an Earth-being. There was also a subtle feeling of recognition – almost familiar, as if it had been experienced in a dream. He immediately tried to dismiss these thought patterns and concentrate on the purpose of his mission.

"I thank you for your kind hospitality." The master spoke slowly as he struggled to regain his composure.

"Sir, I assure you, it is with sincere gratitude that we receive you, Master, along with your men. We, here at Ulonica, hope that your very presence will deter the Alicupions from intruding upon the spiritual development of our people." The princess bowed as she spoke, and then clapping her hands; she summoned the servants to escort the guests to their quarters.

The great hall was empty now, except for the Master Kyate and the Princess Zeidra. The energy sizzling between them was electrifying.

Zeidra turned from Kyate and walked over to a very large ceremonial table. The top was a huge slab of jade, encrusted with various types of precious stones. Upon the table was a golden pitcher filled with grape nectar, and there were two beautifully engraved golden chalices nearby. Zeidra kneeled before the table. She lifted her arms toward heaven and gave thanks to the Galactic Council of Deis for sending the great Master Kyate to assist her in her plight.

At that instant, the two perfectly clear crystal teardrops, on each end of the table and supported by silver standards studded with the purest lapis lazuli, turned smoky blue and began to radiate golden sparks into the air. The display continued for a few minutes followed by a profound celestial peace, which filled the entire expanse of the enormous hall. A voice spoke in stereo from the two crystal teardrops, which were still a smoky blue color. "This... Kyate... the great master and leader of men, is a true son of the Deis Confederation. We are honored that he accepted his mission. He is pure. His wisdom is supreme. His allegiance is with you, Princess Zeidra, as is ours."

The teardrops turned back to their original crystal clear color, and Princess Zeidra arose from her kneeling position, tears welling up in her pale blue eyes. She blessed the wine and poured some into each of the priceless golden chalices.

The Master Kyate stood quietly in the center of the hall, watching the Princess Zeidra as she crossed the reception area, carrying the two cups of wine over to where he was standing.

Kyate was an impressive figure of a man. He looked to be in his late thirties. He was tall and muscular. His eyes were a riveting steel gray color. His hair was a rich brown; sun-streaked with gold. He had a strong jawline; as if chiseled from marble. He carried himself with the boldness and confidence of a warrior. His voice was deep and throaty, yet he spoke slowly and softly. He was a contradictory blending of brutality and tenderness, even visible in the expression on his face. He was dressed in a plain white uniform with a black silk belt, which held a large silver laser sword. He wore no jewels, except for a golden medallion, and he was magnificent in his simplicity.

Zeidra was standing before Kyate, held motionless by his piercing gaze. She felt as if she were being absorbed into those intense gray eyes. It was a feeling she had no control over. As she surrendered to the silent questioning, she realized that there was, in this man, a more profound source of purity and strength than she had ever encountered in her life. She was being read, interpreted, devoured and energized all in the same moment of time, by a man who was closer to being a god than a human, and she understood.

Finally, Kyate released his hold on her psyche. Slowly she raised the cup to offer him the wine. He accepted. There was no need for verbalization. They stood in the center of the hall, partaking of the blessed nectar, recovering from the energy surge which had drained them and revitalized them; the experience that enlightened them and confounded them.

Suddenly, the massive copper doors to the great hall swung open and a man burst in. It was one of Kyate's men. "Master, come quickly, we've spotted an Alicupion scout ship on the horizon!"

Kyate thrust his cup into Zeidra's hand and left the room without saying a word. Zeidra was left alone with her thoughts, glad for a few minutes to consider what she had just undergone.

Outside, the men had assembled and were hastily readying for departure. The humming of the ships vibrated the air.

Zeidra appeared on the balcony of the Temple of Ulonica. She was there to give her blessing to the Galactic Monk Warriors who were about to embark on a mission to destroy the Alicupion scout ship, which had been spotted in the area. As she stood there, appraising the scene below, her gaze was immediately drawn to the bronze figure about to board the lead gun ship. At that instant, he looked up at her. There again, silently and powerfully, was the unspoken communion defying all human comprehension.

In a flash they were in the air and fading into the violet mist of the fog, which hung ominously over the land of Ulonica. One by one, four Deis gun disks slipped out of sight and into the velvety dusk, which was quickly enveloping the hills surrounding the landscape.

Flying in tight diamond formation, the four Deis ships slipped above the clouds. In the lead ship, Kyate signaled the others to engage the electromagnetic shields. Instantly, the diamond formation became invisible. Using the Earth's magnetic ley lines for the silent propulsion, the ships accelerated into warp nine, sweeping back and forth across the heavens like a metal detector over the sands of a deserted beach.

Suddenly the detector systems' alarms were going off. There, directly below the invisible formation of Deis gunships, appeared an unsuspecting Alicupion scout vessel.

With deadly accuracy, Kyate locked his laser fusion amplifier onto the target below. Three, two, one... engage. All that was left of the Alicupion ship was a misty cloud of misplaced atomic particles that soon dispersed into oblivion along with the current threat to Princess Zeidra's kingdom.

'*This was too easy,*' Kyate thought to himself. Wiping a few droplets of perspiration from his brow, Kyate signaled to the other three ships to remain in formation and to resume scanning.

Nothing... the sky remained empty, except for the Deis warriors who commanded the heavens over Ulonica.

The ships headed back to the Benjai complex. The crew members were aware now, that this was only the beginning of something more dangerous than they had originally anticipated.

Kyate rubbed his chin thoughtfully. "The Alicupions are sure to retaliate," he said, speaking into the communications module. "It's hard to believe they could have been taken totally by surprise." He paused, tapping his finger pensively against his left temple.

"Our arrival couldn't have gone unnoticed by those guys," Meno answered back.

Jason joined the frequency. "Maybe this was a ploy to lull us into a sense of false security?"

"You've got a point, Jason" Kyate said. "That scout ship we just destroyed may have been unmanned." Kyate led the ships into a steep dive down through the clouds.

The temple of Ulonica came into full view as the gun ships made their descent. It was an architecturally brilliant complex of white and blue marble edifices, gardens and fountains arranged geometrically throughout the expansive grounds. In the very center of the complex, which encompassed forty-two acres, stood a huge pyramid faced with polished blue and white marble with a pure crystal capstone on the top. It was in this pyramid that the sacred instruction and initiation rites were performed. There, in the chamber of the Meditation, in the heart of that pyramid, Princess Zeidra confers with her oracle. She waits for the return of the Deis fleet; she knows all has gone well.

CHAPTER 3 – A Morning Encounter

It was a glorious sunrise. The air was heavily scented with the fragrance of freshly mown grass, damp from the morning dew. The sun sparkling on each droplet of moisture, made the courtyard and gardens appear to be studded with tiny multicolored jewels.

'Aw! What a glorious contradiction – this world!' Kyate mused.

He surveyed the landscape in awe. He took a deep breath of the cool moist air. The cold, wet grass under his bare feet felt exhilarating. He had awakened early and couldn't resist the temptation to explore the dawn alone. Dressed only in his trousers, he quietly strolled across the courtyard and into the gardens on the north side of the Temple of Meditation.

Kyate began his stretching exercises.

It was his first morning, here in Ulonica, and he knew that he would need to make the most of this invigorating solitude as he would soon be deluged with meetings, briefings, tours, conferences, and other military processes. He secretly wished he could stay hidden here in the garden; yet as much as he appreciated the beauty of nature, he loathed the ugliness of the greed, which was the basis for the conflict at hand; and he was duty-bound to remedy the situation. Kyate was first a spiritual master; and secondly he was a warrior monk. His vow from the beginning was to eradicate the destroyers of freedom and to uphold the good, the truth, and the free will of the created spiritual beings of Earth. The much-needed solitude would have to wait until the mission was accomplished. For now, a few moments of tranquility would suffice.

Kyate lay down upon the soft carpet of moss under a very old redwood tree. The fog was beginning to clear away from the valleys in the distance, and he could hear the chirping of sparrows as they were also discovering the dawn. He stretched out on the ground with his arms comfortably supporting his head. He could feel the dampness of the earth beneath his bare back as he lay there with his eyes closed – listening, feeling, inhaling life; experiencing the awakening. It was a private observation. He was participating as a lone observer in the birth of a new day.

The sound of movement interrupted his meditations. He opened one eye. Kyate was surprised to see the Princess Zeidra standing there, above him, smiling as she gazed down at him.

"Good morning, Master Kyate," she said bowing slightly. "Surely you didn't sleep out here last night?"

Kyate rolled forward and up onto his feet in one easy movement.

Now, Zeidra had to look up. She was dwarfed in this man's shadow. He was tall and very muscular. He was a mighty oak, standing solitary here in the grove of redwoods.

"Actually, no," Kyate said, brushing debris from his bare shoulders and arms, "I wasn't asleep. I only discovered your beautiful gardens at day break, and I thought I would meditate here." He bowed respectfully to Zeidra. "I'm sorry that you caught me in this present state of undress." He noticed her cheeks had turned a bright crimson.

"The gardens *are* lovely... and you're right... this is a serene place to contemplate." The princess turned her back to Kyate as she spoke. "I'll leave you to your peace, Master Kyate. We'll talk later... Please... continue your meditation." Zeidra turned toward Kyate again, and bowed quickly to him. She retreated hastily; back through the grove of redwood trees toward the pathway that led along the perimeter of the gardens.

Kyate finished with his stretching and movement routine, and then decided to do some running.

He sprinted along the path for some distance, when he spotted the princess leaning against a stone wall. She was holding her hands against her temples. She was in obvious pain. Reaching out a hand to steady the princess, he immediately released his healing energies into her aura.

"It's a headache," she said quietly. "I have this pain now and then ... I'm all right, really."

Kyate helped the Princess Zeidra over to a marble bench. Placing his hands just above her head, Kyate examined Zeidra's energy field. He was surprised to detect an energy source emanating from the left front quadrant of her skull. Immediately he suspected an implanted transmitter. *'But why... who...?'*

"When did you begin having these headaches?" Kyate asked, trying not to alarm Zeidra. He wondered if she was aware of the device.

"Three, maybe four years ago. I don't get the pain often, though." She continued to massage her temples; her eyes remaining closed.

"May I excise your pain, Princess Zeidra?" Kyate asked cradling Zeidra's face in his massive hands.

"You can do that?" she asked, opening her eyes wide.

Assuming her permission, he knelt down in front of her, still holding her head between the palms of his hands.

"I want you to look deep into my eyes ... concentrate on only my eyes. Look as deeply as you can .... Deeper and deeper ..... Deeper and deeper .... Relaxing your body ... ... forgetting the pain ..."

When Kyate was certain that Zeidra was securely in trance, he took three deep cleansing breaths, and then he released one massive volt of pure white energy into the area of Zeidra's skull that he was positive contained some sort of transmitter. Suddenly, Zeidra's body began to convulse in seizures. Kyate dragged her lurching body down onto the ground, and he held her securely as the shuddering continued for five minutes. Finally she lay quietly. Checking her vitality sources, he was assured that the device had been deactivated, and that Zeidra would be free from those headaches; along with whoever was monitoring her activities.

Kyate knew that it was customary for the Drothuarians and the Alicupions to use implanted tracking devices on humans, but he couldn't believe that the Princess could have been implanted without being abducted; that would have been counterproductive to whichever group was responsible. Kyate pondered the implications as he scooped Zeidra's unconscious body up into his arms and headed back toward the temple complex.

As he neared the garden gate, Zeidra began to regain consciousness. Moaning softly, she reached her arms up and clasped her hands around Kyate's neck; like a child being carried sleepily to bed. Kyate stopped and looked down at the princess. She looked so vulnerable there in his arms. He enjoyed her warm softness against his bare skin and the smell of gardenia in her hair. He stood there, enjoying a long forgotten sensation. He watched as her breasts strained against the silk of her blouse with each breath she took. He rested his cheek against the silky soft mass of ringlets falling down upon her forehead. His hands were beginning to pulsate beneath the warmth that they held. Zeidra stirred.

At that moment, Kyate heard the central alarm blasting. He collected his senses and quickly headed for the main courtyard. Upon reaching the residences, he was met by several guards

"Master Kyate!" one of them cried out, "Thanks be to the supreme that you found our princess. Minister Niporo issued an Alicupion alert, and then we discovered the princess to be missing!" The man was nearly in tears.

"We were sure she'd been taken this time!"

Niporo was rapidly crossing the courtyard, waving his arms and shouting obscenities as he approached.

Zeidra, who was dazed, but awake, wriggled in Kyate's grasp, indicating that she wanted him to let her down. Kyate held her tightly against his bare chest, antagonistically eyeing Niporo who was now in a rage.

Kyate couldn't help wondering why Niporo had issued the Alicupion alert. He must have done so at about the same time that the transmitter in Zeidra's skull had been deactivated. There certainly was no evidence of Alicupion ships in the area.

"What the hell is going on here?" Niporo demanded, throwing his notebook onto the ground at Kyate's bare feet. "What's wrong with the princess? Where did you find her? Where are your clothes?!" He reached out to Zeidra, trying to snatch her away from Kyate's strong arms, but to no avail. "Did you see Alicupions?" He barked the questions disrespectfully.

Kyate gave Niporo a searing glare. "... Nothing but a headache. We were in the garden. My clothes are in my quarters. No Alicupions." Kyate stated the facts quietly, walking toward Zeidra's chambers, leaving the guards and Niporo behind him. Zeidra was still wriggling, trying to free herself. Niporo followed along hurriedly trying to catch up with Kyate. He kept hurling questions left and right. Kyate ignored Niporo and continued on defiantly, heading across the green to the royal chambers. When he reached Zeidra's chamber door, Niporo was right at his heels. Kyate reached down with one hand and opened the door just enough to squeeze inside with the princess. Kicking it shut behind him, the heavy door narrowly missed hitting Niporo in the face; he was left standing outside still ranting and raving.

"Will you please let me down?!" Zeidra demanded, frantically trying to free herself from Kyate's iron grasp.

"Your wish is my command," Kyate said quietly as he loosened his hold on Zeidra and allowed her body to slide slowly down his torso until her feet were firmly on the floor. The feeling of her body against his was astonishing. It felt like warm fluid, flowing from his chest down to his thighs. It was delicious. He released her.

"Why did you do that? Why didn't you put me down out there?"

"I wanted to make sure you were strong enough to stand. You were in so much pain you passed out. You were weak." Kyate was convincing. "Don't you remember the headache?"

"I don't remember anything... uh. Oh

well, I do recall having a headache... but I don't remember passing out!"

"Of course you wouldn't!" Kyate chuckled. "That's why it's called *lost consciousness*." He led her over to the lounge. "Why don't you relax, and I'll get your maid to see to you."

Zeidra sat down wearily. She watched Kyate cross the room to ring for Shanta. She became acutely aware of his confident movement, his very masculine physique; the broad expanse of his bronze colored back was breathtaking. She watched the muscles ripple on his arm as he reached for the bell. When he turned to face her, she caught her breath sharply. It was obvious that there was nothing between his trousers and his flesh and not much room for anything else. For a long moment she found herself mesmerized by the beauty of Kyate's entire being. She couldn't help fantasizing, wanting to just touch him. Her cheeks flushed again at the thought.

There was a knock at the door. Kyate opened the door. It was Shanta.

"Your lady is distressed. Would you be kind enough to draw a warm herbal bath for her, and then see to it that she isn't disturbed for the rest of the day?" Kyate leaned over and whispered in Shanta's ear, "I specifically mean .... Don't allow the minister Niporo near her."

It was a stern command, and Shanta shook her head, indicating that she understood. She proceeded into Zeidra's private salon to draw the bath.

Kyate returned to the lounge where Zeidra was recovering. He sat down beside the princess and looked deeply into her eyes. "I understand confusion." He spoke quietly, yet his voice was husky and full of authority. "I understand fear. I'm here to protect you... you are *my* charge. This is my mission." He placed his massive hand reassuringly over Zeidra's. "I would never hurt you, Princess Zeidra ... and I won't let anyone else hurt you. Do you trust me?"

Zeidra lowered her eyes, unable to meet Kyate's piercing gaze. He reached over and tilted her chin up, forcing her to look at him.

"Yes, I trust you."

"Is your head feeling better now?" he asked. His sincere concern was obvious.

"Yes, thank you. It's much better," Zeidra answered quietly.

Kyate opened the chamber door to leave, hoping Niporo had given up by now and would be gone. It was a relief – but not for long.

Before Kyate was safely in his dormitory chambers, Niporo was there at his door.

"Master Kyate," Niporo began sheepishly, "I want to apologize for my rude behavior this morning." He pulled a handkerchief from his pocket and blotted at his brow. "But I had no idea it was you... I mean I just didn't recognize you. You know... I would never purposely behave so disrespectfully. Will you accept my apology?" Niporo extended his hand to Kyate in friendship.

Shaking Niporo's hand, Kyate acknowledged the apology. "Niporo, I remember you well. We met yesterday." Kyate turned to enter his rooms, cutting Niporo short again.

"Wait, sir!" Niporo demanded. "I want to ask you some questions if you don't mind. You and I..."

"Well I do mind." Kyate turned slightly, giving Niporo a scowl. "I have much to attend to. You and I will talk later." With that, Kyate entered his room, closing the door abruptly behind him; once again leaving Niporo standing there, his mouth open in mid-sentence.

CHAPTER 4 – A Space Picnic

From the beginning, there were a few Drothuarian colonies established covertly on the Earth, infiltrating governments, corporations, and influential societies. These agents, because they looked exactly like humans, were able to pass as Ulonicans, anytime and anywhere. It was a dangerous situation, and now that the hour of reckoning was at hand, it was the beginning of the end of an era.

In the confines of the temple complex, resting comfortably in his plush quarters, Niporo was dreaming of the day he would no longer be posing as a temple executive, but would be in charge of the temple treasury instead. He had held the position as temple cabinet minister for nearly five years, and he had become a close and trusted friend to many of the Ulonicans who believed him to be one of their own.

Niporo was, however, a Drothuarian. He had breached the temple service some years ago, in order to keep the Drothuarian Command posted on the comings and goings of the Princess Zeidra. She was the ultimate *prize*; the carrier of the "God gene" that empowered the *enabled soul*; which none of the Ulonicans, the Drothuarians nor the Alicupions possessed.

Until the Alicupion problem escalated, it was the Drothuarian plan to simply trick Zeidra into choosing a Drothuarian to father her royal child when the time came. The Drothuarian that was selected for the mission, of course, was Niporo.

Niporo had become a very close friend and confidant of the Princess Zeidra. Even though Niporo was placed in the temple to manipulate policy and to deceive the princess, he had learned to love her, and he felt a protective jealousy toward her.

He was feeling particularly threatened by the presence of the Master Kyate; not only because the covert operations of the Drothuarians might be detected by the Deis warriors, but also because of the fact that the Benjai princesses seemed to prefer choosing men from the Galactic Council to father their children. This could prove to be a real problem, both to the Drothuarian plan and also to Niporo's own personal interest in the Princess Zeidra.

Niporo was a patient man. He was cool and calculating. He was the type of man that once his mind was set on a goal, nothing but *nothing* would discourage him, or distract him from his plan. He always had a plan – and a backup plan. Niporo was seldom taken by surprise, and he was always sure of his alternatives.

He had worked hard for the past few years, earning the trust and affection of the Princess Zeidra. He had learned everything he could about her likes, her dislikes, her strengths, and most of all he had studied her weaknesses. However few, the princess did have some weaknesses, and Niporo had played on them to the hilt. He had, in the past year, convinced Zeidra, that he alone could be trusted with her innermost secrets. He had used her fear of failure to manipulate her into leaning on his advice more and more. He saw himself, at this time, as totally indispensable as far as the princess was concerned. She seldom made a move without consulting him first.

Niporo was a handsome man who looked to be about thirty-five, although his true age was anyone's guess. He had an athletic body, but he also had the intellect of a genius. He was well schooled in the mystical teachings; or so it appeared – the truth being that all Drothuarians were naturally superior, preternatural beings, and their mental powers were impressive.

Niporo possessed most of the desirable

qualities any Benjai princess would approve. The one thing that could cause a problem, however, was his sexual escapades, which he carried on outside the temple complex. It was common knowledge among the temple services. But thankfully, Zeidra had never mentioned Niporo's personal indiscretions

Getting up from his resting-place, Niporo strolled across the room to look out onto the courtyards. Everything was in motion. People were rushing from one wing to another preparing for a special strategic conference, organized by the Master Kyate and his group.

Now Niporo realized he would be forced to intensify his efforts in charming Princess Zeidra. He desperately needed for her to perceive him in a more affectionate way. He also felt the necessity of trying to distract her as much as possible during the coming days, so that she wouldn't be allowed the opportunity to become well acquainted with the Lord Kyate.

He stood at the window for a long time, not seeing the commotion now, but staring into space, lost in his thoughts. He would face the competition, if indeed there was competition, and he would prevail. He would win the princess, and he would be the one to father her first child.

Niporo walked over to the dressing table. Placing his hands on the marble to support his weight, he leaned closer to the mirror.

Studying his reflection, Niporo saw the face of a Drothuarian staring back at him, but he also saw the eyes of a fool. He instantly realized he had become too emotionally involved in his mission. It would be better for him to divorce his emotions and concentrate on the goal. *'Is it too late?'*

"... Niporo, sir?" There was a soft thump against his door. It swung open, and a woman from the laundry lurched into the room carrying a heavy bundle of Niporo's clothing.

"Here's your stuff," she said, peering over the top of the huge pile of garments she was struggling to carry. "Where'd you want 'em?"

"Just put them on the bed," he said.

"God-awful load of clothes," she said, muttering as she unloaded the burden.

Niporo was standing with his hands on his hips, and his legs spread just enough to comfortably support his massive weight. He was enjoying the view as the maid leaned over the bed. Her skirt was hiked high in the back, not leaving much to his imagination.

"Now that's an incredible ass," he said, in an almost inaudible voice as he wiped his mouth with the back of his hand.

"I'm sorry – What'd you say?" She looked

at Niporo and raised one eyebrow, giving him a knowing look.

"Someone, who works so hard, would deserve a reward, don't you think?" he said.

"Yes, indeed I do," she quipped as she finished with her chore and turned to Niporo, "but I've heard about the rewards you have to offer, and I'd just as soon settle for my regular wages, if you don't mind." She smiled at him and winked.

"Llana, you've cut me to the quick!" He rocked back and forth on his heels, retaining the same position – his hands on his hips, his legs spread. He loved to watch that twinkle in her bright green eyes. She was a dark haired beauty with voluptuous curves and an incredibly sensuous mouth.

"No need to play innocent with me, Niporo." She imitated his stance. "Your secret's out!" She teased him as she began rocking back and forth on *her* heels.

"OK," he said, "you win, but you don't know what you're missing!"

"Sure I do, honey," she said. "I've heard my share of firsthand accounts. I do spend some time outside of these walls, you know." She tossed her shiny black hair back over one shoulder.

"Is that so?"

"Yea, and some of the stories I've heard!" She laughed, winking at Niporo again.

"Anything you particularly liked?"

"You're crude, Niporo!"

"Yes I am, Llana, and that's exactly what you love about me!" He walked over to the bed. "Did you get me that schedule sheet like I asked you to?" He mumbled, sorting through the clothes, and selecting a suit to wear to the conference.

"Indeed I did, and I copied everything... just like you said."

"Well why the hell didn't you say so?!" he said, dropping the suit, and spinning around.

"Well why the hell didn't you ask?!" she mocked, reaching into her pocket and pulling out a folded sheet of paper.

"Let's have a look." Niporo brushed past her, snatching the paper from her hand, and heading for his desk.

"My, My, little Llana," he said, unfolding the note, "you definitely do deserve a reward."

"I'll take it in currency, thank you."

"Come on, don't be so hard on me." Niporo finished looking over Llana's notes, and then put the sheet of paper into his desk.

Getting up, he walked over to where Llana was standing, and pinched her on the cheek. "There's just one more favor I need to ask of you," he said.

"Oh, no... What now?" She folded her arms and shifted her weight to one foot, tapping her toe impatiently.

"Damn you're hard to deal with!" He teased back, laughing.

He returned to the desk and pulled a large envelope out of the drawer. "Take this to our man Cole, and tell him that I said to pass the word."

With that, he tucked the envelope into Llana's folded arms and gave her a fast kiss on the cheek.

"OK, but just remember, I don't work for free," she said, turning for the door.

Niporo gave her a hard swat on the bottom as she passed by, on her way out.

"You'll get my bill in the morning," she called as she disappeared down the hall.

Niporo smiled and shook his head in amazement.

'Trouble is,' he said to himself, 'she never really wants to play!'

Niporo dressed quickly for the conference. He carefully attached the crystal recording-transmitting device to the back of the heavy gold ring, which he always wore on his right hand.

He took the route past the government committee room, on his way over to Princess Zeidra's wing of the complex. As he passed the huge double doors, which were standing open, he quickly inventoried the seating arrangement and noted the participants who had already arrived. He didn't see Kyate, although it looked as if most of his men were seated on the south side of the conference table. He was hoping that would be the case because he had already tuned his transmitter for that specific location, and he wouldn't have time to return to his quarters to change coordinates without running late. He was turning the corner on the esplanade when he nearly collided with Princess Zeidra and the Master Kyate.

"There you are," Niporo said, plainly surprised. "I was just on my way to your chambers." He bowed politely to Zeidra and then again to Kyate.

"Master Kyate was kind enough to escort me." She gestured toward the meeting room. "I wasn't sure you were coming, Niporo."

"You didn't think I would neglect you?"

"Of course not," Zeidra said, "I only thought that something important might have come up."

"Nothing is more important than your safety, my Princess," Niporo said.

"Never you mind Niporo," Kyate said. "Your Princess is in good hands." Kyate was goading Niporo. He placed a firm hand behind Zeidra's elbow, a cue to move on.

"Excuse me, Lord Kyate," Niporo said, "but you never know what dangers may be lurking around the next corner." They walked on. "I committed myself to Princess Zeidra's security a long time ago." Niporo's voice was deepening as he spoke. "You surely wouldn't expect me to breach my commitment just because you're here for a short time."

"One never knows how long it will take to choke a serpent," Kyate said cryptically.

"I assure the two of you … I now feel doubly safe," Zeidra said quietly.

"I'm more familiar with the situation here, Lord Kyate," Niporo said calmly. "I know who belongs and who doesn't. I would recognize an intruder on sight. Can you say the same for yourself?"

Kyate stopped and turned to Niporo. "You've made a good point, Niporo. I'm sure you do rely on your sense of sight," he said, looking Niporo straight in the eye, "and you should know … I don't."

The friction was icy hot. They continued on in silence.

When the three of them entered the conference room, Zeidra was seated first, at the head of the great table, and then the others took their places.

On the huge table, in front of each person, were small video display modules and keyboards. The meeting was conducted via maps, charts, schedules, and listings of military groupings displayed on the screens. The business was done mainly in silence, as each participant could key in questions, answers, or vote using his keyboard and screen. Each response or question would immediately flash upon all the screens simultaneously, which would then elicit answers or rebuttals from any or all of the others. The communication was being directed to everyone at the same time.

On the west wall, at the end of the room was one single screen. This screen served as a direct link to the Galactic Council of Deis, which was also monitoring this strategic conference.

When the schedule for planned reconnaissance missions over Drothuarian territory, was placed on the screen, Niporo noticed that it didn't exactly match the schedule that Llana had retrieved from Kyate's personal papers. It was just as he suspected; the Deis group was conducting some sort of covert operations in the southern part of the galaxy – in Drothuarian space. *'Why wasn't the Ulonican military being informed of these extra maneuvers?'* Niporo pondered the reasoning for the Deis secrecy. He needed to determine if the Galactic Council might also be unaware of the extra activities. If this were so, he would feel better. If, however, the Galactic Council was fully advised of the situation, it would mean that they had some reason not to trust the Ulonican military machine... *'Where did that leave him?'* He was already calculating an alternative methodology in the event he was discovered.

As the last microwave transmissions from the Galactic Council were being summarized, Niporo inconspicuously switched the tiny crystal amplifier from "record" to "transmit". In one tiny chip, all the electronic information from the video screen had been picked up by small electrical impulses and stored. Now it was time to transmit the information back to the Drothuarian headquarters.

Kyate, sitting on the opposite side of the table, further down from Niporo, suddenly heard a very high pitched tone in his right ear. He recognized it as a form of Piezo electricity, using a form of wave impulse, and he tuned his ear in that direction. He immediately realized that the source of the wave impulse was Niporo, who was sitting there very innocently, with his right hand resting on the VDT in front of him.

Kyate concentrated harder, focusing in on the emanation.

He observed Niporo closely, but could see nothing unusual. Kyate turned his head the other way, pretending to be interested in the conversation to his left, so as not to alert Niporo.

Princess Zeidra stood up to give her

blessing and adjourn the conference. It had been a long three hours. When she crossed the room to the door, Kyate and Niporo were both watching her. She approached one of the Temple guards and asked for an escort to the Pyramid of Meditation and she left the room hastily.

Kyate and some of his men were left behind in the conference room discussing some of the strategic operations that had been outlined during the meeting.

"I'd like to speak with you in private, Kyate," said Jason.

Jason was Kyate's best navigator and one of his closest friends.

"Very well, men," Kyate said, "that's about it for now. We'll meet in the morning, at the landing pad... Six sharp. Jason, you and Meno come with me."

The room cleared quickly.

Kyate, Jason, and Meno walked out and across the green to the military area. An XRT-probe was sitting on the launch pad in the middle of the air command complex.

"Let's have some peace and quiet," Kyate said, motioning toward the small silver craft.

"You get her fired up, and I'll be right back," Jason said, as he jogged off toward the dormitories.

Kyate and Meno climbed inside, and after

manipulating several control devices, the propulsion system engaged. There was a soft "whirring" sound that settled down to a low hum after a few minutes.

The inside of the craft was smaller than the scout ships, but large enough to comfortably transport four or five officers. The main control room was a clear dome, set atop the disc shaped body of the XRT-probe. The body housed the propulsion generator core, which was a very small area, considering the amount of power produced from that hub. Other lesser facilities were also situated in the body – a galley, bath facilities, and a lounge, which was actually quite plush for a military probe.

"Now we're ready." Jason had returned and was climbing into the craft. "Look at this .... Anyone up for a space picnic? ... Just thought I'd bring along a little sustenance." He was holding up a large, box shaped thermal container in one hand, and a bottle of wine in the other. He displayed them like a champion flaunting his trophies.

Kyate and Meno looked at each other and laughed.

The three friends settled into their contoured seats, fastened the shoulder harnessing, and all gave the "thumbs-up" sign at the same time.

Kyate ran the palms of his hands over the

colored controls on the console in front of him. The hum became a pulsation. The craft lifted off the ground, rising slowly, and then hovering for fifteen seconds. He slightly rotated his left palm over the green key and in an instant the probe was arcing out over the horizon toward the north, climbing at an incredible rate.

In seconds, the three of them were looking out at the individual multi colored bands; the different levels of the atmosphere appeared to be a huge round rainbow encircling the Earth. The ship glided silently through the layers of colors; one after another, and then it passed through the last one. It was like slipping through a glowing silver curtain into the vast jeweled expanse of space.

Kyate moved his hands over the keys again, and the probe settled into a smooth, silent orbit above the Earth. He unfastened his harness and stood up. He stretched. Jason and Meno followed suit.

There was a sense of freedom here. They could relax and unwind, away from the military mentality, which forced them to keep up a type of front that wasn't necessarily an indication of the spirit of their long and deep friendship.

Kyate set the automatic warning sensors and locked the electromagnetic shields, just in case they were detected by an enemy craft.

They were always prepared.

Kyate, Meno, and Jason descended the spiral walkway into the body of the craft. Crossing the bridge over the core, they entered the lounge.

Kyate sank down into a large overstuffed circular chair, and Meno collapsed onto a lounge. Jason was busy preparing the food and pouring wine for all.

"Well men", Jason said, "we've escaped!" He handed Kyate and Meno, each, a glass of wine. "How long do we get to stay this time?" he asked looking at Kyate, who was sprawled out all over the chair; his arms and legs going in all directions. "Kyate, how long has it been since you took some time out? Looks like you sure need this. Maybe ... as much as I do." Jason looked over at Meno, who was dreamily gazing up at the ceiling of the lounge. – Just gazing.

They sat in silence for a long while.

"I'd sure like to have some quiet here, if you don't mind," Jason said, teasing his silent friends. He passed each of them a plate of fruit, meats, and cheeses.

"You know what I wish I could have right now?" Meno said.

"Brace yourself, Jason .... Meno speaks," Kyate said, sitting upright and leaning toward Meno in anticipation. Kyate liked to tease Meno because he was the strong silent type.

He didn't usually talk a lot; that is, unless he had something important to say.

"I wish I had my wife here with me … …." Meno paused, and then added, "Instead of you guys."

"Uh oh, Kyate," Jason said, "You hear 'him? Meno doesn't like us anymore!"

"Don't take it personally," Kyate said, winking at Jason, "you're just not built right, and I don't smell good enough."

"Well, I really love her … my wife; just gets to be a part of you I guess."

"You know what," Jason said, "I don't know if you'd call it love, but I sure do find that little Temple maiden, Shanta, attractive. I mean I haven't known her long enough to be in love – have I?" He paused thoughtfully. "Anyway we've been spending some time together and …"

"So that's where you've been," Meno interrupted, "I thought I'd lost my shadow. … guess I never thought much about where you were slipping off to. I was just happy to have you out from under my feet."

"Well, now you know," Jason said. "I really care about her."

"Don't worry son," Meno said, "your secret's safe with us, isn't it Kyate?"

Kyate was frowning, that awful thoughtful frown.

"Come on, Kyate," Jason said, "I've only

seen her during off-duty hours. Hey, I haven't done anything you would disapprove of. Honest!"

"What did you say, Jason? I'm sorry... I must have been somewhere else."

"Kyate, just exactly where were you?" Meno demanded to know.

"He's probably back there with the Princess," Jason teased.

"That's enough of that sort of talk," Kyate became suddenly animated, "why would you say something like that?"

"Because she's gorgeous, that's why," Jason said.

"She's definitely more than that!" Meno frowned at Jason.

"Well, old Kyate here, isn't getting any younger," Jason said, "... think he'll ever find a wife?"

"Well that's *forbidden fruit* if there ever was any .... The Princess I mean," Meno said, in a low serious tone.

Kyate took a piece of bread and began building a sandwich. "You two are talking about me like I'm not here. I can assure you that there's nothing between the Princess Zeidra and myself except those damnable Drothuarians." He took a big bite of the sandwich. He smiled to himself as he managed to tell the truth so well; he was thinking of Niporo.

"What would happen, Kyate, if you and the Princess ... you know ... realized you were maybe made for each other? What if it really happened?" Jason asked.

Kyate looked angry, then thoughtful, then confused. He put down his plate and stood up. He walked over to one of the portholes and peered outside. He stood there quietly for a minute.

"First of all," Kyate said, "I barely know the Princess. Secondly, she is, as Meno said, *forbidden fruit*." He turned to face his friends. "And have you forgotten my vow of celibacy." He looked distressed. "But beyond all of that, there is something ..." Kyate rubbed at his chin as he struggled to choose his words carefully. "... A distraction, or a type of chemistry... it seems like a recognition of some kind .... It's hard to explain – Not wholly physical, yet not totally spiritual. I don't know .... It's different, and it seems to have a life of its own."

Meno jumped up and slapped Kyate on the back. "Don't take it so seriously, my Lord. Just sounds like love to me."

"No, Meno, my friend," Kyate said, struggling to find the right words. "It's not love. It is however, something I must contend with and conquer. Maybe it's just the *forbidden fruit syndrome,* as you said before." He looked up at the ceiling and sighed. "I wouldn't admit this to another living soul," he said, twisting the chain of the golden medallion suspended from his neck, "but you two are my dearest friends ..."

"You know you can trust us," Jason said, gathering up the plates and glasses. "We only have each other to confide in – and thank God for that!"

"If you feel that this is some kind of a test or a trial, Kyate," Meno said, "I have no doubt in your superiority. You'll overcome it, so don't worry. After all, the greater the spirit, the greater the tribulations... But then, you're the Master. You know what I'm saying." Meno punched Kyate on the shoulder and returned to the control room.

"Jason, I know you are honorable enough not to say anything of this to Princess Zeidra's attendant, Shanta, but... I wouldn't consider it dishonorable if you repeated anything she had to say about her mistress. Understand?" Kyate winked at the young man. With that, he also returned to the command room, leaving Jason to clean up the mess.

With all three finally strapped into their flight seats, Kyate manned the controls, and the probe slipped silently out of orbit and began the descent back to Earth.

CHAPTER 5 – A Forgotten Kiss

Several weeks passed and there had been no serious confrontations with the Alicupions or the Drothuarians.

The servants had been instructed to prepare the baths for the warriors and to make ready the feast room for the special banquet. The entire complex was in a mood of celebration.

Her maidens attended the Princess Zeidra with special affection on this particular occasion. The servants seemed to have a specific intention for the Princess this evening. There were whispers and gleeful smiles as the handmaidens readied the Princess to receive her dinner guests.

Zeidra stood in front of her full-length mirror watching her servants as they weaved small white and violet flowers into her silky, golden hair. She obediently allowed the girls to adorn her with the best amethyst in the land. The perfumed oils were lovingly massaged into her skin. At last she was prepared.

All of the attendants left the quarters

except Shanta, who was Princess Zeidra's favorite. Shanta was relieved; they were finally alone.

"You look beautiful," Shanta said, helping Zeidra into her gown.

"Thank you Shanta, are you admiring your own handiwork?" Princess Zeidra laughed.

"... My handiwork?" Shanta exclaimed, "Only God himself can take the credit for this creation!"

Princess Zeidra straightened the front of her gown as Shanta fastened the tiny buttons in the back.

"I need for you to escort the Master Kyate to the banquet room," Zeidra said, turning to look at Shanta. "Will you do that for me?"

"Oh my, Zeidra," Shanta backed away as she spoke, wiping her hands against her skirt nervously, "I will do as you ask, but I am so in awe of the man."

"Are you?"

"Aren't YOU?"

"I?" Zeidra said, trying to sound surprised. She laughed and then Shanta laughed, both watching the other's face in Zeidra's mirror.

"Well he's just so ... he's just so .... Overpowering, yes, that's the word. It's his presence. It makes me nervous," Shanta confessed.

"Are you frightened of him?"

"It's just that I wouldn't want to make a fool of myself, you know ... say the wrong thing. Besides, I feel so inferior to him; I've heard so much about his being a mystic."

"I see," Zeidra said, walking over to her jewel case to select a ring.

"Well, what do YOU think of the Master, Princess Zeidra?"

"I think it was a blessing for us that he decided to come."

"That's not what I mean. – I'm talking about the MAN."

"Oh," Zeidra stopped to think for a minute. "Well .... I don't think it's a wise idea to think of the Master in terms of his PHYSICAL presence. After all, he is a very high spiritual being. I think what frightens you, may be his very powerful SPIRITUAL aura."

"He can read one's mind you know," Shanta said. "At least that's what I've heard .... That bothers me a lot."

"Why Shanta, what could you have to hide?" Zeidra laughed a quiet knowing laugh. "Don't worry about it, or you'll be sure to give your secrets away. After all, we both know, if someone acts like they have something to hide, then it's in our nature to become curious .... And thus ... to find out what it is that's being hidden."

In the west wing of the complex, Kyate was impatiently pacing the floor of his suite wondering what had become of the scouts he sent out earlier to find the Alicupion base station. Knowing that the *Grays* had to have a base relatively close to the Ulonican territory, the scouts should have been able to locate it and report back within four hours. His assistants hadn't had contact with the scouts for over three hours.

There was a soft knock at the door. "Master Kyate, dinner is being served in the feast room." It was a female voice speaking from the other side of the door. "Do you wish to be escorted to the table, sir?"

Kyate picked up his laser sword as he crossed the room to answer the door. He opened the door to find the petite young maiden standing just outside. He stood silently looking at the young woman as he fastened the sword to his belt. "I would be flattered to be escorted to the table by such a delicate beauty." A faint smile crossed his lips as he continued to inventory the girl.

She lowered her eyes, and her cheeks glowed with a soft flush as she felt his eyes examining her from head to toe. Unlike Princess Zeidra, Shanta's caste was not allowed to look into the Master's eyes; it was considered disrespectful.

"Follow me please, sir." She spoke quickly, still refusing to look up. She started toward the hallway.

"Wait!" Kyate caught hold of her wrist, stopping her in her tracks. "Are you ill at ease in my company?" he asked, releasing his hold on her.

Withdrawing her hand slowly, she glanced up into the handsome face of the great master. "Yes, I am ... I have no right to even walk in your shadow." She spoke almost inaudibly.

Kyate reached out and took both of her hands in his. Although his hands were massive and strong, his touch was gentle and warm. "Shanta ... you are sincere, honest, and loving ... you have every right to be proud of whom you are, and I am truly honored that you would escort me to dinner!" Kyate released Shanta's hands and waited for some reply.

"Thank you, sir, for sparing me the embarrassment of revealing to my consciousness what my unconsciousness perceives. Now, Master, would you like to partake of the feast?" She turned and started again for the hallway.

Kyate knew exactly what was distressing the maiden, and although he tried to have her believe he didn't know her secrets, his reputation had preceded him. He had been fully aware of her racing pulse, the beads of perspiration that trickled down between her breasts, and the excitement that raced through her entire body, when he spoke to her. He had read her past and present like an open book, she would have been a fool to believe that he didn't know how his presence affected her – and not spiritually, but in a very human and physical way. And he knew about her infatuation with Jason. No wonder she was concerned!

Having to deal with this physical aspect of human existence was awkward for Kyate. Too often, his outward appearance seemed to be a distraction to women and even to some men. More often than not, people tended to expect a great master to be something less than a man – let alone secure in his masculinity. Women were either afraid of him or blatantly trying to seduce him, while men were often jealous and suspicious of his intentions.

The truth of the matter was, Kyate the great Master had vowed to himself to remain celibate in order to retain his secret power over the physical plane. There was no place in his present mission for any preoccupation with the opposite sex. He had no interest at all in *it*, and he didn't care to be involved with *it*.

Kyate followed the maiden Shanta down the long corridor, across the gardens, and into the feast room where the others were already gathering for the reception and dinner.

He was seated at a long table along with his entourage, which was seated to his right. Looking to his left, he saw many of the nobility, which resided at the temple complex. Across from him, were seated the military officers and cabinet members. To his immediate left, there was a vacant seat.

The temple guards stood at the door on the east. The Captain made the announcement in a strong voice, "Ladies and gentlemen, the Princess Zeidra!" Immediately, all of the guests rose to their feet.

At that moment, a hush fell over the crowd gathered at the long tables. All eyes were fixed on the door at the east end of the room.

Zeidra appeared in the doorway, looking like a goddess. She stood for a minute as the purple colored fog rolled into the room from the outside, surrounding her feet and progressing on past her as if a royal purple carpet were being laid out before her. She was dressed in the purest white silk robes, draped loosely over her shoulders and falling in graceful folds across her breasts. Her skin was nearly as white as the silk that covered it. Although the robes were cut very low, her soft golden curls with the delicate flowers interwoven into the ringlets, covered her shoulders and flowed over the soft white curves of her uplifted bosom. The silk was caught tightly at her tiny waist and held in place by a belt studded with amethyst. From her waist, the shimmering silk hugged her hips down to her ankles in cascades of iridescence. The faint shadow of her feminine outline was teasingly visible under the skirt. Her ankles were delicate and shapely, and she wore an amethyst ankle bracelet on her right ankle. Her silver sandals were studded with amethyst and pearls.

The Princess Zeidra bowed to her guests and proceeded into the room. Taking her place next to the guest of honor, the Master Kyate, she turned to face him. Looking up into that fascinating face, she was, at this point, closer to him than she had been since that day, after her liberation from the implant, in the garden. She could even feel his breath on her face as she stood there with her head tilted upward. She was dwarfed by his size.

Zeidra couldn't help but notice that the healthy bronze glow of his skin was what made those intense gray eyes stand out even more. His broad, determined jaw with his large mouth and full lips were terribly appealing. He had a deep cleft in his prominent chin. His neck was muscular and his shoulders were very broad and strong looking. At eye level, she could see through the opening of his satin vest. The muscular swell of his tanned chest was covered with tiny golden-brown swirls that seemed to continue down onto his stomach. She wondered if she buried her face in his chest, if he would smell of warm cinnamon. This was indeed a beautiful man!

Kyate bowed politely to Princess Zeidra, and she bowed to him. Then she motioned to her guests to be seated.

During the course of the dinner, Kyate was courteous and amiable, conversing easily with the military figures seated across from him and even more comfortably with his own men. To his left, however, there was a tension that was almost tangible.

"Do you think your men are enjoying the banquet?" Zeidra asked Kyate, trying to ease the tension.

"They seem to be," he replied glancing at her, then turning quickly back to the conversation with the officers.

"I think your commander Jason is a fine young man, he seems so mature for his age, don't you think?" she tried a second time.

Kyate had just taken a large bite of the

beef. His mouth was full. He turned to the princess and studied her face intently while he finished chewing the meat. "He's one of the best," he said, swallowing hard. Turning back to the men, Kyate continued the conversation with the men.

"Excuse me, Master Kyate," Zeidra said, reaching across in front of him to take a bun from the breadbasket. Her breast barely brushed against Kyate's forearm as she leaned his way.

Kyate recoiled at the contact, as light as it was; it was an instant and automatic reaction. He collected himself immediately, and turning slowly to the princess, he smiled broadly. "Well you certainly know how to get *my* attention," he quipped.

Zeidra's eyes were wide with embarrassment mixed with some other emotion she refused to acknowledge. The Princess quickly turned away, and pretended to busy herself with the bread, which she was now trying to slay with her butter knife.

The seating at the long table was crowded, but no one seemed to mind it as much as Master Kyate and Princess Zeidra. A kind of static electricity danced between their bodies, yet went undetected by the rest of the guests.

Every time Zeidra looked into Kyate's face, she could see that his jaw was set, and his mouth was drawn into a tense line. She wondered if he was as uncomfortable as she was, and she worried that she had offended him. It seemed as if he was smiling and talking freely with everyone but her. Whenever he spoke to her, his face took on a stern, tense look. The tension was too much for the Princess. She removed her napkin from her lap, and rising from her seat she placed the purple linen on the table. Her guests looked surprised. She motioned for them not to stand. "Blessed be the citizens of Ulonica and the house of Benjion." She continued in a soft voice, "I beg your forgiveness for my departure, but I feel the need to meditate upon the events of the day. Please continue the celebration in honor of our revered Master Kyate and his Deis warriors. Not one of us is more grateful for their protection than I." Zeidra turned to Kyate; she looked him straight in the eyes, "Master," Zeidra lowered her voice so that the others couldn't hear, "I will serve you reverently and respectfully, and I beg you to forgive my lack of grace this evening." With that she excused herself and left the room.

Niporo excused himself, too, and rushed out after her, to see her safely to her private temple.

Kyate was seated across from Niporo at

the banquet table and had been acutely aware of his dark energy field. He was also disturbed by Niporo's aggressive manipulation of the conversation during dinner. The Master had observed Niporo's eyes literally riveted on Princess Zeidra. Kyate knew that Niporo's intentions may actually be something other than devotion to his mistress, or even devotion to the Drothuarian cause.

A strange uneasiness moved through Kyate's psyche when Niporo followed the Princess from the room. The Master was sure that something was out of balance, but his own energy seemed to be in a state of flux, so he couldn't be clear at this moment what was actually making him uncomfortable.

The dinner continued, and the guests all managed to enjoy themselves. When the company departed the banquet hall, Kyate was escorted back to his quarters, once more by the maiden Shanta.

Grateful for some solitude, Kyate sat down to try and center his concentration on everything that he had perceived during the evening. Taking inventory of his own emotions, he felt the need to go to the Princess and prove to himself that things were actually in their correct and balanced order.

With the boldness expected of a Deis Warrior, Kyate left his chambers and strolled confidently across the green to the temple of meditation.

The moment he entered the great hall, Kyate knew Zeidra was aware of his presence. He heard her pulse racing, and he watched as her aura retracted. He was confounded by her reaction, and that awkward sensation he felt earlier was returning. He was conscious of Zeidra's fear. But unlike Shanta's fear, Zeidra's fear was more dangerous.

Quietly Kyate strolled into the room; his eyes were fastened on the delicate figure kneeling before the altar at the other end. He didn't speak because he didn't want to interrupt, but it was already too late.

Zeidra rose slowly to meet his gaze. Even at a distance of some fifty feet, the energy emanating from Kyate's eyes seemed to have a paralyzing influence on her.

"My Princess, I'm sorry to inconvenience you," Kyate said, moving toward her, "but I'd appreciate your company for a few minutes. I have an apology to make, and I have some questions that need to be answered."

As he drew nearer, he could sense her growing apprehension. This *one* wasn't an easy earthling to read, and he couldn't be sure just what it was that was frightening her, but he knew that he could calm her.

Kyate took a long deep breath, and in one amazing movement, he had surrounded Zeidra with a tranquil energy field.

With that, he proceeded across the sanctuary and reached out his hand to her.

"Will you walk with me in the garden?" he asked.

Zeidra accepted his hand. "Your desire is my pleasure, and I would love to show you the gardens, Master," she said. "They're as lovely in moonlight as they are by day."

Kyate led her out of the temple and into the night.

As the two of them walked through a maze of flowering shrubs, Kyate couldn't help thinking to himself that the princess was much like the gardens; she was as lovely in moonlight as by day.

"I want you to know I'm sorry if I embarrassed you at the banquet," Kyate said, looking straight ahead as they walked.

"I thought it was I who embarrassed *you*. I thought you were returning the sentiment. I'm sorry as well."

"I made light of the incident .... In error. I shouldn't have done so at your expense."

"We were both on edge. I'll accept your apology .... If you accept mine."

"Good! Now we can get on with business."

Kyate led Zeidra down a path he felt must lead to a fountain because he could hear the water singing in the distance."

"How well do you know your ministers?" he asked.

"I would hope that I know them well!" She stopped abruptly. "I confide much to them, and I certainly respect their counsel. But why would you ask that question?" She looked directly into his eyes.

"Please don't take offense," he said, giving her hand a reassuring squeeze, "I merely need to know if you trust every one of them."

They began walking again.

"In fact, I do," Zeidra said, "especially the minister Niporo, who is one of my most loyal cabinet members." She reached over and broke off a sprig of Night Blooming Jasmine. "He's also a very good friend," she added, holding the flowers up to her nose and enjoying the fragrance. "Isn't this lovely?" She held the cluster of Jasmine up for Kyate to smell.

Her innocence was disarming, and Kyate couldn't help but laugh as he inhaled the perfume from the flowers. "It certainly is lovely," he said, taking the flowers from her hand and inserting the stem in his belt. "I think I should need these on my ship to freshen the air when my men become tense in battle."

"Your courageous Deis Warriors actually would allow flowers on a war ship?" She joked as she picked some more Jasmine. "What would the enemy say of them, if the craft were captured?"

"The enemy would say that the Deis Warriors must have a most sensitive nature."

Zeidra laughed.

They had come to a stream trickling over a waterfall. The place was enchanting. The moonlight was dancing on the water, and the air was rejuvenated by the smell of pine, enhanced by the mist rising from the pool. There was a terrace there, with a bench partially surrounded and covered by a grape arbor.

"Shall we sit?" Kyate was already sitting down, not really giving the Princess a choice.

She sat down beside him.

"Tell me more about Niporo." The Master peered into her face. He wanted to find some hidden truth in what she would say.

"Well, he's been with the Temple for about five years. He's honest. He's responsible, and he's quite brilliant ...."

"What kind of a personal relationship does he have with you?" Kyate was blunt. He regretted it immediately. "What I mean to say is ... does he advise you on your personal affairs as well as affairs of Temple policy?" Kyate continued to watch Zeidra's expression.

"Yes," she admitted, "I do occasionally consult with him on personal matters." She stood up. "He's wise and caring. Is there any reason why I shouldn't heed his counsel?" She walked over to the waterfall. Her back was turned toward Kyate.

"What about his personal reputation?"

"What about it?" Zeidra turned back quickly; she was facing him now, and she spoke with a tinge of defiance in her voice. "What a minister does on his own time is really no concern of mine."

"Well, I happen to know that your friend Niporo, although he may be wise, and brilliant, and responsible as far as his Temple duties go, has another, quite elusive side to his nature."

Kyate rose from the bench because he knew he would meet with opposition on this subject. *'Was the Princess going to defend her minister's honor'?* Kyate wondered.

"Master, please don't force me to slander a friend's character!" Zeidra was being evasive.

"Then you condone it?"

"Of course I don't! – I mean, I'm not sure what you're speaking of!" She stammered. "Kyate, what is your point?"

"Well ... tongues wag in the Temple complex, and I've overheard much in a few weeks," he said. "You should also remember, Princess Zeidra, that I have my own source of uncovering the true nature of a being. So ..." he said it sharply, "if you don't condemn it, then you must condone it."

Zeidra's cheeks flushed a radiant pink, in the moonlight. "Master Kyate, I don't want to be disrespectful, but I find your attitude arrogant and difficult to endure."

"I'm sorry. I just call things as I see them." Kyate knew he'd crossed an invisible line. "I didn't intend to offend you, Zeidra." He leaned down to get a better look at her flushed face. "But you really are lovely when you're angry." Kyate grinned; it was a roguishly handsome grin, catching the princess off guard.

"I'm so sorry. I shouldn't have said that, Kyate!" She placed her hand on his chest.

What the Princess didn't know, was that Kyate hadn't really heard any gossip about the minister Niporo, but had instead, finally gained the information from Zeidra herself. His powers of perception being superior to others, he was able to glean what he needed to know just by observing and feeling. With Zeidra, however, staying centered and objective was at times impossible. Kyate felt a foreign vulnerability, at times, while attempting to decipher her thoughts.

Zeidra lowered her head in humility. "I cannot justify Niporo's lack of discipline, Master." She turned back to the waterfall. "It's just that he is my friend."

"Do you honestly believe he's your friend, when he's an embarrassment to the integrity of the Temple?" Kyate said, catching Zeidra by the arm and turning her around to face him.

"Could it be that he has been able to cloud the judgment of a Benjai princess?"

"I feel some truth in what you're saying, but I really want to deny that reality!"

Kyate took both of Zeidra's hands in his. "Denial is not the way to remedy the problem. But there is a more serious threat regarding your Minister Niporo. Princess Zeidra, take care not to be deceived, for if what I fear is true, you could be in very grave danger."

Zeidra shivered as a chill ran down her body.

Kyate knew her anxiety. He wrapped his arms around her and held her close to his chest as a parent comforts a frightened child.

"Come, I fear that I've ruined your evening," Kyate said, looking down at Zeidra, still holding her against him. "Would you consider forgiving me for that much?"

"So ... You want me to forgive you for making me feel betrayed, but you care not for forgiveness in slandering my friend?" She spoke into Kyate's chest, her words barely discernible.

Kyate was silent. He felt a strange restlessness stirring in his psyche, and he knew it was time to return to the green. There was some sort of chemistry at work here that amazed and excited him; yet he understood instinctively that this type of energy was nothing to toy with.

Equally as much as he wanted to release Zeidra and return to the complex, he also wanted to prolong the moment. She felt so warm and soft. Her body was emanating the most delicious vibrations. Those pulsations seemed to penetrate his being. He tightened his hold on the Princess as all of his muscles tensed. She gasped as he involuntarily pressed her closer to his body. If only for an instant, Kyate recognized his need. He released Zeidra immediately.

Kyate took her arm and they walked back to the green in silence. The night air was growing chilly now, and a light fog was enveloping the complex.

When they reached the Princess Zeidra's chamber doors, Kyate hesitated briefly, looking deeply into her eyes; searching for some explanation for the disconcerting affect this woman had on him. He decided it was time to deal with it. He needed to conquer this provocative distraction, and prove to himself that he alone *controlled* his actions.

Kyate wrapped his arms around the princess, and pressing her body tightly against his, he continued to look down into her eyes. They were glazed with what he recognized as fear and anticipation, but she didn't fight him. He could feel that delicious pulsation emanating from her body again. It had a maddening effect on him. He held her there, savoring the sensation. He wanted to kiss her. The urgency was growing. He fought the reckless need beginning to burn in him. This he had to do. *HE* would choose *WHEN* he would kiss her. *HE* would control.

He slowly lowered his head, brushing his lips lightly across her cheek. His blood felt like rivers of fire running through his veins. Something explosive was stirring in his soul. He broke. He jerked her body into his so violently and abruptly, that she let out a little cry. He kissed her on the mouth, first gently then hungrily. Kyate was sure Zeidra had never been kissed before, but her body seemed to respond on its own behalf. He kissed her deeply. Zeidra melted into Kyate's kiss, surrendering her body willingly to his strength and his demand. She didn't try to escape. The world was reeling, and Kyate continued to allow it to happen. Just when it seemed that the situation would explode out of control, he stopped.

Slowly, he released his hold on Zeidra. As she stood there dazed and breathless, he placed one finger on her lips, as if to say, '*don't say a word*'. He then began the hypnotic trance that would cause Zeidra's experience of her first kiss to be lost forever in forgetfulness.

Instantly it was gone. Kyate was squeezing her hand and saying 'good night.' Zeidra watched as he crossed the courtyard walking toward his suite. She closed the door to her chambers and prepared for sleep as she would on any other night.

CHAPTER 6 – Cloak and Dagger

The shadow quickly passed over the louvered shutters of Kyate's parlor. A dim light flickered, and then was extinguished. Silently Kyate drew his laser sword and crept stealthily onto the veranda outside his chambers. The double doors were slightly ajar. He crouched and waited. Poised like a leopard about to make his kill, Kyate surveyed the darkness inside, waiting for movement. Suddenly a black-clad figure appeared at the doorway. Without warning Kyate sprang upon the intruder, and with one deadly blow, the phantom lay motionless on the cold marble floor.

Kyate bent down to remove the cloak from across his victim's face when a rustling sound caught his attention. Dropping the garment he whirled around in time to see the glistening dagger. Grabbing the wrist of the second assailant, in one swift move, Kyate braced his elbow against the man's shoulder; still holding his wrist, he deftly executed one quick twist – a snap, a scream, and the knife fell to the ground.

The attacker immediately caught Kyate off-guard, thrusting an elbow into his ribs. Kyate staggered back, and then spinning one hundred eighty degrees, landed a heavy kick to the man's throat. He went down, but spotting the dagger close by, he snatched it up in his left hand and stumbled to his feet, dazedly. Kyate waited. The stranger raised the dagger, and with a blood curdling scream, rushed at Kyate who was now in a defensive stance and ready for his assailant.

Before the man could reach Kyate's body with the knife, he ran straight into a right blow to the throat, followed by a left foot in the groin that sent him careening over the veranda wall and onto the green below. Kyate jumped off the balcony after his opponent, only to find him fallen on his own dagger, which was now buried deep in his neck; fountains of blood were rhythmically showering the white marble wall. Kyate didn't recognize the stranger's face. Checking his clothing for some ID, he found nothing.

Remembering the first victim, he leaped back up onto the veranda. The body remained motionless. Kyate knelt down, and removing the covering from the intruder's face, was shocked to see it was a woman. She was still breathing, much to his relief. He picked up the limp body and flung it over his shoulder.

Once in his rooms, Kyate dumped the woman onto his bed. He checked her energy source, which revealed that all was in balance.

"You'll stay put like a good little girl," Kyate said, "while I dispose of your friend outside." He lightly touched the base of the woman's skull with his right index finger while breathing into her aura a paralyzing anti-energy beam.

Kyate retrieved the molecular accelerator from his locker and disappeared outside.

"Now my friend, we'll just leave your body for the vultures in some other dimension," he said, dialing the specific frequency on the black box he held in his hands. A quiet hum and a pale green strobe light began to emanate from the apparatus. Kyate aimed the light at the blood soaked body lying there on the ground in front of him. Within seconds, there was nothing to be seen. No trace of the violence that had taken place – not even a drop of blood – nothing but the dagger left on the grass. Remarkably, the dagger had remained.

"I should have suspected something like this," Kyate growled. He picked up the dagger and examined it closely. Although it was dark, he was able to determine the molecular weight of the metal. *'I know this material,'* Kyate thought to himself. *'X-15 – from the Drothuarian region of Urampa! So now we know what we're dealing with... The Drothuarians ARE working from the inside'*

Kyate tossed the dagger into the air, and catching it in his other hand he jumped back up onto the veranda and returned to his hostage.

By this time the paralysis was beginning to wear off, so Kyate took out his demobilization gun, pulled a chair up to the side of the bed, sat down, and waited.

Her eyes began to flicker. The woman weakly raised her arm and rubbed the back of her hand across her swollen cheek. Slowly she turned her head to look at Kyate.

"Why didn't you kill me?" she asked coldly.

"What would I have gained by doing so?"

"You may find it dangerous to your cause if you don't."

"Um, I believe the danger lies with your comrades. I'm sure they'll be much harder on you than I .... When they find out that I let you live .... They'll probably wonder why I did."

"I shall have to kill *myself!*" She spat out the words bitterly.

"Oh no ... You won't kill yourself ... you're mine now." Kyate stated it calmly. "From now on you'll be working for me."

"I won't work for your cause! I'd die first!"

"Are you Drothuarian?"

"Go to hell!"

"Well, I've been there and I really don't care to return. Do you have a name?"

The woman jumped from the bed and ran for the door. In one swift move Kyate caught her around the waist.

"Let me go! Let me go!" She pummeled him with both fists – kicking and scratching as she fought to free herself.

Holding her tightly by both wrists, Kyate walked her back over to the bed and threw her onto it. "Now ... I want some answers and I want them straight, or I may be tempted to forget your gender!" Kyate raised one eyebrow and smiled sarcastically.

Reminded of her femininity, the woman softened abruptly. "You know, Master Kyate ... if you were to consider releasing me .... I would be most appreciative. I would be willing to ..." She began unbuttoning the pearl buttons on the dress she was wearing beneath the cloak. "I know how to make a man feel really nice ..." She opened her bodice, exposing her breasts and looking Kyate straight in the eye the entire time.

Kyate was amused. "You don't have to do that," he said, laughing. "You can't bribe me with something I could simply *TAKE* if I wanted it." Kyate turned the chair around, and straddling the chair, sat down again. Folding his arms on the back of the chair, he leaned forward, resting his chin on one forearm. "Llana ... That's your name. You're not Drothuarian!" Kyate was reading her.

"How do you know that?!" she demanded.

"What's your connection with the Drothuarians here?" Kyate studied her intently.

Pulling the cloak over her naked breasts, Llana cowered back against the wall, at the head of the bed, trying to escape Kyate's interrogation. She was silent. She looked scared.

"You really don't have to be frightened of me," Kyate said. "But you'd better rethink your allegiance to the Drothuarians ... whatever that is. They'll chew you up and spit you out. You're not one of them ... they're only using you for a time. When they're finished .... *YOU'RE FINISHED*!" Kyate threw up his hands in exasperation. "Do you understand what I'm saying?"

Llana began to sob uncontrollably. She pulled the cloak up over her head, clenching it so hard her knuckles were white with the pressure. "It's only money," she choked. "I only work for the money." She collapsed in a heap on the mattress.

"How high a price would you put on your soul?" Kyate got up and walked over to the double doors. He locked them securely and closed the louvers. "Your allegiance, then, goes to the highest bidder, is that correct?" Kyate didn't wait for an answer. Keeping one eye on the woman, he went to his trunk and took out a velvet pouch. "Tell me Llana, do you work for diamonds and golden nuggets as well?" he asked, emptying some of the contents into his hand. He returned to the bed and sat down beside Llana, holding the handful of treasure for her to inspect.

She slowly raised her eyes, peering into the glittering array of gems and golden clusters.

"Is it enough, Llana? Is this enough to entice you to swear allegiance to me?"

Llana reached over and touched the jewels with her finger, stirring them around in Kyate's palm; she was silent.

"All you have to do is tell me what you were after here tonight. I want to know who your companion was, and I want to know who you're working for. That's all." He looked at Llana intently. "Is this enough? What more would it take to have the answers I need?"

Kyate threw the handful of diamonds and gold onto the bed; he waited for an answer. Llana remained silent. In frustration, he opened the pouch and emptied out the entire contents into Llana's lap. "Is it enough?" He repeated the question.

Llana didn't answer. She sat quietly just looking at Kyate. Minutes passed. After a while, Llana picked up one of the diamonds and examined it closely. "Well, Master Kyate .... How can you buy me if I'm already yours? That's what you said, you know. You said I was yours." Llana barely whispered the words.

Surprised, Kyate stiffened. "I must admit to you Llana, I have already gleaned the information I need from your mind, now that you've relaxed. The truth is ... you're free to go. You can take the jewels with you, too. Maybe that will keep you from cavorting with the wrong people. Monetary wealth means nothing to me, although I see it holds much value for you."

"Master Kyate!" Llana jumped up onto her knees. "I don't want to go! It's not safe for me to go! I will serve you .... As God is my witness ... I wish to serve you! I need your protection ... *PLEASE* Master!" She flung her arms around Kyate's neck, and sobbed into his flesh.

Kyate wrestled himself free from her grasp and stood up. He walked over to the vanity and poured some wine into a goblet. Taking a kerchief from the table, he returned to the bed.

"We need to attend to that nasty bruise on your cheek. I've never struck a woman in my life, but then I've never been so viciously attacked by one either!" he said dipping the cloth into the wine and dabbing it against

Llana's cheek. He then placed both of his thumbs on the wound, closed his eyes, and taking a deep breath he projected white healing energy into the tissue on her face. Immediately the swelling disappeared and the discoloration vanished. "There," he said, "good as new. Don't ever try to attack me again, or I'll put it back the way it was!" he teased, trying to lighten the moment. "You're not so tough after all. I'm not sure what we need to do with you. Since you were looking for my weekly schedule to deliver to Niporo, I guess I should produce one." Kyate sat down at the desk and began to write.

Llana watched him intently.

"Here's what you and I are going to do," Kyate said, getting up from the desk and going to the wardrobe. "We're going to deliver the schedule to your man at the tavern. I'm going to disguise myself as your Drothuarian companion, Ullo. We'll get your job done, and no one will be the wiser." He put on a large black hat and a full-length cape. "Are you ready to go?"

"Are you just going to abandon me after we deliver the schedule?"

"Llana, I'll reprogram your memory banks. Your life will continue as normal, but you won't want to work for Niporo again. You'll perceive your life in a whole new light. Fair enough? I just need your help tonight.

You will have the jewels, the money, and a *new vision.* You will also have my help whenever you need it. Don't you think that's fair enough?"

"Master Kyate, it will be as you say!" Llana smiled as she fastened her dress. She climbed down off the bed, gathered up the jewels and adjusted the cloak. "I'm ready when you are."

Kyate walked slowly over to where Llana was standing. He reached out for her and pulled her into his massive arms. She looked up at him in amazement. Brushing the long dark curls away from her face, he studied her clear green eyes as she relaxed in his embrace. "Now you will have a new life-path," Kyate said, pressing his forehead against hers.

Kyate was concentrating on new thought patterns; instilling in Llana's mind the new reality of this evening's events and changing her perspective on life. He would now (in her mind) become her companion, Ullo. The schedule would be delivered as if nothing had gone awry.

He withdrew slowly, steadying Llana until she had regained her equilibrium.

Kyate then placed his hands over his face, tensed his muscles, and proceeded to convert his bone structure and facial features to those of the Drothuarian spy, Ullo.

"Let's go," he said.

Llana rubbed her eyes and shook her

head, still trying to collect her senses. She followed Kyate out into the darkness.

The two cloaked figures made their way through the night to the tavern.

The door stood open, and hazy shafts of light illuminated the silvery colored pavement of the street in front. Kyate and Llana moved to the side of the building and peered in through a window.

"Ullo, look .... There's Niporo – there at the table with Cole. He better have the money!"

"You go in and bring them out here," Kyate said.

Llana disappeared around the side of the tavern and went inside. Kyate could see the three of them talking. Niporo grabbed Llana, pulled her down into his lap and began groping at her breasts. It was obvious that he was intoxicated. Kyate decided to join the trio.

He stepped into the dank, smoke filled room. The smell of stale beer and sweat permeated the air. Shadowy figures lounged around tables, oblivious to Kyate's entrance. He walked slowly and deliberately up to the Drothuarians' table.

"I thought this was to be a business meeting," Kyate said as he approached Niporo, taking hold of Llana's arm and pulling her off Niporo's lap and onto her feet.

"Ullo, Sit! Have a drink," Cole said,

apparently believing Kyate's effective disguise.

"How'd it go?" Niporo asked, still eyeing Llana, and running his tongue over his dry lips.

"We got the schedule," Llana said.

"What we really need, is to get on the inside of that Deis group. Got any suggestions, Ullo?" Cole poured himself a drink from the half-empty bottle on the table.

"Sounds like a good plan, but it won't be easy getting anything by the Master Kyate." Kyate was enjoying his new identity; he leaned lazily against the column behind the table. "Tell you what .... I've got some connections .... Some guys in the fleet ... what exactly do you need to know?" He crossed one boot over the other.

"We need to be sure that the Deis Command isn't sending any more ships into this area. We need to eliminate Kyate. – That's really what we need. Without him, the Deis fleet doesn't amount to much. The Benjai will be our reward! If Niporo can't get to her, maybe you'd like to try, Ullo! You've been in command there in the guard long enough to have her confidence. You look better than old Niporo here, too. That's it, maybe little Zeidra would have the hots for someone younger .... More virile ... you're not a bad looking guy, Ullo. Why not make a play for her?"

"Maybe I will," Kyate said caustically, looking intently into Niporo's eyes, enjoying the obvious jealousy he saw there. "Bet I could have her in less than a month if I set my mind to it." He was goading Niporo again.

Niporo slammed his goblet down hard on the table. "Would you like to make a little wager on that, Ullo?"

"It would be like taking candy from a babe." Kyate leaned over placing his hand on the table beside Niporo and supporting his weight on it. He leaned a little closer to Niporo. "Want'a put your money where your imagination is?"

"OK guys," Cole broke in, "let's not fight over who gets the virgin. I just hope one of you *CAN*! Now, let's see the schedule."

Kyate pulled the paper from beneath his cape and handed it to Cole.

Taking it, Cole studied it carefully, squinting his eyes in the dim light. "Take a look at this Niporo," he said, laying the document on the table.

Niporo snatched it up quickly, and running his finger over the paper from left to right, raised one eyebrow. "This sure isn't what we expected is it? I thought those Deis bastards were smarter than this! Looks like they don't think we're interested in the Benjai at all. All they're concerned with are those Gray monsters!" He handed the schedule back to Cole.

"If you can get a copy of the next planned transmission, there'll be more in it for you next time, Ullo," Cole said, slapping Kyate on the shoulder.

Niporo poured another drink, and offering the bottle to Cole, said, "Let's drink to the victorious ... he gets the Benjai .... Let's drink to the loser .... He can have Llana ... and ..."

"Let's have our money!" Llana interrupted, extending her hand under Niporo's face.

Niporo reached up and grabbed Llana behind the neck, pulling her face down close to his. "Let's have a kiss," he demanded gruffly.

In one stealth move, Kyate slid his massive forearm around the front of Niporo's neck while bracing his other arm on the back of his head. Applying slight pressure, he said, "Pay the lady!"

Niporo released his hold on Llana who instantly jumped back behind Kyate. "Thank you, Ullo – nice to know someone cares!"

"Damn!!" Niporo snarled in indignant resignation. Reaching into his vest, he pulled out a small leather pouch and counted out the coins onto the table. Kyate collected the money with one swath of his hand across the surface.

"Next time, Cole – we'll have that drink next time." Kyate guided Llana toward the door, hoping she wouldn't instigate any more trouble.

Safely outside, Kyate poured the coins into Llana's hands, laughing at her surprised expression.

"Ullo, half of that money's yours! What's wrong with you anyway?" she said, shoving a handful of silver at Kyate.

"Happy birthday, honey ..." Kyate laughed. "This is your lucky day."

Not being one to look a gift horse in the mouth, Llana happily accepted the prize.

Kyate and Llana parted company near the temple complex as if nothing unusual had occurred.

"Good night, Ullo," Llana whispered, then hurried off across the courtyard.

Kyate was satisfied that the reprogramming had indeed been effective.

"Sweet Dreams, Llana." Kyate amused himself, wondering how Llana would justify having *ALL* the money *AND* the diamonds and gold. He chuckled softly and he disappeared into the night

Back in his quarters, he sat down in front of the portable command console. Manipulating the dials to facilitate the secret Deis frequency channel, he began to encode the transmission:

"DROTHUARIAN PLANTS IN BENJION GOVERNMENTS. CONFIRMATION

RELIABLE. SEND REINFORCEMENTS. AT LEAST 40 FLEETS. STAY ON PERIMETER UNTIL FURTHER NOTIFICATION. MICROWAVE REPULSAR SHIELDS NECESSARY FOR NON-DETECTION. 99674 END TRANSMISSION."

CHAPTER 7 – One Bond Established - Another Bond Broken

Over the next few weeks, Kyate occupied most of his time touring Ulonica, revising aerial maps, training and perfecting tactical maneuvers with his men, and doing background research on the cabinet ministers and other Temple officials.

Through it all, he managed to keep silent in regard to his knowledge of Niporo's identity and plan. He skillfully masqueraded as Ullo from time to time, in order to keep abreast of the Drothuarian strategy.

There were numerous meetings with the Princess Zeidra concerning Temple affairs and the status of the Alicupion conflict. Kyate made sure to keep all contact with the Princess centered on his mission to Ulonica. He also managed quite well in keeping his personal inclinations in check.

The disturbing factor in all of this, was whenever Kyate made an appointment to speak with Zeidra, he could be sure that the minister Niporo would be present. Niporo had become Princess Zeidra's shadow. Wherever she was, there also was Niporo. Kyate found that he was never alone with Zeidra, although he might be thankful for it at some level. He ran the risk of being seen, the night he gave into his physical curiosity, and he admonished himself for not exercising more restraint – yet he had been in total control of the situation, and had not allowed it to progress further than it did. Kyate felt that he was in no need of a chaperone.

As far as Niporo was concerned, Kyate desperately wanted to expose him – with Niporo's reputation being what it was, Kyate was uneasy in accepting the cabinet minister's close association with Zeidra. The Master had discounted rape, but he feared that Niporo's deceit might lure Zeidra into something more acceptable. Kyate could not, at this time, reveal the truth about Niporo. It was out of the question. Forcing the issue would undoubtedly place the Princess in jeopardy. A man like Niporo would be capable of any atrocity if trapped in a desperate situation. Kyate continued biding his time.

The Alicupions had been extremely elusive during this time, with only a few skirmishes in the border regions of the province.

Kyate was sure that something was going on between the Alicupions and the

Drothuarians, which hadn't been discussed in his meetings with Cole. Several Drothuarian reconnaissance ships had been seen, just in the last two days. The Deis pilots had also discovered several disintegrated Alicupion craft just over the mountains that separated Ulonica from a province called Jalequaria.

It occurred to Kyate, that there was probably an Alicupion base somewhere in the Jalequarian region, and it was imperative that the Deis star group check the area as soon as possible.

The Drothuarians had made no offensive move on Ulonica for the last three or four years; however Kyate had already discovered Niporo was the key to that mystery.

The afternoon was sweltering hot and still. Kyate decided to lie down and try to calm his mind. He pulled his shirt off over the top of his head, tossing it over onto a nearby chair. Stretching his arms high above his head, it felt good to feel free from the heavy material. He walked to the window and closed the shutters, blocking out the intense afternoon sun. Strolling lazily across the room to the bed, he collapsed onto it, relaxing back against his pillows with his arms behind his head and his legs crossed at the ankles. He closed his eyes and concentrated on his breathing, taking him deeper and deeper into rest. He slept.

At the same time, on the other side of the complex, Princess Zeidra was conferring with her ministers in the government court. They had been discussing the political climate of the province in regards to organizing a military effort to incarcerate or eradicate the Pfystron population in Ulonica.

The military had a weapon that could single out Pfystrons by DNA detection, and then destroy the molecular structure, thereby rendering them sterile. It could also be fine-tuned to completely destroy the creatures. The question before the cabinet of ministers was: which was more desirable, a sterile Pfystron or a dead Pfystron?

The decision was unanimous among the cabinet members, and the meeting was adjourned. The officers and ministers filed out of the room quietly, leaving Zeidra alone with her introspection.

"You appear distressed, my dear." It was Niporo. "Is there anything I can do to help?"

Zeidra was surprised as she hadn't noticed him standing there.

"Oh, Niporo ..." She stood up and walked around the desk. "I find killing to be vile and distasteful," she said, "and I so wish I didn't have to be associated with it." She clasped her hands behind her back.

"Well then, don't think about it! Put it out of your mind and let's talk about something else." Niporo picked up a picture of a group of Pfystrons and frowned. "You *do* realize, Zeidra ... those ugly creatures are breeding like flies in a dung hill. They're only partly human, if that." He tossed the photograph back onto the desk. "So I wouldn't worry much about their demise. They're barbarian heathens ... just an unfortunate experiment gone wrong."

"I suppose you're right as usual, with your *logical* approach .... But I intend to veto the cabinet's decision .... We'll sterilize – not kill! You can accept that as *MY humanitarian* approach."

"Of course I'm right! And if you exercise your veto, Zeidra ... you'll live to regret it!"

"Well, I'll just take that chance, Niporo. Don't forget, the decision is ultimately mine to make."

"Of course, Zeidra. Now... let's talk about something pleasant."

Zeidra walked across the room and looked out the window. She was quiet and thoughtful for several minutes, and then she turned and approached Niporo.

"Niporo, where is your family?" she asked.

"Why would you want to know that?"

"We've known each other for a long time, yet I realize how little I actually know about your past," she said, brushing a piece of lint from his shoulder and smiling innocently. "I've never heard you mention your parents or any relatives, and I was just curious as to your descent?" Zeidra peered inquisitively into Niporo's eyes. She saw them turn mysteriously dark, as she waited for him to answer.

"Why Zeidra, could it be that you've taken up genealogy as your latest hobby?" He teased, but it was clear that he was being evasive.

"Is your ancestry here, or are you from some other star system?" She pressed him for an answer, sauntering about the room with her hands still clasped behind her back, watching him intently out of the corner of her eye, tilting her head back toward him coquettishly.

"Look here, my sweet," Niporo said, taking her hand, "I have an appointment and I shall be late if I don't leave now. I would definitely like to continue this conversation this evening." He pressed her hand to his lips, giving her an intense demanding look. "I'll meet with you in your chambers at, say, nine? Is that agreeable with you? I'll see you then." He left quickly. He didn't give her chance to decline.

Zeidra stood there for a long moment trying to ascertain the meaning of that look in Niporo's eye. No bother ... she would entertain him tonight in her chambers as he had requested, and maybe she could uncover some of his ulterior motives, if he actually had any, as Master Kyate had implied.

Zeidra thought it would be wise to inform The Master Kyate of her plans to interrogate Niporo tonight in her chambers. She quickly left the government court and slipped across the complex to the dormitory where Kyate was residing.

There was a soft knock at his door. Kyate opened one eye and tried to decide if he had dreamed the sound. He listened. There was another knock.

Drowsily he swung his feet off the side of the bed and struggled to sit upright, still half asleep. Wrestling himself to his feet, he found his way to the door and opened it. It was an unexpected surprise, or was he still dreaming? Kyate shook his head quickly, trying to clear the sleep from his brain. On his lips, there was the faintest glimmer of a smile, and he blinked his eyes hard trying to focus them. Zeidra stood there, outside Kyate's chamber door, looking in at the Great Master Kyate, half naked, hair tousled, glassy eyed, and trying to wake up.

"Are you all right, sir?" Zeidra asked.

He was supporting his weight with the door, which he was holding open. He opened it wider, and motioned for her to enter. She brushed past him and into the room. Kyate closed the door behind Zeidra, and then turned to her with an inquisitive look on his face. "I'm fine," he answered, "but what matter of importance brings you to my chambers?" He noticed that she was staring at his nakedness, but he wasn't much in the mood for modesty in this heat.

"I've come to inform you that tonight, Niporo wants to meet with me in my suites," she said. "I'll find out, then, what exactly his background is." Zeidra repeated the conversation with Niporo, describing his body language and expressions. "You'll see," Zeidra said, "he really isn't a threat .... I will prove your misgivings wrong!"

Kyate, jolted fully awake now, was suddenly overpowered with a sense of ominous foreboding.

"Princess Zeidra," Kyate interrupted her as he sat down heavily on the bench at the foot of his bed, "I feel that it wouldn't be in your best interest to press Niporo for details pertaining to his past." He rubbed his hands roughly back over his head from his forehead, frowning as he watched her. "I have additional information on your minister

Niporo that confirms him to be part of a Drothuarian plot to attain their goal from the inside." Kyate spoke in a slow low tone and watched her carefully as he divulged the specifics of the sinister Drothuarian plan, not sure how she might react.

Zeidra stood there motionless for a moment, and then she rushed across the room and stood squarely in front of Kyate. Planting her feet firmly on the floor, she looked him straight in the eyes. "Surely, Master, this can't be true ... you must have obtained some sort of bogus information!" Her pale blue eyes were wild with disbelief. "Tell me, please ..." Zeidra begged, falling down on her knees at Kyate's feet, "Tell me this is just a trial; that you're only testing my reactions, or my courage, or ... or ..." She lowered her head and became strangely silent.

Kyate felt his soul stir in his gut. He reached out for Zeidra's upper arms and raised her to her feet. As he sat there holding Zeidra in front of him, he became aware of how delicate her arms felt in his huge hands. Steadying her, he watched a single tear slip down her cheek and onto her breast, which was barely exposed by the dainty white silk bodice she was wearing. Kyate watched the tear slide across the rounded flesh and disappear into the cleavage. Her bosom was heaving now with stifled sobs, and Kyate knew she was struggling to control her very real fear, and come to terms with her disappointment.

Kyate was certain that Zeidra was well aware of the implications of the plot, along with the various nightmare scenarios the Drothuarians might employ in order to usurp her authority.

"Do you think they'll try to kill me?" Zeidra asked in a quiet voice.

"I believe they will just corrupt the gene, Zeidra."

"What does that mean?"

"It means they intend to impregnate you. If they aren't successful in that ... then they may very well exterminate the source."

"Exterminate *ME*?!! ... Or my ovary?"

Kyate drew her closer to him, between his knees where he was sitting. He enfolded her in a warm, comforting energy field, which immediately seemed to calm her. Zeidra looked down into Kyate's upturned face, and one last tear dropped onto his lips. Instinctively he retrieved it with his tongue. He marveled that instead of tasting salty as would be expected, it tasted sweet, like the nectar from a honey suckle flower. He had an impulsive desire to reclaim the other tears, wherever they had fallen.

Frozen in time, Kyate sat there comforting Zeidra, and yet Zeidra was comforting him – A silent and unspoken bond was being established between them. He held her there, his face buried in her soft, sweet smelling flesh. Kyate had never felt such tenderness for another being in his entire life. This experience seemed to happen so naturally, that for a long while the two just languished in the solace they provided one another. It was a sincere nurturing affection culminating in an implicit union of friendship, of loyalty, of trust, and understanding.

Returning to the reality of the danger at hand, Kyate gently moved Zeidra to the side, and rose from the bench.

"Zeidra, you can't meet with Niporo tonight." It sounded like a direct command, yet Kyate softened it a bit. "It's just too dangerous," he said. "Make an excuse, tell him you're ill." He rubbed his forehead with the back of his hand. "Tell him anything!"

Kyate moved to the window and cautiously opened the shutters, just enough to see across the courtyard in the direction of the Temple Service quarters. He had full view of most of the comings and goings in the Temple complex. At this moment, all was quiet on the grounds. The sun was beginning to sink below the horizon, and the purple and pink sunset cast a warm glow across the pyramids and the rooftops. Kyate couldn't help thinking that most of the beauty on this planet was only to camouflage the ugliness. He felt a very deep sadness in his spirit.

Zeidra slowly approached Kyate. She laid her hand on the bareness of his muscular back; it was a reassuring gesture.

"My Lord, I will do as you say." She turned toward the door.

"Wait!" Kyate turned after her. "No matter what," he said, "you can't afford to take any chances. Niporo isn't stupid enough to try anything, unless he knows or thinks his scheme has been discovered." He caught hold of Zeidra's arm to stop her. "I know you're strong enough, and brave enough to handle this. You only need to make him believe that nothing has changed in your relationship with him." Kyate released Zeidra's arm and paced back over to the window. "You have to be convincing! Do you understand what I'm saying?" He turned and walked back to where Zeidra was standing. "If you need me, I'll be there. It's too obvious for me to post a guard at your door, or I would." Kyate ran his hands through his hair in frustration. "We'll set a trap when it's time, but for now, it's basically up to you … to lull our Drothuarian friend into a false sense of security." Kyate shook his head, eyeing Zeidra critically. "But *NOT* tonight, Zeidra – and don't you dare meet with him in private – *EVER!*"

Zeidra reached out her hand again and

placed it on Kyate's chest this time. "I will do what I must do." She looked sweetly up into his eyes, her hand lingering on his warm skin. "Niporo won't find out from me that he's been discovered." With that, she opened the door and left Kyate's room, leaving him there with a warm spot on his chest that penetrated all the way through to his heart.

When Zeidra returned to her rooms, she immediately summoned a messenger to deliver the note to Niporo. In the letter, she told him that she was sorry, but just didn't feel up to a meeting tonight, and that maybe another time would be better. The messenger took it and left. It was 8:30 p.m. when Niporo received the message from Princess Zeidra

Princess Zeidra settled into a soothing, warm, herbal bath. Some esoteric music was playing in the background, and a cool breeze was blowing into the room from the opened vents in the walls. In one corner, a fountain was cascading down over some jeweled rocks, and the sound of the waterfall was as refreshing as the breeze that cooled Zeidra's perspiring face. As the steam rose all around her, the Princess slipped lower into the bubbles. She felt the tension melting from her body. She inhaled the fragrance of the herbs, and she felt safe and warm. She let her thoughts drift. She dozed.

She was abruptly jolted back to reality by a loud knocking at her door.

"Who is it?" Zeidra called, jumping out of the bath and throwing her purple satin robe around her.

There was no answer, just another knock, this time harder.

"Who's there?" she demanded as she stood with her ear to the door.

"It's Niporo, open the door!"

"Niporo, didn't you receive my message?" Zeidra spoke through the door, struggling to find an acceptable reason not to open it.

"I wanted to know if you're alright. Please open the door." He was being quite insistent, and Zeidra didn't know how to answer his demand without making him suspicious.

"Niporo, it's only a headache, I'll be fine, please don't worry. I was just going to bed. I'm not dressed!"

"For god's sake, Zeidra, open the damned door!"

Slowly, Zeidra unlocked the door and opened it just enough to see Niporo's face. He was obviously upset, and she didn't want to upset him more.

"Don't you understand how I worry about you?" he said, pushing the door open and walking straight away into Zeidra's room.

"Niporo, I'm honestly sorry, but you can't

stay. I'm not dressed, and I really don't feel very well."

Niporo, was an aggressive, earthy type of man who was unimpressed by modesty and seldom took "*no*" for an answer. He walked over to Princess Zeidra and put a finger on her forehead.

"You have no headache," he announced bluntly. Arrogantly he went over to the bureau and poured two glasses of wine, returning to hand one to the Princess. "Drink this, you'll feel better if you do."

"I'm not used to being spoken to this way," Zeidra retorted, "and I don't much care for your attitude either!"

Niporo enjoyed the spice in her anger, which he had never seen before. He was stunned by Zeidra's natural beauty as she stood there clutching her robe tightly around her. Her face was aglow – a combination of anger and just being freshly scrubbed. Her hair was pinned up on the top of her head in a crown of golden curls. Wispy tendrils fell in unorganized ringlets down the back of her neck, some over her cheeks, others fell across her shoulders. The sight of the Princess looking so vulnerable enchanted Niporo. He had never seen her like this; it provoked his desire to *have* her.

"Come now, Zeidra." He reached out his hand. "I apologize if I upset you ... please forgive me." When Zeidra didn't accept his hand, he reached down and took hers. "Come on Zeidra ... let's sit down and talk about this," he said, leading her over to a lounge, where he sat down, and gently pulled Zeidra down beside him. "If you drink your wine and relax, you really will feel better." He paused. "We've been friends too long to let a little misunderstanding ruin it." He turned to Zeidra and tried to look hurt.

"Alright, Niporo," Zeidra said, "I don't know what's gotten into you this evening, but you are certainly in a distasteful mood." She took a sip of her wine. "I will forgive you," she continued, "but only this one time .... Do we agree?"

Niporo pressed her hand to his lips and kissed it.

"Thank you, for being understanding. We've been so close for so long, I guess I just forgot my place. I'll make this up to you. You're more important to me than you know. Besides ... didn't you want me to tell you about my homeland?" He took another drink of the wine.

"It doesn't seem important now," Zeidra said, withdrawing her hand from his. "It must have been just a passing curiosity." She took a sip of her wine. "I didn't mean to pry, you know."

"It's not a mystery, I'll tell you whatever

you want to know," he said. "In fact I want you to know ... you know?" He laughed a deep husky laugh that made Zeidra laugh, too. "I know that you know what I know I'm saying .... This is *your* kind of conversation, isn't it?!"

They both laughed easily.

"Well, then .... Tell me about your mother." Zeidra pulled one leg up under her as she turned to face Niporo.

"A feisty winch, she was!" Niporo chuckled.

"Is that all? Where was she born?"

"If I'm not mistaken, she came from the star system of Xylos."

Niporo got up and went to fill his glass with more wine.

Zeidra watched him as he moved across the floor. Niporo was a very good-looking man. He was mature and confident. It showed in his fluid movements and his arrogant style. He was wearing a tunic type shirt made from some kind of lightweight material. It clung to his broad back and shoulders. He was squarely built with massive muscles, which could never be hidden by his clothing. Even the muscles on the calves of his legs seemed to strain against his trousers. Although not as tall as Kyate, he was broader and more massive.

Niporo returned to the lounge with the

wine decanter. He filled her glass, which was still more than half full.

"Are you feeling better, yet?" he asked, putting the decanter down on the table in front of them.

Taking a drink of the wine to keep it from spilling, Zeidra nodded.

Niporo drank the entire glass of wine in one long drink, and he set the glass on the table beside the container. He sat down again, beside Zeidra, but this time he turned and put both hands on her shoulders, turning her slightly so that her back was facing him. He began to massage her shoulders and her neck.

At first Niporo felt her stiffen, but then she relaxed. As he continued manipulating the tight muscles around the back of her neck and across her shoulders, he rambled on and on about his family history. Zeidra's tense muscles were becoming pliant in Niporo's strong, sensuous hands. Now and then, she took a drink of her wine, or made a comment. She sat quietly, and made no effort to stop him.

After a while, Niporo gently eased Zeidra back against his muscular, warm chest, and began kneading her arms and her hands. She was compliant and peaceful.

He moved his lips against her ear.

"You know Zeidra, you and I have more in

common than you may think," Niporo said, his voice low and husky. He ran one finger up her arm and around the nape of her neck. She shivered.

"I want you to remember one thing," he said, and then he paused for a long moment. "No matter what might happen between us ..."

"What's that Niporo?" Zeidra interrupted, turning lazily to face him.

Gently cradling her face in his massive hands, he looked deep into her eyes. "I love you Zeidra," he said, "and I have for a long time."

Zeidra's body tensed. She tried to move away.

"Don't pull away ... this is hard enough for me to say." Niporo spoke slowly. "I don't want you to trust me, because I don't want to hurt you. You have to believe that I never want to hurt you."

In an instant he was kissing her, it was an insistent, demanding kiss. She was trapped in his massive arms. His kiss was brutal and unrelenting. She fought in vain to free herself.

Suddenly Niporo realized what he was doing. This was no village "harlot" he was trying to seduce! This was a royal Benjai Princess. He stopped himself.

"Get out!! Get out now!!" Zeidra screamed. She glared at the drunken Niporo, rubbing her bruised mouth with the back of her hand.

Fearing that she might call the guards, he obeyed her adamant command to leave, and he staggered to the door. He left.

Zeidra collapsed in tears, her body trembling with sobs and chills. She straightened her robe and tried to collect her thoughts. She ran her tongue over her lips; they felt sore and swollen. She couldn't quit thinking about it.

'What would she say to Niporo the next time she saw him? How could she be civil to him after this? It was all true!! Everything Kyate had said made sense now. Niporo had too much to drink and he'd all but confessed to Kyate's accusations.'

She sank down onto the lounge ashamed that she had allowed the scenario to escalate.

'Kyate shall NEVER hear of this! NEVER, – no matter what,' Zeidra vowed.

CHAPTER 8 – Passion's Price

It had been a long exhausting evening. Kyate was checking out the maintenance schedule for the fleet and plotting next week's maneuvers. He was glad to be finished.

Reflecting back on the events occurring earlier in the afternoon in his chambers with Zeidra, he was worried and concerned for her safety. Was he wise in telling her he had verification of Niporo's involvement in the Drothuarian plot? But then, if he hadn't, would she have been at risk by being deceived by the cunning Niporo? He would just have to stay as close to her as possible for the time being and try not to arouse Niporo's suspicion. When the time was right, he would confront Niporo and catch him off guard.

Walking across the Temple complex, on his way to his quarters, Kyate mauled it over in his mind. It was very late and the stillness was audible. The faint aroma of Night Blooming Jasmine caught his attention and stirred an immediate and intense association with the Princess Zeidra – the walk in the garden, the brief embrace, the kiss. But that had been weeks ago. And then, there was that inexplicable tenderness they had shared that very afternoon.

His stride quickened, as if to escape the scent of Jasmine in the air, and those forbidden emotions – those unholy thoughts Princess Zeidra seemed to arouse in his psyche.

Alone in his suite, Kyate removed his sword and his vest and began his evening ritual of movement, meditation, and prayer. He soon realized that he was having a hard time focusing; this preoccupation made it impossible to continue. He, the great Master Kyate, couldn't master his own concentration! It was her face, her hair, her eyes, her body, the smell of gardenia and jasmine – the Princess Zeidra was invading his solitude! He was off to the baths; an ice bath should do the trick! Kyate grabbed a thick towel and left his room heading straight for the complex spas.

When he reached the spas, Kyate literally tore off his clothing and lowered himself abruptly into the icy water. The shock was exhilarating. After a few minutes, his body adjusted to the low temperature, and he was able to relax. He lay back against the wall of the spa with his arms outstretched on the side of the deck. The night sky was luminous with the twinkling of stars everywhere. It was totally quiet except for a faint, fragrant breeze blowing across from the gardens, and rustling through the pines.

Kyate surveyed the courtyard, the great expanse of greens, and the gardens that surrounded it. Then he looked over toward the palaces where Princess Zeidra's chambers were located.

Immediately, a movement in one of the windows caught his attention. The figure was pacing back and forth past the window. Kyate instinctively interpreted the body language of Princess Zeidra, who was obviously distressed.

The Master stepped out of the ice bath, dried his body and slipped into his clothes. He sat down in a nearby lounge chair and began his relaxation breathing.

Quickly, he put himself into an altered state of consciousness. Leaving the confines of his physical body, he moved toward the window and into the room where he had seen the Princess.

Kyate was briefly immobilized, gazing upon this enchantress standing before him. Suspended in time, he surveyed Zeidra's body, which was scantily clad and fully feminine beneath the semitransparent garment she wore.

She grabbed the robe, which was lying across the chair, throwing it around her shoulders in an attempt to cover her flimsy nightgown. She kneeled down onto the floor, head bowed low in frustrated humiliation.

Kyate knew she sensed his presence. In his compassion for the anguish of a human in emotional pain, Kyate enfolded Princess Zeidra in his energy field. He intended to comfort her and warm her; to calm her and reassure her. He tuned into her emotions and understood what had happened here. He wanted to let her know she was safe.

What happened next was unexpected and inexcusable.

In an instant, the healing, calming energy field that Kyate had projected around Princess Zeidra changed into an electrifying, sensual pulsation, encompassing the princess and holding the source (Kyate) fast. What he had feared most, had happened – and at the worst possible moment. He had let his concentration wonder for only a second. That torturous, tempting sensation he had gone to the ice baths to rid his physical body of, had entered his consciousness in that one split second; when he had purposefully encircled the Princess Zeidra with his energy field.

Zeidra was unprepared for this extraordinary sensation. Confused and afraid, she struggled with the specter's energy, trying to counter the force. Unable to extricate her aura from his, the powerful entanglement was engulfing her being. The contradictory combination of pleasure and pain confounded her consciousness. The potency of Kyate's emotional energy was overwhelming her body, her mind, and her spirit. She was unable to fight the sensations. She was being inundated with Kyate's passion; she was now experiencing *it*, being possessed by *it*, and surrendering to *it*.

The intensity of the energy was rising. The Master was agonizing in the torment of the delirium. Kyate tried desperately to regain his concentration and center the energy field on healing and comfort. It was to no avail. Just witnessing the event taking place heightened his sexual desire and increased the ferocity of the sphere; it encircled and enveloped the Princess Zeidra.

In the drama of the moment, Kyate was able to feel every emotion and every physical sensation going on in Zeidra's body. He was becoming lost in the sensuality of his own indiscretion.

Zeidra began tearing at her nightgown. She was moaning and writhing.

"Please," she begged. "Please Master, stop this torment!" Ripping the material from her body she was sobbing and moaning more loudly. "Please, Master, I'm begging you!"

The Princess was trapped in Kyate's energy spiral; it was growing into a furious fever pitched passion.

Kyate felt that he was about to explode, and as he watched, Zeidra's nude body began convulsing in agony and she was screaming now, begging him for relief.

'What relief?!! If he had been able to control his energies, he would have stopped this already!'

He struggled with his spirit. The Princess was in torment. *'What relief could he offer, when even HE was caught up in this escalating vortex!'* He couldn't stop this insanity no matter how hard he fought it! Kyate wanted desperately to stop Zeidra's torture – and his own.

Without warning Kyate snapped. He allowed his very soul to enter the energy field; his astral body mounted the Princess and with a very tangible intensity, he entered her physical body and her astral body simultaneously. Kyate gave to her, that which had *NEVER* been given before. The desire was insatiable.

Kyate couldn't get enough! He was lost in Zeidra's passion and in his own. He realized that now Zeidra was feeling *his* feelings and experiencing *his* desire, as he was *hers*. They had become *ONE*. Kyate and Zeidra were united in *one* mind, *one* body, and *one* unrestrained intensity.

It kept building and building - passion fueled by passion. It was amazing; Kyate could feel her pleasure and his own concurrently. It felt as physical as it was spiritual.

For the first time, Kyate understood that the intensity of *sexual* energy in an astral body is just as tangible as in the physical, yet much more complex and even more explosive when reciprocal.

The intensity of the pleasure was reaching that explosive point of no return. Kyate desperately wanted to materialize his body. He compromised. He materialized all but that which he was forced to deny.

Catching Zeidra's face between his two muscular hands, he covered her mouth with his, to silence her cries. Zeidra was being devoured by Kyate's eagerness. As she melted into his kiss, Kyate released her face and began caressing her entire body, memorizing every inch of it as his hands explored her flesh.

Zeidra was right on the brink of fulfillment. She was screaming. Kyate reached deep inside her with his own soul. He bore into her very being, to bring forth all the pent up feelings and emotions of a lifetime, in one convulsive, climactic surge.

Zeidra shuddered. Kyate braced himself,

pounding his passion into hers. Suddenly, the entire universe exploded; taking with it two souls locked in *oneness*. It was the dance of the spirit – two completely merged souls dancing out across the cosmos in an erotic ballet seldom experience by mortals.

It was over. Princess Zeidra laid half-conscious on the floor. Her face flushed and her naked body limp and wet with perspiration. Kyate gazed at her lovingly for a long time. He decided that the kindest thing he could do, at this point, would be to eradicate her recollection of the entire episode. Otherwise guilt and embarrassment would devastate her. Another very good reason to remove her memory would be to erase the event for his own sake. – The "Great Master" had permitted the circumstances to evolve into a physical frenzy – sexual passions out of control – and no one must ever know this truth.

Kyate placed his forefinger on Zeidra's invisible spiritual eye, and injected a thin tendril of energy directly into her most current memory center. It was done. She was unharmed, her virginity intact. '*She would probably think she had experienced a bizarre dream.*'

He knew, in his soul, however, that there was nothing he could do to alleviate the erotic connection he had made with her astral body.

He could only surmise what repercussions to expect from her carnal awakening. He could only pray that it wouldn't happen!

There were sounds outside the chambers, and fearing that he would be discovered, Kyate decided to protect himself by disappearing as quickly as possible. He paused, realizing he should remove Zeidra's self-inflicted lacerations, but he dared not take the time!

Allowing himself one last look at Zeidra's sensuous form; unconscious there on the floor, he hesitated. Kyate wanted to scoop her up into his arms and tuck her into her cozy bed, but knew that he couldn't risk it.

Taking a deep cleansing breath, the Master de-materialized the body he'd created in the throes of passion.

He retreated slowly back to where he left his true physical body. Nearly drained of all energy, he melted into the resting form stretched out on the lounge. Slowly the movement began in the extremities. After a few moments, Kyate was able to stand and walk.

CHAPTER 9 – Earth Is Under Attack

The sky pulsated with brilliant white and red flashes. The Earth trembled beneath the explosive impact of the enemy assault. Dawn was breaking over Ulonica. The Earth was under siege.

This time it was the dreaded Drothuarians. They had come to claim what had always belonged to them. Their first military priority was to destroy the Alicupions; their second objective was to control the sacred house of Benjai. The Deis fleet, present in the vicinity, posed no threat to the mighty Drothuarian forces. The Drothuarians were blatantly disregarding the few ships that had been deployed to Ulonica by the Galactic Council.

All inhabitants of the Earth were considered expendable, save the Princess Zeidra. Some others, however, would be saved, in order to use them as *breeders*. It all depended on the genetic code – their DNA.

The Drothuarian destroyer ships were sweeping across the planet using a variety of death rays and poison gasses, selectively eliminating all humans not carrying the DNA considered desirable. The ships hovered over cities and villages using scanning equipment that could zero in on an individual human, from miles above the clouds. The scanner would systematically read the DNA coding, as the cryptograph passed over the source. If the subjects passed the scan, they could live. If not, they were destroyed.

At the same time, the heavenly battles were being waged against the *Grays*. The Drothuarians were mercilessly seeking out all Alicupion bases, scout ships, and mother ships, in hopes of totally annihilating the entire force of *Grays* stationed anywhere within the star system.

Niporo sat bolt upright! He was receiving a telepathic message from his command. "Increased security is now necessary. Invasion implemented. You're immediate attention to be directed at keeping Alicupions from the Benjai. End transmission."

Niporo knew the invasion was due to take place, but he wasn't prepared for it to be implemented so soon. These events would mean a more desperate attempt by the Alicupions to capture the temple, and be the first to control the genetics of the House of Benjai. This was a serious situation. The Princess Zeidra was to be protected at all costs.

Leaping from his lounge, Niporo dashed through his suite and out into the courtyard, pulling his jersey over his head as he sprinted through the gardens toward the quarters of the Princess Zeidra.

When he reached her doors, Niporo stopped to catch his breath and compose himself. He couldn't afford to alarm the Princess, although it was important for him to keep her in his sight for at least the next forty-eight hours. His mind was racing, struggling to find just the right excuse to disturb Zeidra at this early morning hour; especially considering his behavior the last time he saw her.

He knocked softly on the door. No response. He knocked again, this time a little louder. No response.

'For god's sake Zeidra, get the hell up and open the damned door!' Niporo literally pounded on the door.

He felt apprehensive; something was wrong. He tried the door. It was locked. He knocked again. No answer. Taking a deep breath, he engaged his source, and with the strength of five men, he literally ripped the door from its hinges.

Inside the royal apartments, all was quiet. Niporo rushed through the reception chambers as he called out Zeidra's name. No reply. Outside the bedroom door, he took a deep breath, not knowing what to expect, he slowly lifted the latch and the door opened easily.

Time stood still. Niporo stood at the doorway desperately trying to make some sense of what he was seeing. His first impulse was to rush into the room and over to the nude body of the princess lying in the middle of the floor … *Was she dead?'*

He collected himself, in the cool manner of a Drothuarian; he divorced his emotions, and silently drew his high frequency amplifier weapon from the leather pouch on his hip. Slowly – cautiously, he entered the room, using his three hundred sixty degree vision as he carefully approached the lifeless form of his beloved.

All Niporo's special senses were now engaged. He was picking up life energy. *'Was there someone still in the room, or was Princess Zeidra actually alive?'* He realized as he came closer, that Zeidra was breathing easily, her life signs were normal. She appeared to be in a deep sleep.

There was no sign of forced entry. All windows were locked tightly. There was no sign of a struggle. All of the furniture and accessories were neatly in place.

"What the hell is going on here?" Niporo spoke aloud as he noticed the huge draped bed, which hadn't been slept in.

He turned his attention back to Princess Zeidra. Returning his weapon to its pouch, he knelt down beside the princess and ran his hands over her energy field to test its strength and balance. All was normal. She looked, however, as if she had been attacked. Her nightgown was lying in shreds beside her. Her hair was a tangled mess, still wet with perspiration. Her cheeks were flushed and swollen as if she had been slapped again and again. She had long scarlet scratches running length wise from her neck, over both breasts and down her stomach.

She didn't move.

"Zeidra," Niporo whispered, trying to rouse her gently.

He suddenly realized that he was gazing upon the naked body of the Princess Zeidra, who had for so long been the object of his fantasies. Right now, however, it almost seemed sacrilegious to look at her. At this moment, Niporo only cared that Zeidra was alive. He couldn't even allow himself to touch her, although he couldn't leave her there on the floor.

"Zeidra, wake up." He spoke louder this time as he gently brushed the hair away from her face.

She moaned softly and turned her head ever so slightly. She did not open her eyes.

Niporo scooped the nude body up into his arms and rose easily to his feet. Zeidra's skin was warm and fragrant and moist. Her body was limp. He carried her over to the bed and gently laid her across it. He felt the rage welling up from deep inside his being. A feeling of betrayal was seething into his consciousness.

"Who did this?!" he shouted hoarsely, turning on his heel and pacing over to the window then back to the bed. Grabbing both of Princess Zeidra's shoulders, he shook her violently. "Wake up, goddamit!" he snarled. "Tell me who the hell did this to you!" Zeidra felt like a rag doll in Niporo's hands.

Awakening to the violent shaking and trying to focus her eyes, Zeidra's head was snapping back and forth with the force of the abuse.

Realizing that Zeidra was waking up, Niporo instantly regained control of his emotions and released her shoulders. Zeidra fell back heavily onto the bed as if she'd been dropped five feet.

Her brain felt fuzzy. She couldn't think. She seemed to be numb all over. Her mouth was so dry. Her body was too heavy to move. She tried to focus her eyes on the figure looming in front of her. She tried to speak but couldn't.

Niporo disappeared from the room briefly,

returning with a glass of cold nectar. He raised Zeidra's head from the bed and held the glass to her lips. She took a few sips and then sank back on his arm, too weak to hold her head up.

She tried to speak, again. This time, finding her voice, she whispered faintly, "Niporo .... What are you doing here? I don't know ... what happened .... I feel as if I've been drugged."

"That's it!" Niporo said. "Some sonofabitch drugged you, then attacked you! I'll kill the bastard!" The veins on his neck were bulging, and his face was practically blue with rage. "Who was it?" he demanded loudly. "Who were you with last night?"

He hurled the glass across the room. It smashed against the wall and disintegrated into a million pieces, raining glass everywhere. "Who the hell did it?" His voice was suddenly very low and husky with passionate jealousy as he spoke through clenched teeth.

Frightened, Zeidra managed to turn over to bury her face in the softness of the bed. She tried hard to think, to remember. She was afraid Niporo would surely strike her if she didn't give him the answer to his question. She still wasn't thinking clearly.

"Did what to me?" she cried into the mattress. She couldn't understand his anger.

That rage was terrifying to her. She had never seen him this upset.

Without warning, Niporo snatched Zeidra from the bed and set her feet down hard in front of the full-length mirror standing beside the divan.

"This is *WHAT!*" he yelled, pointing to the reflection in the mirror. His throat was tight with emotion.

The jolt seemed to bring back Zeidra's senses, somewhat. She stood there looking into the mirror, at a totally bare body, covered with ugly bloody scratches all the length of the torso. It occurred to her that it was *her* body. She caught her breath and cried out softly as she saw her matted hair and her swollen face.

She gasped out loud. Suddenly the room began to spin and she could hear a roaring sound in her ears. The light was fading and she felt as if she were falling. Collapsing into Niporo's strong arms she lapsed back into semi consciousness.

Niporo lifted her, holding her tight against his chest, he carried her once more, back to the bed. He stood for a moment just staring off into time, clutching that soft warm body closely against him. Finally, he lowered his head and buried his face in her hair. A tear slid down his cheek. He laid her on the bed and pulled the sheet up over her nakedness.

He numbly went to the intercom and

summoned the temple physicians.

When they arrived, he gave a full report of what he had discovered. He then gave orders for the temple guard to be posted at all entrances to the chambers. He asked to be notified when the physicians had made their diagnosis. He left.

The first rays of morning light shown through the louvers of the shutters, casting long gray shadows across the floor and up over the bed in the room where the Master Kyate was sleeping.

The sheets on the bed were tangled and knotted by perpetual tossing and turning. The restless sleeper had been granted no reprieve from his troubled spirit. He fought an endless night, desperate for sleep which finally came just as the first misty-white glimmer of dawn crept over the horizon.

Even in sleep, Master Kyate was unable to escape the mental anguish inflicted by his self-imposed guilt. He demanded of himself perfection in all areas of his life – spiritual, emotional, mental, physical, and moral superiority.

This past evening, Kyate had violated every one of his personal convictions; and he had, without sanction, victimized and defiled the spiritual and emotional virtue of the only living princess of the House of Benjai; the princess he had vowed to protect with his life!

Even if the Princess Zeidra didn't remember the events of the nighttime visit in detail, she would never again be the same. Although physically intact, fervid emotions and carnal desires had been awakened. Those feelings, once aroused, seek their own consummation. That primordial, primitive instinct becomes a living entity, demanding its own exploration and perpetuation.

In a sense, Kyate had opened *Pandora's Box.*

Somewhere a million miles away, an alarm was sounding. Kyate rolled over onto his back and flung his arms out to his sides. As he lay sprawled on the bed, he was vaguely annoyed at the insistence of the irritating sound.

Kyate felt the Earth tremble, and a flash of light swept across the sky outside.

Suddenly he realized the alarm was emanating from his own portable Command Control Unit, and it was alerting him of enemy attack vehicles detected in the immediate vicinity.

Leaping from the bed, not yet fully awake, he wrestled with the tuning aperture on the unit to determine the source, destination, and identity of the incoming threat ...'*Who was staging this attack?'*

The readout was on the screen – two Alicupion gunships, headed due north at 556.8, four Drothuarian inter-dimensional destroyers headed due north at 972.5. The distance between the two, 790.2 with the Drothuarians closing fast. Location – Ulonica.

Kyate deciphered the readout and discovered that the Drothuarian and Alicupion ships were only six hundred miles out of Ulonican territory at this time; and the Drothuarians were deploying offensive weapons against the Alicupions in seven separate sky grids.

'What could this mean?' Kyate rubbed his hands hard over his brow and back over his hair. He shook his head, trying to clear his brain. *'If the Drothuarians are staging an offensive strategy against the Alicupions, my god, we're in for a three-way conflict!'* Kyate's mind was racing now.

He promptly tuned the frequency of the control unit to the Deis Command communiqué band to brief headquarters of the new twist of events. Then he enacted the red alert, which would call all Deis warriors in the area to report immediately.

Kyate quickly encoded orders for his generals into the command unit, with instructions that they be carried out upon reception, and that he would stay behind just long enough to establish contact with the reinforcements from Deis Command – the squadrons that had been secretly stationed within the star system.

Only moments later, the fleet was assembled and ready for an emergency deployment.

The reconnaissance division was ordered out first, followed by twenty-seven Deis antimatter accelerator craft.

Dressing hurriedly, he mentally assessed the situation, planning alternative strategies depending upon what would develop once the enemy was encountered. The problem at hand was in determining what the reaction would be when the Deis war ships appeared in the middle of a two-way battle; and which group would react first – the Drothuarians or the Alicupions?

Kyate decided not to wait to see who would attack first. He ordered the generals to attack the Drothuarians and the Alicupions simultaneously. The plan was to try and catch both groups by surprise.

Pulling on his boots and grabbing his laser sword, Kyate bolted from his chambers. He headed toward the temple's military wing to brief the officers there. Emergency procedures needed to be implemented; and it was imperative to initiate a plan to seal off and defend the temple complex in case of any infiltration attempts by the Drothuarians or the Alicupions.

At the same time, Niporo was in the process of contacting the Drothuarian command ship to warn the squadron of the approaching Deis destroyers.

Just as he was finishing his transmission, there was a knock at his door.

"Enter," Niporo barked impatiently.

A temple surgeon entered the room. "She's intact, Sir."

"Are you telling me she wasn't raped?"

"No sir .... No rape ... we're not sure what happened, but she definitely wasn't sexually molested."

"Come on, man .... How do you explain her condition when I found her? What about the scratches ... the bruises? You can't tell me she wasn't attacked!"

"Her virginity is intact."

"Well I'll be damned ...," Niporo sat down thoughtfully on the lounge. "I would have sworn some sonofabitch got to her!"

"No sir, we're sure of it."

"Very well, you may go .... No wait. Is she conscious?"

"Not right now. We administered a sedative."

"Very good, thank you," Niporo said, motioning the man out. This was it. He knew what he had to do.

Niporo waited until the man left the building, and began implementing his plan. Rummaging through his belongings, he packed only the necessities that he needed for a trip.

Slinging the heavy bag over his shoulder, Niporo ran across the green and onto the tarmac. Spotting a small Deis scout ship, he checked to see that no one was looking, then climbed aboard, tossing the bag in, ahead of him. Once inside, he powered up the propulsion mechanism and set the throttle to idle. Hurriedly he programmed the coordinates needed to guide the ship to the area of Urampa. He was sure he could safely hide the princess there.

Niporo jumped out onto the rim of the ship, looking around cautiously. He descended the ladder and headed for the royal chambers.

"Niporo, where are you off to?"Niporo turned to see Llana coming around the other side of the craft.

"Taking a little trip, are you ... Don't I get to come?"

"There's an invasion taking place here! Don't waste your time talking .... You'd better get your little ass to some safe place. All hell's going to break out here!" Niporo called over his shoulder as he sprinted across the green.

Niporo came to an abrupt halt at the

Royal Chamber doors, and face to face with one of the court's armed officers.

"I'm afraid the princess can't be disturbed," the guard said curtly.

"Get the hell out of my way," Niporo screamed, smashing the man on the side of the head with his laser; dropping him to the pavement.

Niporo stormed into Zeidra's chambers, packed some things as quickly as he could. Then, scooping the princess up into his arms he quickly rushed out the rear entrance heading back to the tarmac and the waiting ship.

As he neared the craft, he noticed one of Kyate's men inspecting the controls inside the cockpit. Quietly he laid the princess down on the pavement below the hull, and he crept up the ladder engaging his laser weapon just as he reached the hatch.

"Looking for something?" he asked, pointing the gun at the surprised Deis Commander.

It was Jason. "This ship isn't authorized for transport!"

"Sorry son... It is now!"

With one burst from the laser, Jason lay bleeding on the floor of the cockpit. Niporo dragged him to the door and rolled him out. His body bounced down onto the tarmac with a dull thud. Niporo hurried down the ladder and over to the princess. Lifting her limp form up and over his shoulder, he picked up the bag and climbed back into the craft. Within moments the craft was humming and hovering above the ground. Niporo switched on the electronic navigation system and the ship streaked up into the heavens and out of sight.

CHAPTER 10 – Heartbreak and Desperation

The geo-sphere was illuminated with red points indicating the Drothuarian positions, and yellow points indicating the Alicupion targets. Several of the Deis ships had already been dispatched to the area of activity and were being monitored by flashing white points on the grids.

"Now take heed, men," Kyate said, drawing a series of rings around the grid where the combat was most concentrated, "your main objective is to keep the areas outside of these perimeters secure. You've got to apply every bit of cunning you possess; you've got to think like a Drothuarian. Second-guess their each and every move on the Alicupions – Beat 'em at their own game." He whirled around to face the warriors. "If they succeed in defeating those gray monsters and make a run at our forces, in the confusion, they could very well breach the confines of the complex here. If that were to happen, and we aren't able to route the enemy ... then our primary concern would then be the Princess... *ONLY* the princess." Kyate's right hand was twitching on the handle of the sword that rested against his hip. He rubbed his chin hard with his left hand. He was thoughtful for a moment, contemplating the consequences of a direct Drothuarian assault on the complex. Beads of perspiration were appearing on his brow. The Master slammed a heavy fist down on the table in front of him. "That's it men, do your best! You know what the mission is. We will accomplish this mission at *ALL COSTS*. Are there any questions?" He studied the tense faces of his compatriots. There was no response – just a strained silence. "All right then, get on with it!"

The command had been given. The room emptied hastily, and Kyate quickly returned to his rooms to check in with the Galactic Council. His secret call for backup needed to be confirmed, especially now.

With the last transmission finalized, and the entire fleet of Deis warriors mobilized, Kyate bolted through the doors and out across the greens toward the Princess Zeidra's residence. Halfway down the corridor and in sight of Zeidra's chambers, Kyate knew something was terribly awry. He could see the huge double doors standing wide open, and an inanimate body sprawled out on the marble floor at the entrance. His heart rate doubled as he ran toward the guard. He had a sinking feeling in his gut; he vaguely remembered that gut-wrenching knot in his psyche – he'd had it only one time before.

"What happened to the Princess?" he shouted, nearly choking on the words.

The guard tried to sit up, but lost his balance and fell back onto the white stone floor. "Niporo," he moaned, struggling to stay his consciousness, "Niporo took her ... I ... tried to stop him ... no use... I know not where ..." His voice evaporated into the air as if being pulled along with his spirit, which was leaving his body at that moment. He was dead.

The Master dragged the guard's body inside Zeidra's quarters and closed the doors behind him. Standing outside, looking across the courtyard, he felt the panic clutching at his core. An eternity seemed to pass before his mind's eye. He had no time to waste. He quickly pulled his emotions into the confines of his iron will and directed his energies into the ether to try and gain some sense of direction. *'Which way had Niporo taken her? How could they have escaped?'* Breathing deeply, Kyate began walking toward the military complex; then he was running. The essence of the Princess was faint but still lingered, and Kyate followed it with the insistence of a lion stalking his prey.

There was screaming; '... *not Zeidra ... who was screaming?*' Kyate could see the tarmac now.

"Master Kyate! Oh my god! Master Kyate!!" Shanta screamed hysterically when she saw Kyate approaching. "... My god! Jason, Oh my god!" She sank down into the pool of blood on the gray surface, beside the body of Kyate's best friend Jason.

Kyate felt his spine turn to ice as he approached the body, and realized that in fact it *was* Jason. Nearly paralyzed by the shock, he stopped beside Shanta and stared down at her blankly.

"He's dead, Master!" Shanta was wiping her eyes with her blood soaked skirt. "I don't know what happened... I just found him here ... like this ..." She was choking between sobs. "Oh my god, Oh my Jason ... How could this happen?!" Shanta started to scream again in hysterics. Kissing Jason all over his face as if she thought that would revive him; she was suddenly oblivious to Kyate's presence. "I want to be with you, my Jason... Oh Jason I will be with you... Oh please, God, let this not be true!!!" She continued the kissing and caressing; she was virtually covered with Jason's blood; it was a gruesome and heart-wrenching spectacle.

"Shanta ... come girl." Kyate spoke

numbly, trying to pull the maiden off his dead friend's body. Shanta clung on to Jason's limp corpse like a lost child clinging to her tattered rag doll.

"You can't bring him back … you've got to get to safety …" He lifted her, bodily, and held her fast. The girl fought Kyate's hold, grasping for her dead lover.

"Jason would want you to go to safety … come on now, pull yourself together!" He spoke firmly now.

Something about the authority in Kyate's voice seemed to jog her senses. She stopped struggling and looked up into the Master's eyes. His face appeared to be gray steel frozen solid; his expression was devoid of all emotion.

"I loved him, too," Kyate stated quietly, feeling his world sinking as he spoke, yet managing well, to conceal his pain. "I need you to be strong. I need your help." Kyate spoke gently as he brushed the crimson stained curls away from Shanta's bloody, tear-streaked face. "Princess Zeidra's gone. Niporo took her. Nobody else knows – only the two of us, right now. We've got to work together and find her, but you can't tell a soul she's missing. We just can't risk the widespread panic it would cause." Kyate scooped the weakened girl up into his arms and turning toward the dormitories, he didn't allow himself to look back. Shanta wrestled to free herself from Kyate's strong arms; not wanting to leave her beloved. It was no use.

In his chambers Kyate laid Shanta's weary form on his bed. She sobbed intermittently while he attempted to wash the blood from her face and hands. He read her thoughts and felt her emotions: *'The cool cloth felt like sandpaper on her irritated skin. The vision of Jason lying there dead, all bloody and still; it kept invading her mind, each time to elicit the pain and grief all over again.'*

Kyate's heart was heavy. *'How could he comfort her when he needed comforting himself? He must remain strong."*

Precious time was being lost while Kyate attended to Shanta. He knew full well, it was imperative to proceed with finding the Princess right away. He had to get a reading on her. With his left hand on his solar plexus, he placed his right hand on Shanta's heart. Taking a long, deep breath, he expelled the calming, healing energy necessary to accelerate Shanta's sense of wellbeing. She sighed, and then peacefully drifted into a deep and tranquil sleep state. Kyate desperately wished he could accommodate himself in the same way.

With no time to waste, Kyate raced back to the tarmac, relieved to find that Jason's body had been removed. He quickly surveyed the area for an available craft. He needed urgently to get up above the Earth atmosphere where the ethers were more stable. He wanted to get a fix on Zeidra's and Niporo's location. He spotted an XR-28 just ahead, and he wasted no time getting aboard and firing her up. The hum of the propulsive inner core was a comforting sound to Kyate's psyche. Slowly the ship rose from the tarmac. It hovered and then shot straight up into the misty, colorless heavens. Kyate was alone – alone as never before.

He left Earth below. He could see the combat forces engaged in the distance. The bright, white-blue flashes of pulsed phasers were distinctly contrasted against the gray canopy shrouding the Earth. He knew his warriors were literally in the fight of their lives, but he was unable to dwell on their predicament. He was directly responsible for the welfare of the Princess Zeidra; and he had failed her, along with his sacred Deis Command. He was bound by honor and duty to retrieve the Benjai, no matter what the sacrifice; even if it meant his own men.

Kyate's soul was frustrated with sorrow. He tuned into the ethers and could feel nothing – no sense of the Princess – no essence of her left. He was too late. He ventured out into the void further and further. He continued his search, while the war in the heavens above Earth escalated.

"Get a fix on the gray to your right!" shouted Meno, rotating the cube to get a closer look. "You better get him or we're *gonners*!"

"This one's in the bag, SIR!" the first gunner yelled back.

"Well then fire it! What in blazes are you waiting for?!! You want us to meet our maker today, or what?!!!!" Meno rushed over to where the gunner was stationed and in one determined lunge hit the firing node on the console, releasing the lethal ray that immediately disintegrated the Alicupion ship. Watching the gigantic bursts of blue-green, and white exploding particle beams meeting matter, the entire crew breathed a sigh of relief in unison; the immediate threat to the Deis fleet was over.

The first gunner just looked at Meno and shook his head.

"I would've handled it, Sir!" he said, "I was going ..."

"Sir, the Drothuarians are undetectable!" The first mate moved in a frenzy, trying to locate the group of Drothuarian gunners that he'd been tracking. "I swear I had them in range just a moment ago! Check the scouts on the perimeter and see if they've got 'em!"

Meno moved to the command unit. He booted up the scanner system and took a real-time reading on all coordinates. – Nothing. "Boost the amplifiers! I'll contact the periphery!" Meno dove into the pilot seat, locked the harnesses and programmed the craft for an acute dive. "Hold onto your hats. – Here we go, men!"

Messages were pouring in on the console.

"Sir – Word from periphery is in!" the communications officer yelled, "DROTHUARIANS HAVE BREACHED PERIMETER... DEPLOY ALL AVAILABLE BACKUP TO COMPLEX AREA... ULONICA NOW UNDER SIEGE... BENJAI AT RISK... REPEAT ... BENJAI AT RISK ..." He read each word slowly as it crossed the screen in front of him.

"Good god! We've let 'em through!" Meno screamed in rage. "Those devils'll be hard to stop once they set those ships on Ulonican soil!!" He swiveled the chair around to face his crew. "It's serious! I've been in this situation before!" Meno's face looked tense, and his words were catching in his throat. "Let's take 'er in, boys! Let's see if we can beat 'em to the ground!" Meno turned back to the console and set the course directly toward the Drothuarian fleet.

"I'm getting a message, sir!" The communications officer was impatiently watching the video display terminal in front of him. "Our guys on the edge have lost nine! Twelve Drothuarian ships breached the perimeter and are approaching the Temple Complex. Twenty of ours are in pursuit – seven are holding the remainder of the Drothuarians, but need help *FAST*!!!" he screamed across to Meno.

"OK! Get on the horn and reroute the rest of our group to intercept those scoundrels! We sure as hell don't want to lose any more of our ships!" Meno barked.

"If they get into the complex what'll we do?" the first mate asked in an ominous tone, looking over at Meno.

"Well, I'd hope to hell Master Kyate has that situation under control by now!" Meno's demeanor was intent. He prayed under his breath that Kyate had a plan, although he'd had no communication with him for hours now. This was most irregular.

"Another message, sir!" The communications officer yelled out the message, "FIVE ON THE GROUND... ALL HAVE BROKEN THROUGH... TEMPLE COMPLEX UNDER SIEGE ..." Suddenly, the young man jumped to his feet. "... Oh god! I've lost 'em! My transmission was interrupted!! Oh NO!! They're gone, sir!! They got the surveillance craft!"

"No choice any more, men ... We're going

in. This'll be a ground fight now. Radio the others! Get 'em all in there *FAST!!! – DO IT, DAMNIT!!"* Meno's apprehension was tangible. He wiped the sweat off his face with his forearm.

The Deis Warriors were going in. They had annihilated the Alicupions in the air, but failed to deter the Drothuarians. This was the very worst scenario. Now they had to be concerned with the civilian population as well as their own men. This complication should have been avoided. Meno, as commander of the Deis fleet, knew that his responsibility had now escalated.

'Please Dear God... don't let me fail this time!' Meno silently pled with his Creator.

CHAPTER 11 – The Sacrificial Flames

Shanta stirred. She could hear muffled explosions outside. The intense flashes of light permeated the darkened room. She sat upright on the bed, trying to make out the voices coming from the corridor outside the chamber. She remembered. Jason! She turned and swung her legs over the side of the high bed. It all came flooding back to her consciousness. – The war – Princess Zeidra. She remembered what Kyate told her about Niporo taking Zeidra, and that not one living soul would know, save she and Kyate alone. *'Jason ... her beloved Jason was dead! How could she go on?'* Shanta ran her hands back over her matted hair. Sliding down off the side of the bed, she dazedly tiptoed over to the shuttered windows and peered through the louvers. She rubbed her eyes with the backs of her hands and strained to see out into the courtyards. Every now and then an explosion would light up the entire area, and she could see the chaotic activity; people seemed to be running in all directions.

She heard two men talking excitedly, right outside.

"They're here! The Drothuarians are coming over the walls as we speak!" the one man said nervously.

"What'll we do ... they're after the Princess! I pray she's hidden well by now!"

The two ran off toward the military quarters leaving Shanta alone, and frightened, and confused.

'Where is Kyate? Has he found Zeidra? What am I to do? Poor Jason!' Shanta questioned herself. She paced back and forth across the room wringing her hands, stopping now and then to listen for sounds outside. She felt dizzy. Making her way back to the bed, across the darkened room, she climbed back up onto it and lay down on her stomach. She buried her face into the soft comforter and cried quietly. She pounded the mattress with her fists in frustration.

"They're searching the complex! Those Drothuarians are looking for the Princess!" a voice yelled from the corridor.

"Is she hidden?!" another voice called out. "No one's seen her for hours!" The voices faded out of hearing range and were gone.

Rolling over on her back, Shanta stared blankly at the ceiling. She felt a peculiar calmness, which seemed illogical under the circumstances. In her mind she was formulating a plan; it was a plan that would possibly end the war, put her spirit to rest, possibly reunite her soul with Jason's, and may in fact save the revered Princess Zeidra.

"I'm a genius!" Shanta whispered to the dark.

The girl quickly jumped from the bed and ran quietly to the door. Opening it just a crack, she peeked into the hallway to make sure no one was there. Assured that she wouldn't be seen, the maiden slipped out into the corridor and made her way to the giant doors leading to the courtyards beyond. The chaos had intensified. People were oblivious to what was happening; each trying to find safety as the Drothuarians invaded the complex.

Silently and unnoticed, Shanta crossed the courtyards, making sure to stay close to the growth of vines and shrubs that lined the walkways. Every now and then, one of those explosive bursts of light illuminated the heavens and Earth. Stopping, she crouched beside the vegetation. She waited until all was safely dark; then she continued on. She scurried across the green in the direction of the Royal Chambers.

Upon reaching Zeidra's residence, she carefully crept up to a window. She saw several Drothuarian officers milling around the inner chambers. She moved to the rear window and looked into the dressing area. No one was to be seen. Shanta silently opened the dressing room window and very carefully climbed through. Once inside the room, she knew exactly where to find what she needed.

Moments later she escaped undetected and bolted across the esplanade to the Temple of Meditation; she disappeared inside. The girl hurriedly ascended the inner spiral staircase, climbing to the top of the pyramid to the "Plateau of the Bells". She dropped the bundle, which she had smuggled out of Zeidra's rooms. Opening it up, she withdrew a long purple satin, hooded cloak, the drug, and a large jar of holy oil.

Shanta raised the vial of concentrated opiate, and emptied it into her mouth. She consumed every drop. Squirming quickly into the cloak, she pulled the hood up over her head, and then down as far as she could, to conceal her face.

Carefully, she lifted the container of oil up over her head. Tipping it slowly, she allowed the oil to run over the hood and down the entire length of the garment, fully saturating the material. The musky scent of the oil was warm and pleasant, soothing her wounded senses. She dipped her hands into the puddle of oil, which was accumulating at her feet.

Ever so deliberately, Shanta massaged the pungent oil into her skin, applying it liberally to her face, her neck, and her arms. When she had finished, she knelt down and prayed a simple prayer:

"Heavenly Father, please accept this selfish sacrifice that it might benefit those whom I love and reunite my spirit with that of my beloved. Forgive me for my weaknesses, but acknowledge my courage also. I pray that in my death there may be the hope of life for this people, an end to the fighting, and a renewed peace on this Earth. Into your hands I commend my spirit."

The drug was beginning to take effect. Struggling to her feet, in the heavy, oil-soaked attire, Shanta removed one of the torches from its holder and walked over to the bell tower. She took a long deep breath and swallowed hard. Fighting back her tears, she reached for the cord attached to all five of the huge bells, which were housed in the tower. These bells were rung only during times of special significance to the Benjai people.

Taking the cord in her hand she gave a hard pull. The bells barely began to swing – no sound was made. Again she tugged hard on the cord, this time using her entire weight; she struggled with the ropes. The swing was gaining momentum. She pulled a third time. This time the bells began to ring. One last time she strained at the end of the bell cord. The bells were tolling loudly now and continued after she released her hold. She ran through the doors of the tower and emerged outside on the gallery of the great central structure. Carrying the torch with her, she lit the great beacons, which stood on either side of the balcony. With the bells pealing, and the huge beacons lighting the entire complex, Shanta was clearly visible at the summit of the temple.

In awe, everyone stopped and looked up. Not one person moved. Not the civilians – Not the military – Not the Drothuarians. An unearthly silence overtook the entire complex. The bells had stopped ringing. Even the gunships had stopped firing. Everything appeared to be in a state of suspended animation. The entire world seemed to be focused on the purple clad figure at the top of the pyramid. Everyone watching was convinced the figure was, in fact, the Princess Zeidra. A crowd was gathering on the esplanade, staring in silent apprehension.

Standing there with the torch in her hand, Shanta surveyed the incredible scene below and above.

Slowly she brought the torch ever closer to her garments. A dreadful uneasiness gripped the populace. There were gasps and horrified screams, and several men ran to the temple, frantically scrambling up the steep steps, uselessly trying to reach their princess; to stop her.

Shanta touched the flame of the torch to the oil soaked cloak, and the material ignited in a fury of blue and red fire.

Shrieks of terror echoed through the crowd gathered near the base of the temple pyramid. There was a profound sense of panic, helplessness, then loss and sorrow for all of those witnessing the sacrifice. For all intent, it appeared to be an act of desperation, in order to safeguard the sacred gene, and keep the Benjai line free from the defilement of the Drothuarians and Alicupions.

The flames continued to burn white hot, consuming the frail figure wrapped inside what was once purple satin. No one could get close enough to extinguish the conflagration. It was all consuming. It was the infallible eradication of an identity.

As the inferno transformed itself into a mound of smoldering ash, a melancholy hush seemed to fall upon the land of Ulonica. Without the Benjai succession, what would become of Ulonica?

CHAPTER 12 – The Stowaway

Llana shifted her body restlessly in the cargo bay of the craft. She crawled out from behind some crates and quietly raised the hatch to peer into the cabin. All was quiet. She could see into the lounge area and quickly inventoried the scene. Niporo was sprawled out over a berth, sleeping peacefully, while Zeidra lay in a drugged stupor on a couch next to him. Beyond the lounge, was the control room; housing the communication equipment. It was Llana's nearly impossible destination.

She snaked her body through the hatch and wriggled along the floor of the craft until she was close enough to the Princess Zeidra to touch her. Slowly reaching toward Zeidra, Llana's attention was suddenly drawn to Niporo. She stopped short and immediately withdrew her outstretched arm. Niporo rolled over onto his right side and moaned hoarsely. He flung his left arm over the side of the berth. Llana could feel his heavy breathing on her cheek now as his left hand dangled ominously in front of her face. She flattened her body against the cold metal flooring. Sliding backward, she cautiously retreated back to the cargo bay hatch, and disappeared down through the opening.

She crawled to the far corner of the enclosure and sat down cross-legged behind a huge container. Burying her face in her hands, Llana sighed with relief. It was a close call ... too close. Wearily, she leaned backward and relaxed against the wall. She would wait. She slept.

Llana awoke with a start. Someone was rummaging through the boxes that were strewn around the cargo bay. She curled up into a ball on the floor behind the big container and held her breath in anticipation.

"Those damned incompetents!" Niporo cursed as he knocked cartons out of his path. "Where the hell are the supplies on this ship?!" He was making his way closer to Llana's position. "I know there's got to be some food on this piece of tin!"

Llana heard the sound of wood splintering. Then she heard the rustling of paper.

"Ah ... Hah!" Niporo sounded satisfied. "This should hold us for the duration!" His voice trailed off as he climbed the ladder, back up toward the lounge.

Llana peeked around the side of the crate just in time to see Niporo disappearing through the hatch with his arms full of packaged food supplies. She was relieved to know she wouldn't starve either.

Quickly, she scrambled over to where she had heard Niporo collecting his find. There was an open crate full of food and drink. Llana hastily gathered what she could carry and quietly returned to her hiding place. Settling back to enjoy some nourishment, she was aware of Niporo's voice directly above her. She strained to hear what he was saying. He was talking to Zeidra. She could hear Zeidra crying. Her curiosity was peaked.

Surveying the ceiling of the cargo bay for an air vent, Llana spotted one just to the right of where she was sitting. She strategically arranged some boxes directly beneath the vent, and she climbed up onto them hoping to see through the screening, as well as discern the conversation. She was successful.

"For god's sake, Zeidra, stop crying and listen to me!" Niporo shouted.

Llana could see Zeidra curled up on the couch, looking frightened and confused.

"Your Kyate is a fraud! I'm telling you ... I never trusted that sonofabitch! Last night, someone drugged you and raped you. My guess ... it was him. He probably had it planned all along! The bastard is a Drothuarian! He's an imposter. Don't you see? He's impersonating the great Master! It's the god's truth, I tell you!"

"No ... No! NO!!!" Zeidra was holding her face between the palms of her hands and shaking her head *"no"* furiously. She dropped her hands and looked up at Niporo defiantly. "It's not true! None of it's true! He wouldn't do that to me! He's not a Drothuarian! IF anyone raped me, it wasn't *HIM*! You're a liar, Niporo! How could you accuse the Master of such a heinous thing?" Zeidra jumped to her feet and stumbled drunkenly to one of the small round windows to look outside. "Where are we?!" she demanded. "Niporo, where are you taking me?"

"I'm taking you somewhere; where I'm sure you'll be safe!"

"You're kidnapping me, Niporo! That's what you're doing!" Zeidra whirled around to face Niporo. "I demand that you return this ship to Ulonica immediately!" she screamed furiously.

Having never seen this side of the Princess, Niporo broke into a fit of raucous laughter. Crossing his arms to support his ribs he collapsed into a chair directly next to where Zeidra had taken her stand. Catching her wrist, he wrestled her down into his lap.

"Zeidra, I'm astonished! You've actually lost that righteous, calm demeanor of yours. What has happened to the Princess? Was your serenity attached to your virginity?" Niporo mocked the Princess.

Zeidra fought to free one hand. With surprising strength, she jerked her right wrist from Niporo's grasp and immediately delivered a deafening blow to the side of Niporo's face.

"Zeidra, dear, the fire in your spirit has aroused my passions," Niporo said matter-of-factly. He rubbed his flushed cheek, which still stung from the slap. "This is definitely your better nature!" Niporo caught Zeidra's chin in the palm of his massive hand.

Still struggling to free herself, Zeidra grabbed Niporo's hand away from her chin and sunk her teeth deep into the muscle. Niporo shot up out of the chair in acute pain from the bite, sending Zeidra crashing to the floor in the process.

"Damn! ... girl!" Niporo swore. He shook his arm violently, and then grabbed his wrist as if to support the wounded hand. Blood was beginning to ooze from the punctures in his flesh. "Now look what you've done, Zeidra... you should know better than to bite the hand that will feed you!" Niporo was teasing again. A faint smile crossed his handsome face.

Zeidra was dazed; the impact had knocked the wind out of her. She slowly looked up at Niporo who towered above her.

"Oh god, Zeidra," Niporo said, bending down to take a closer look, "is that my blood or *your* blood on those sweet lips?"

Zeidra wiped the back of her hand across her mouth and was startled to see the bright red trail left on her ivory skin. Her lower lip stung as she ran her tongue over it.

"I'm honestly sorry," Niporo whispered in a low, hoarse voice. He reached down to help Zeidra to her feet. "I would never hurt you purposefully! I swear it, Zeidra. I didn't mean to hurt you. "

Niporo's sincerity was obvious, although Zeidra refused to be lulled into fully trusting him, ever again. She did, however, allow him to help her up. Zeidra ripped her arms away from his hold and walked back to the couch; then she turned and looked at him for a long time. She studied his face intently.

"Niporo, please take me back to Ulonica." She spoke calmly this time.

"Zeidra, why won't you believe me? What if you're pregnant ... and you *could* be ... what would you tell your people? That you're carrying a Drothuarian child? How do you think that will sit with the elders?"

Panic flickered in Zeidra's eyes. She sat down heavily on the couch.

"Why do you insist on trying to make me believe I've been raped? Don't you think I would know it ... if something like that happened to me?" She hesitated for a moment. "What proof can you offer, if you're telling me the truth?" Zeidra tilted her head to one side, raised her eyebrows and waited for Niporo's reply.

"How could I expect you to remember?" Niporo grumbled. "You've been drugged so heavily... First last night and then again this morning ..." Niporo was slowly moving closer to where Zeidra was sitting, inching closer to her as he spoke. "The temple physicians examined you, Zeidra. You're hymen is no longer intact! Is that proof enough?" He lied.

"I want *THEM* to tell me that! I won't just take your word for it! You must think I'm a fool! Niporo, you've insulted me enough. Now take me home!"

In one unexpected movement, Niporo brought a heavy right hand down onto the crown of Zeidra's head. Kneeling down in front of her, he placed his left hand behind her skull and held her there in an iron grip. Her eyes were wide with fear. Her body was immobilized. She began to lose consciousness. She wanted to speak, but couldn't. She fainted.

In a split second, Niporo had scanned Zeidra's recent memory centers and had detected two blocked portions, which he immediately released. Reading the events like an open book, Niporo became incensed with jealousy. He could see the events taking place within his mind's eye. He could even feel the passion between the two. Carefully he re-blocked the first memory center, using his innate Drothuarian mystical skills. As for the memory center containing the blocked recollections of the previous night's erotic encounter, Niporo chose to leave most of the memory complete. He was sure that Zeidra would then be convinced that he was, indeed, telling her the truth.

'Wish the hell I had the Crionnachtian ability to implant a false memory ...' Niporo complained to himself as he released his hold on the princess, *'I'd make sure she HATED the sonofabitch!'*

The princess's limp body fell backward on the lounge.

The communications alarm was sounding. Niporo left abruptly to check for the messages. To his amazement, the news about the suicide of the Benjai Princess Zeidra, of Ulonica, was flashing across the screen.

'Unbelievable ... this is unbelievable ...' Niporo kept muttering to himself and rubbing his arm thoughtfully.

Zeidra struggled to gain control of her senses. She sat up; disoriented. The memories of Kyate began exploding into her consciousness. A chill ran through her trembling body, and she felt tears well up into her eyes, clouding her vision. As the passion re-ignited in her soul, she embraced herself and allowed those memories to come alive; she relived the moments, experiencing the pleasure and the pain. She was perplexed by the contradictory feelings. She was being overwhelmed by the ordeal. She felt ashamed and yet fulfilled; she was frightened and yet relieved; the act itself seemed to be so brutal and yet so tender. The princess had no doubt now, that the incident had actually taken place; there in her chambers, in the darkness, Kyate had breached his holy vow. He had taken from her, that which could never be replaced. She held herself tightly and rocked back and forth on the couch, weeping silently. Yet, in her sorrow, confusion, and shame - she could not *HATE* Kyate. She could only admit to herself, that Kyate had essentially surrendered to *her* unrelenting passion. She realized that *he* was as much a victim as she was.

"Well, my sweet," Niporo said softly,

returning from the communications room to face Zeidra, "you may have no home to return to... It seems you are officially dead. Nobody will search for you because nobody knows you're still alive. Seems the Princess Zeidra ignited herself on the Pyramid, making it impossible for any race to claim the Benjai *god gene*. It was quite a valiant act to save the *seed* from the Drothuarians who captured the temple complex." Niporo bowed low from his waist and gestured toward Zeidra, "... You are the most beautiful corpse I have ever laid eyes on! Allow me to reinstate your honor, madam .... Marry me and I'll be a father to your little bastard."

Zeidra grabbed a heavy vase from the table beside her and hurled it at Niporo, barely missing his head. Infuriated, she collapsed into a heap, and sobbed uncontrollably.

Niporo realized he had gone too far. He was used to a coarser grain in a woman. Zeidra was made of *finer* stuff. He regretted his cruel jesting.

"I'm so damned sorry! Zeidra, I'm sorry! ..... I'm damned sick of saying I'm sorry!" Niporo turned on his heel and stormed out of the lounge.

This was Llana's cue. She quietly

removed the metal louvered cover from the vent located on the floor under the table. It was right beside the sofa where Zeidra was sitting. Zeidra was distracted by the faint sound and looked down, catching her breath in surprise.

"... Shhhh!" Llana held a finger to her lips, warning Zeidra to be quiet.

Zeidra quickly moved the table from over the vent and extended her hand to help Llana out from the opening.

"No... I can't risk it right now!" Llana whispered to Zeidra, motioning for her to back away. "I just want you to know that I'm going to try to help you, but you must promise not to tell Niporo... honestly ... He would kill me! *HE'S* the Drothuarian! I know ... I worked with him against the Master Kyate!" Llana whispered rapidly.

"My god!" Zeidra shrieked, and then slapped her own hand quickly across her mouth, looking frantically in all directions, and hoping Niporo hadn't heard her. All seemed to be safe. "You're not .... You're not Drothuarian?" Zeidra whispered hesitantly.

"Hell no I'm not!!" Llana was emphatic. "Listen to me, Zeidra – as soon as it's safe, I'm going to try to send a message to Deis Command to let them know our position. If we can get old Niporo, distracted somehow ... I think I know a way. It's just that you will have to do it ..."

"I believe I know exactly what you're talking about!" Zeidra spoke in a low exacting tone.

"Well, not to worry. I'll keep an eye on what's happening ... If I don't get caught first! God, I hope I can figure out that communications stuff!"

"Just leave Niporo to me ... uhh ... what's your name?"

"I'm Llana"

"Well, I know this man's weakness, too, Llana. I'll keep him occupied and pray that you can get through to the Deis Command." Zeidra breathed a deep sigh. "I can't tell you how relieved I am to know you're here! ... Oh no! He's coming!" Zeidra hurriedly placed the screen over the vent and moved the table back to its original position. She sat back down on the sofa and looked toward the doorway innocently.

Niporo came lumbering into the lounge, carrying a tray of meat, cheeses, bread, and fruit. He pretended not to look at Zeidra, but she caught him glance at her from the corner of his eye. She tried to look dejected. She didn't say a word.

With his back to her, Niporo busied himself with the food, while every now and then stealing a glimpse back toward her to see if she was looking. She sat quietly with her eyes cast down at the floor.

Frustrated, Niporo slammed a bottle of wine down hard on the bar. Turning to face Zeidra, he threw his hands up high above his head.

"I give up! You win! Whatever you want ... I'll do it!!" Niporo sat down heavily in the chair across from Zeidra. "What's become of our friendship, Zeidra?" He leaned forward with his hands on his knees. "Why have you let that imposter come between us? ... Like a hot knife through butter?! I've never done anything ... not intentionally ... to harm you! You know how I feel about you!" He shifted his muscular body back against the chair, letting his arms drop limply over the sides. "I love you." He choked on the words.

Zeidra looked at him in amazement. "Do you mean what you're saying, Niporo?" she asked quietly.

"Anything ... You name it!" he said, staring up at the ceiling.

"Then you'll take me home?"

"Well, uh ... do you think that's a good idea? I mean what about Kyate?" Niporo chose his words carefully, hoping not to start another scene.

"Oh, I don't know. I don't know if I could face him." Zeidra squirmed in her seat. "I know you were being truthful with me. I remember what happened ... at least some of it." She clasped her hands tight on her lap. "Niporo, I'm so confused ..." Her voice trailed off as she fought the onslaught of emotions welling up from deep within her psyche. Tears began spilling down her cheeks.

"Please ... Please don't do this to me!" Niporo half shouted as he left his chair and sat down on the sofa beside Zeidra. He gathered her into his arms and held her warmly against his massive chest while she released the pent up frustration. For a moment, she almost believed she was safe.

"Come on, Zeidra, you're stronger than this," Niporo whispered, taking Zeidra by her upper arms and gently moving her away from his body. "What we need is some food and drink. I know you don't approve, but I think some wine would do you good!" He looked at her and grinned broadly, hoping that she would lighten up.

Zeidra tilted her tear-streaked face upward to meet Niporo's gaze. She tried to smile. "You know, Niporo ... I think that's exactly what we need."

Niporo caught Zeidra's face between his powerful hands and leaned toward her, almost touching his lips to hers. She could feel his warm breath on her face as his breathing became heavy. He held her there, alternately looking deeply into her pale blue, sad eyes; and then lowering his gaze to study her sensuous mouth.

Zeidra didn't resist. She relinquished her will to his intense contemplation. She wondered what was going on in his mind. The anticipation was maddening.

One last time, Niporo's gaze was drawn to Zeidra's mouth. He moved even closer. Zeidra's apprehension increased; she trembled. Her senses were overloading. Niporo's seductive lips parted slightly and Zeidra closed her eyes, straining upward, succumbing to the enticement. Niporo silently withdrew his mouth; back away from Zeidra's, leaving the princess quivering with expectation. She opened her eyes in disbelief. Niporo was grinning that disarming broad grin of his. Releasing her face from between his hands, he winked at her.

Zeidra felt a red hot flush spreading out across her cheeks. She was speechless. She just sat there, her eyes wide in astonishment. Her heart was pounding so loudly she was afraid he could hear it.

Niporo got up from the sofa and strolled confidently across the lounge to the bar, without saying a word. He stopped and placed both hands on the surface, supporting his weight on his arms. Smiling back at Zeidra, over his shoulder, he gave her a knowing look and winked again.

Zeidra was furious – more with herself

than with him.

Niporo prepared two plates of food and poured them both a glass of wine. He placed the food and drink on a large silver tray along with the decanter of wine. Picking it up, he turned around, facing the princess. Niporo couldn't help chuckling to himself as he brought the tray over and placed it on the table beside the couch. Zeidra looked like a little girl who had been caught with her hand in the cookie jar. He took one of the napkins from the tray and laid it across Zeidra's lap. She looked up slowly, meeting Niporo's eyes. She felt the flush return. Trying to regain her composure, she straightened the napkin on her lap and reached for one of the goblets containing the wine. She took a long drink.

"Hold on, there, Zeidra... This is potent stuff!" Niporo reached for her glass.

"That's what I need ... Potent stuff!!" she quipped, moving her goblet away from Niporo. She reached over and refilled her glass.

"Now wait a minute. Are we about to have another confrontation, Zeidra? I don't want you to get sick. The drugs and the wine may not interact so agreeably, you know ... and it's obvious to me that those drugs are still affecting your behavior. Or hadn't you thought of that? Besides, I make a damned poor nurse maid!"

"Just eat your food and leave me alone!"

Niporo proceeded to enjoy his meal while watching Zeidra drink half the bottle of wine. He knew, too well, what was going to happen.

"Don't you think you should eat something? Or are you going on a liquid diet?" Niporo refilled his glass, hoping to drink what was left before Zeidra could finish the bottle. "Try this cheese; it's good for the nervous system."

Zeidra didn't say a word. She grabbed the bottle of wine from the table and got up from the couch with her glass in one hand and the bottle in the other. She walked out of the room and across the central bridge area to the sleeping quarters.

Niporo calmly got up and followed the princess, unsure at this point, what to expect.

With Niporo safely out of the way, Llana climbed down from her surveillance position on the boxes beneath the air vent, and ran over to the ladder leading out of the cargo bay. Quietly she climbed out into the corridor and slipped silently through the lounge and into the communications room.

Surveying all the dials and switches, she chose one marked "transmit". Another button read "destination". Llana typed in the words *DEIS COMMAND*, crossed her fingers and punched the key. Suddenly the screen read *searching.* To Llana's relief, the screen was now displaying information on target coordinates and the words: *destination targeted.*

Sitting down at the console, she began to key in the message. Looking up on the display above her, she was easily able to make out the coordinates of the ship's position. She also noticed that the word *URAMPA* was flashing on the VDT in front of the auto-piloting controls.

Just as she had finished typing in all the information, she heard a crashing sound from the other end of the cabin. Immediately, she reached over and flipped the lever to transmit. The screen flashed off and on three times and then it was blank. Llana prayed that the message be received.

CHAPTER 13 – Confession

News of the Princess's demise spread rapidly throughout the provinces of Earth. The Drothuarians had withdrawn temporarily, to regroup and reevaluate their plans for Earth inhabitation and conquest. The Deis Command appeared to have been defeated by default, and the Master Kyate was nowhere to be found. It was indeed a sad time. But there was, however, peace on the Earth – for now.

In another section of the cosmos, one lone scout ship scanned the grids; swooping, diving, searching the heavens for some sign of the vessel which had escaped the boundaries of Earth. A Drothuarian and his hostage, the sacred Benjai, had disappeared beyond the bounds of Master Kyate's perception.

Until now, Kyate had been unwilling to contact the command post on Earth, or the Deis Command Council. He was unable to admit, even to himself, that the Benjai had been lost. Now it was time.

"This is Kyate ...." He spoke slowly,

holding the audio transmitter so tightly in his clenched fist that his knuckles were white with the pressure. "I'm returning to Earth at this time... Unable to locate Drothuarian craft which I believe to have abducted the Benjai Princess, Zeidra .... Respond please ..." Kyate waited.

"Thank god! Kyate! I thought we'd lost you!" It was Meno's voice. "You mean you've been out there chasing *ONE* Drothuarian all this time?"

"Meno, it was that snake Niporo! A dying guard told me that Niporo kidnapped the princess! I had to try!"

"Kyate, listen carefully!" Meno interrupted, and then hesitated, trying to think of a way to break the news to Kyate. "Niporo probably just made a run-for-it, to save his own neck." Meno fidgeted with the ring on his left hand. "Kyate, the Princess wasn't with *HIM*!" Meno waited for some response. There was none.

"Kyate ...? Are you still with me?"

"Where is she ... the Princess?! Where was she when I went to her chambers to take her to safety? Have you seen her? Meno, I couldn't find any trace of her essence in that compound! Nothing! I was positive they had gone. Have my powers failed me completely? What's going on?"

"Easy, son ..." Meno spoke reassuringly. "It's true – Niporo evidently did escape. He's definitely not here." There was a long pause. "The Princess is gone, son... Not with Niporo... but she's gone... Kyate, she's dead."

Kyate wrestled with his confusion. He threw his head back against the seat and closed his eyes, squeezing them tightly shut. He struggled for his voice. He wanted to argue the facts with Meno.

"It's not true!" Kyate stated bluntly. He switched the transmitter to his other hand, shaking the numbness from the fingers that had clenched the apparatus so brutally. "You are mistaken, Meno!" Kyate was insistent.

"Kyate ... Son, listen to me... I was there! I saw it! She's gone!" Meno took a long, deep breath, and then let out a shuddering sigh. "Kyate, she torched herself on the pyramid. I watched it. God help me ... I saw the whole thing ..." Meno waited for a reply. The silence was deafening. The silence was an eternity.

"*NO!!!*" Kyate cried out in a thunderous, resonant voice. He was inundated with anguish and remorse. His scream reverberated throughout the ship. It was as if the voice of God Himself was echoing across the universe, disavowing the death of the Benjai. The transmission was broken.

Kyate slammed his fist down hard on the console; over and over he pounded the metal surface until the flesh on his hand was bruised and bloody. Over and over again, he cursed himself for defiling the virtue of the Benjai Princess. Over and over again, he pled to God to turn back the time. He wanted so desperately to annul that one indiscretion. The sorrow, guilt, and shame overwhelmed Kyate. He dropped to his knees there in the empty cabin of the ship, and he wept bitterly. He grieved openly.

Hours passed. The Master Kyate lay prostrate on the floor exhausted; his spirit broken. Eventually, he struggled to his feet and staggered to the console. Kyate set the coordinates on the auto controls and programmed his vessel to return to Earth.

The sky was gray and it had started to drizzle. It was a completely dismal scene, as Kyate's ship made its graceful landing on the rain soaked tarmac. Kyate wearily unsnapped the harnessing and powered down the craft. Taking a deep breath, he placed the palms of his hands to his temples and closed his eyes, visualizing a state of renewed strength and vitality. He felt nothing; revitalization did not take place. He got up from his seat and opened the hatch. Stepping outside, he surveyed the landscape and breathed in the cool, moist air. It all seemed so alien. *'Had he alienated himself?'* Kyate climbed down the steps to the ground. Thankfully, he didn't see anyone in sight. He proceeded directly to his quarters, bolting the door behind him. He immediately disrobed and fell naked across the bed. He soon fell into a restless sleep; it was a much needed respite.

His reprieve was brief. Visions of Zeidra and Jason soon invaded his slumber. Kyate tossed and turned trying to escape the intrusions. As its only alternative, his spirit left his body.

Soaring into inner space, the necessary freedom released sorrow's hold on his tortured psyche. He attracted the much-needed purple and pink rays, which his being voraciously absorbed. Having satiated his vitality with the recuperative essences, it was now essential to restore the holy blue and white rays. Alone in the rainbow colored void he meditated; he repented. The colors began to move, encircling his soul. The colors whirled around his being, creating a powerful vortex that became *HIM*. The force of the maelstrom created a vacuum on the inside of his astral body, beginning at his feet and sucking them up through his legs, through his torso, and finally exiting at the crown of his head. He had literally been turned inside out. He strained against the excruciating pain, which was as agonizing spiritually as it was in the physical sense. He suffered in solitude. He screamed and nobody heard. The reality that was once *him* was slain; he perished yet no one mourned. And then, in an explosive burst of pure, blue white energy, the ethers ruptured, ejecting Kyate back through the void, catapulting his spirit back into his lifeless physical body with such force that it was thrown from the bed by the impact. The *REBIRTH* was complete.

Kyate struggled to sit up. He was dazed and disoriented. Shaking his head to clear his consciousness, he immediately realized what had taken place. It was an unexpected blessing to know the magnificence of his personal inner universe, in all its complexity, was capable of regeneration. Kyate stumbled to his feet, and he leaned back against the wall to steady himself. He closed his eyes and took a long deep breath, then exhaled in a slow sigh of relief.

There was an urgent pounding on his door.

"Kyate, open the door! Kyate, are you in there?!" Meno yelled from the corridor.

Kyate was slow in recovering his equilibrium. Pushing himself forward, away from the wall, he stood dizzily for a moment.

"Kyate... Open the door, man! I know you're in there ... I saw your ship when you landed. You don't have any more time to brood ... so open up ... *NOW*!!"

Kyate staggered across the room and unbolted the door, opening it slowly.

"It's tough, I know. But we need to talk – you and I," Meno spoke gently now, his expression full of concern for his good friend and master.

Kyate was literally hanging on the door, trying to remain on his feet. Meno took one look at the Master's ashen colored face and rushed in, catching him under both arms from behind. He dragged Kyate's dead weight over to the bed and helped him onto it.

"You don't look so good, chum," Meno muttered, pulling the sheet out from under Kyate. He pulled the bed cover up and over Kyate's nakedness, tucking it in under the master's chin, finalizing his effort by giving Kyate a supportive pat on both shoulders.

Kyate just looked at him and forced a smile. Meno was the only one left now; the only living soul who actually *knew* Kyate *the man*. Kyate was glad to see him.

Meno pulled a chair up close to the bed, turned it around and straddled it, resting his chin on his arms and studying Kyate's face.

"You can talk to me. Let's don't play *Master* right now, OK?"

Kyate nodded weakly.

"You loved her didn't you?"

Kyate closed his eyes, hesitated, and then

nodded again.

"I probably knew that before you did. It showed, you know. She was right for you, too. Being an old man gives me some special powers of my own, old chum. Call it experience ... I'd like to think of it as wisdom ... but I read the signs. I knew it. You know, Kyate ... there's no way I could make light of what you must be feeling right now ... you know how much I cherish my Merisa ... God! Part of me would die if anything happened to her!! There's nothing I can say, my friend ... that can make it all easier for you. But at least you can know ... I understand love."

Kyate turned his head toward the wall, away from Meno's intense gaze. He hoped his guilt wouldn't show; although he desperately needed to confide in someone. But this – this was so serious and so complex. He wondered if even his good friend Meno would stand by him if he knew what an abominable violation this great master had inflicted on the Princess Zeidra, just prior to her tragic death. Kyate squeezed his eyes closed tight. His body shuddered with the low, sorrowful groan that unexpectedly emerged from his very soul.

Meno jumped from his chair and leaned over Kyate, placing a firm hand on the master's shoulder. "Talk to me, Kyate! You've got to talk about it. Why torture yourself like this?! You're tough ... you'll make it ... come on, Kyate ... get the grief over and done with. Once you talk about it you can put it behind you. It's OK to mourn ... even if you are a *GREAT MASTER*, you're allowed to grieve ..."

"AAAhhhhhOOOhhh!!!!" The animal-sounding cry nearly shook the walls. So full of emotion and anguish, that Meno stepped away from the bed in frightened disbelief. Kyate cried out again. Meno began backing away, slowly.

Kyate turned toward Meno, eyes brimming with tears he was unable to hide from his friend. "I took her!" Kyate spat out the words as if they tasted bad. "I loved her, and I took her ... physically ... spiritually ... I possessed her, Meno!" he whispered hoarsely. "I'm responsible!" he shouted now. "She's dead, and I'm responsible!!" Kyate turned back toward the wall and became silent – staring into nowhere – overwhelmed with remorse.

"What are you saying?!" Meno inched forward as he spoke. "What exactly are you telling me, Kyate?!" he demanded. "Did I hear you right, man?! Did you say that YOU raped the Benjai?!"

Kyate didn't speak. His silence was enough of an affirmation.

Meno felt astonishment mixed with intense anger rising up from his gut. He stormed over to the bed without thinking and grabbed Kyate's shoulder hard, jerking him, turning Kyate back to face him. "Now you'd better start explaining, 'cause you just dropped a bombshell on me, and if I've misunderstood anything here … you'd better clear it up before I tear your holy head off your sacred shoulders!"

"I cannot justify my indiscretion," Kyate said numbly.

Kyate respected Meno. He was a decent man; he was a man of high moral standards, and honorable in every area of his life. That's why Kyate admired him so. He wasn't angered by Meno's reaction, nor was he surprised. Had any other person spoken to him in that tone, or laid a hand on him like that, he would have retaliated ferociously. This, however, was his best friend – his only friend. Or had he now destroyed this friendship as surely as he had destroyed the princess?

"The Kyate I know isn't capable of such a thing!" Meno screamed. "My master and friend wouldn't force his affections on any woman … especially one who was specifically in his charge – especially one that he admittedly loved!"

Kyate remained silent.

In his rage and confusion, Meno swung one massive open hand, catching Kyate squarely on the jaw, hoping to knock some insight into him, and a credible explanation out of him.

Kyate sat bolt upright on the bed rubbing his jaw and looking at Meno in total amazement.

"I don't want any more of this *wimp shit*, Kyate! I want to know exactly what happened between you and the princess! Our friendship is riding on this, Bud ... so you'd better give it to me straight! I've *NEVER* had a reason *not* to respect you ... But now ...." His voice trailed off as he walked across the room and poured himself a drink.

Kyate was still rubbing his jaw when Meno turned back to face him. His anger had subsided somewhat, and he felt a bit guilty looking at the puffy red handprint on Kyate's face. *'Who, in their right mind would strike his master?'* Meno wondered silently.

"I choose to overlook this," Kyate stated. His indignation was conspicuous.

"I don't give a rat's ass if you overlook it or not!"

Kyate had seen Meno angry on many occasions, yet that anger had never been directed at him, and he had never seen Meno exhibit this intensity of rage. The master understood that he owed his friend the explanation he was demanding.

"Meno ..." Kyate motioned his friend to sit. "I can describe for you my actions and my feelings ... but I can find no logic in it all, and I can see no justification for my lack of judgment." Kyate paused thoughtfully. "We did discuss my predicament months ago. You said not to worry, that I could overcome any trial. Well, my friend ... it seems you were wrong."

Kyate proceeded to tell Meno the whole story. He detailed every encounter with Zeidra; he honestly and sincerely described all that had happened.

For what seemed like hours, they discussed the affair, and although Meno certainly couldn't condone Kyate's actions, he thought he understood the motivation.

"Good night my friend," Meno said.

"Do you really still consider me your friend?"

"Well, hell ... nobody's perfect, Kyate. Not even *YOU!* Now I won't have to try so hard to measure up." Meno left.

CHAPTER 14 – Close Encounter

The Deis vessel, with the Drothuarian Niporo in command, was streaking across the cosmos in route to the planet Urampa. Undetected to this point, the Deis Command was now receiving a transmission from that craft.

Llana quickly dropped to the floor beneath the console just as Niporo emerged from the corridor and was crossing the lounge. He snatched another bottle of wine from the vault on the wall and headed back in the direction of the sleep quarters.

She tried to still the shaking in her body. She had survived one more very close call. Taking a minute to collect her thoughts, she suddenly remembered the Princess Zeidra, alone with that oversexed Niporo in the sleep quarters, and having had so much wine to drink.

'Oh my god!" she gasped. "He'll take advantage of her for sure ... that SOB was only priming the pump and testing the waters before; this time he'll go for it! ... A plan ... a plan ... what's the plan?!! Come on girl, *think ... think..!'* Llana was frantic; she was talking to herself. She'd been around Niporo too many times; she knew what made him *tick*!

Niporo returned to the bed where Zeidra was reclining, propped up on a mountain of black satin pillows, on a fluffy black satin comforter. A mass of golden curls were strewn up and out, across the fabric in total disarray. She was still wearing the long, white, linen and lace night gown she'd been wearing when Niporo stole her from her own bed. Her cheeks were pink from the wine, and her eyes were glazed and sleepy looking. She rested there, holding the crystal goblet in her hand, seeming oblivious to Niporo's approach.

"My god, Zeidra, you're beautiful!" Niporo said hoarsely. "You have no idea what you do to me?" He sat down on the edge of the bed, unable to take his eyes off the vision of Zeidra – half dressed, half intoxicated.

Niporo opened the wine and refilled their glasses. Zeidra didn't refuse. Instead, she turned onto her left side, and she raised herself up on her elbow to face Niporo. She gulped at the wine while watching Niporo's face.

"What is this?" he demanded, "... don't you know what you're asking for!? For god's sake, Zeidra, put yourself in my situation. I'm only a man, you know!" Beads of sweat were beginning to appear on his forehead.

"Niporo ... all I asked you for was some more wine." Zeidra drew her right knee up across her left thigh as she spoke. She took another drink. She watched Niporo's face. His eyes were dark and serious. The veins on his neck were bulging.

Niporo eyed Zeidra's provocative position. Her leg had moved her gown up, exposing her left inner thigh. The smooth, milky white flesh was more of an enticement than Niporo could resist. Slowly, he reached across Zeidra and drew one finger up along the warm skin, from the inside of her knee, silently challenging her to stop him. She shivered at his touch, her eyes riveted to his. He withdrew his hand abruptly in exasperation and got up from the bed.

The princess watched Niporo as he leisurely pulled his shirt up over his head and tossed it onto the floor. Zeidra finished her wine, watching Niporo intently as she raised her glass higher to empty it. The muscles bulged across his immense chest; they appeared smooth and flowing, while further down on his stomach they were drawn into taut ridges. Zeidra couldn't help admiring Niporo's flawless physique. He stood there before her, his hands on his hips and his legs slightly apart, supporting his heavy frame. The muscles on his huge arms were tense and sculptured.

"Zeidra ... Zeidra, look at me," he motioned toward his face.

Zeidra lifted her eyes to meet Niporo's.

"Is this what you want?"

"I want some more wine."

"You've had enough wine! I'd like you to stay sober enough to know what you want! I promise you, Zeidra ... whatever you want, you *WILL* get! I'm past trying to second-guess you at this point. Tell me you're not drunk, goddammit!"

"I'm not drunk, and I want some more wine," she said lazily, extending her empty goblet toward Niporo. "Please, Niporo?" Tilting her head, she smiled up at him impishly.

"Good god, Zeidra ... how can I say no to you?" Niporo conceded; and he filled her glass. Then he put the nearly full bottle to his mouth and drank the remaining wine in a series of determined gulps.

Zeidra sat up cross-legged, and giggled at Niporo's irritation. Eyeing him over the top of her glass, she gulped her wine down, just as quickly.

"You will be sorry. I've warned you about making yourself sick. Now let me warn you of something more ominous ...." Niporo's stare was fixed on the princess. Her gown had slipped casually off of one shoulder, revealing nearly all of one breast. She had gathered the folds of material into her lap, allowing him full view of her outer thighs and lower hips. "Zeidra, I love you more than you know ... but what you're doing is going to get you into serious trouble. I don't play games, and if you don't stop this one right now, you're going to have to assume full responsibility for whatever happens!"

"Oh Niporo ..." Zeidra whispered, brushing her curls back off of her face. "How you do go on! Are you trying to scare me?"

"No! But you're starting to scare the hell out of me!"

Zeidra resumed her original position on the bed. She was on her left side, facing Niporo, but this time her gown was caught up around her waist. "I'm not scared," she said, looking up at his extraordinarily handsome face.

Niporo just stood there dumbfounded. The curves of her legs, her thighs, and now her hips and buttocks in full view; it was driving him wild with need. The throbbing in his loins was white hot with desire. The material of his trousers was being stretched beyond its strength.

Zeidra caught her breath at the sight of his obvious arousal. She watched.

Niporo looked into Zeidra's eyes; still his

question was unanswered. "What do you want, Zeidra?" His breathing was heavy and his voice was husky with desire. "If you don't want this," he gestured toward the conspicuous swelling under his trousers, "then for god's sake stop me now!"

"I can't stop you, Niporo," she whispered. She could feel a vaguely familiar sensation awakening low in her stomach. Her heart was racing and she felt a strange pulsating, moving through her body, increasing as she watched Niporo. Tiny beads of perspiration were visible on her breast. She ran her tongue over her parched lips as her breathing became more labored.

Niporo knew she was toying with him, and decided to *call her bluff*. He wasted little time unfastening his pants and letting them fall to the floor. Zeidra gasped in surprise, but she pushed her fears out of her mind.

The intensity was rising and the throbbing in Niporo's loins was too painful to deny any longer.

Zeidra was blatantly enthralled by Niporo's nakedness, and he reveled in the admiration. She stretched out her hand to touch him.

Niporo climbed onto the bed next to Zeidra. He took her hand and he placed it on his chest, moving it for her, across the broad expanse. He guided it over his breasts and she marveled at the texture of his skin. He slowly moved her hand down onto his stomach and allowed it to linger there. Zeidra ran her fingertips over and around his navel, savoring the sensations; touching this warm masculine flesh. Then he took the palm of her hand and placed it firmly against his skin. Holding her wrist tightly, he moved her hand lower. Just as he had anticipated, she tried to withdraw her hand. She sucked her breath in hard, and struggled with his hold for only a moment. Then she allowed him to continue to guide her exploration over his body. Zeidra was trembling now.

Zeidra's apprehension was almost unbearable at this point. Niporo rolled over onto his side and pulled Zeidra's body in hard against his. Watching for any sign of fear in her eyes, he was careful and deliberate in all of his actions. Knowing the truth about her virginity, he was trying to retain some control over his physical need. He gently smoothed the hair back away from her face and tenderly tipped her chin up toward him. He could feel the rise and fall of her breasts against his chest, as her breathing became heavier.

She searched his eyes for some reassurance; her need more insistent than her fear. Niporo brushed his lips across her cheek, holding her fast with his eyes. He reached down and raised her gown high above her hips and then encircling her with his powerful arms, he pressed her closer to him. She was soft and warm, and she yielded to his pressure. He probed against the quivering flesh of her stomach. She let out a little cry. He moved his lips lightly around the corners of her mouth. She closed her eyes, and as her lips parted slightly Niporo moved hungrily onto that sensuous mouth. Kissing her deeply he began caressing her body with one hand while holding her hips tight against his with the other.

Zeidra was reeling in the delicious passion that was electrifying every nerve in her body. Niporo continued to kiss her, and fondle her until she felt she would explode. Without warning, something ignited deep in her being. A memory was surfacing. An undeniable yearning was becoming immediate. Zeidra threw her arms around Niporo's neck and she kissed him more passionately than he had kissed her. She moved her hands up onto his head and pulled him ardently into her demanding kiss. Niporo responded.. She was moving rhythmically now; against him. She lifted her leg up over his hip in order to get even closer to that rigid heat. She began to moan softly while Niporo explored her passion. He knew she was ready, but something was holding him back.

He gently escaped from her hold and slid

his face down onto her breasts, which were partially bared and partially covered by her gown. He lingered there for only a moment as he made his final decision. He vowed to himself, not to give in to his need until the Princess willingly agree to marry him. He would use Zeidra's passion against her logic, and thus secure the Benjai legacy for himself.

Niporo adroitly brought about the relief that Zeidra was desperate for; ignoring his own, in order to preserve the girl's virginity.

She appeared to be unconscious, and her chest was heaving as she gasped for breath. Her hair was soaked with perspiration, and her face was flushed. Niporo smiled to himself. He knew he'd done well. He climbed down off the bed and pulled the comforter across Zeidra's body. He stood there a long time, staring down at her, amazed at what love can do to a man – even a Drothuarian man.

Zeidra rolled over lethargically and mumbled, "I love you ..." She rambled on.

Niporo leaned over the bed and lightly kissed Zeidra on the lips. It was then that he was able to make out the one word she'd been murmuring over and over. – *KYATE*.

She moaned his name, a little louder and more clearly, "*K Y A T E .....*"

Niporo was incensed! He could feel the

blood rush to his face. His nostrils flared and the veins on his forehead pushed angrily outward against his flushed skin. He flung his arm across the table by the bed, sending everything crashing against the wall and all over the floor. He covered his face with his hands and tilted his head backward, screaming silently; his spirit was frustrated with the anger and the pain of knowing Kyate had unwittingly defeated him again.

"I'm surprised at you Niporo! I see you *ARE* an honorable man after all. ... Although I can understand why you might be a teeny bit frustrated with your own honor!" Llana was laughing, leaning against the doorway, one foot propped across the other in a nonchalant pose.

Niporo spun around in surprise. "... Llana?! What the hell are you doing here?!" he demanded.

"Becoming extremely horny, for one thing," she laughed. "When you told me to get to safety, back in Ulonica, I climbed in here to hide. Who would've believed I would end up in a bizarre situation like this! I fell asleep, and when I woke up, there was no way to get off this bus ... so ... here I am!"

"How long have you been standing there?"

"Long enough to know you didn't stick it

to her!" Llana quipped crudely.

"Well now, you see honey – I'm not the bad guy you've been accusing me of being. I told you, you didn't know what you were missing."

"Huh! You probably just couldn't get it up!" Llana laughed.

"Llana, my dear, you couldn't have shown up at a better time! Bring that sweet little ass of yours in here!" Niporo said, catching her by the wrist and dragging her into the lounge.

"Niporo, aren't you afraid you'll catch a cold? Don't you think you should at least put your pants on?"

"Honey, if what you just witnessed didn't shock you ... then you shouldn't be shocked by my bare ass!" He moved close to Llana and moved his lips along her neck; catching her earlobe between his lips. "Are you really horny, Llana?" he whispered, breathing hot kisses all over the outside of her ear. "You know I'm in bad shape, don't you? Would you help me out, honey? Maybe we can make a deal?" He put his arm around her waist and pulled her against him. He was becoming aroused again and he wanted her to feel it.

"Niporo, I might consider it. How much are we talking about?" Llana's green eyes flashed as she spoke. Niporo was already aware that her heart was racing, and he could see the desire in those gorgeous emerald eyes.

"I don't believe it! After all these years,

I've been trying to talk you into a little fun and you never would, and now you tell me you might?! I'll give you anything you want, honey ... *ANYTHING!*"

Niporo had always been physically attracted to the maid. What attracted him the most was that he could never have her the way he wanted her.

"Did you get turned on in there? Is that what it's all about ... the change of heart, that is?"

"That may have had something to do with it." Llana blushed.

"You don't have to be embarrassed, honey. That was pretty intense stuff. Not what you need though ... You need the real thing! I've got plenty to give you if you want it. Llana, relax." Niporo took her by the hand and led her into the shower room. Llana didn't resist.

"Niporo, you are a fine piece of masculinity!" Llana ran her hand over Niporo's chest and then down his muscular arm.

"What you see is what you get, honey." Niporo reached in and turned on the shower. "Let me help you out of this," he said unbuttoning Llana's dress.

Niporo slipped the dress down over Llana's shoulders exposing her magnificent breasts. He had always admired her body, but up to now he'd only fantasized about it. He slid the garment down over her hips and it dropped to the floor. Llana now stood before him completely nude. Niporo just stood there for a while, admiring her voluptuous curves.

"Amazing ass, Llana, I've always loved your ass!"

Llana felt a chill go through her body and her nipples immediately hardened. Niporo was quick to observe. Lovingly he gathered her large breasts up into his massive hands and kneaded them until Llana thought her legs would give way; her knees were weak. She was surprised at what Niporo's touch could do to her. She had been curious for a long time, but she would have never guessed that he would have such a profound effect on her. Still, in the back of her mind, she was trying to justify this weakness by telling herself that she was doing it to protect Princess Zeidra; that if Niporo didn't have some relief, he may decide to give it to the princess – and a novice just couldn't handle this one!

Niporo stepped into the shower pulling Llana in with him.

CHAPTER 15 – Crossing The Void

"Hey! HEY!!! ... Kyate!"

Kyate turned to see Meno sprinting across the gardens waving a piece of paper over his head like a flag. By the time he got to Kyate, he was so out of breath the master couldn't make out what he was trying to say. Meno finally gave up and just shoved the paper into his friend's hands; and with such force that Kyate was compelled to take a few steps backward.

"What's this?" Kyate asked, opening up the folded sheet.

"Re.. re.. read it!" Meno was grabbing his sides and bending over gasping for air.

Kyate was silent as he read the encoded communication from Deis Headquarters. Meno excitedly watched his master's face as Kyate's expressions changed from disbelief, to excitement, then to horror, relief, anger, and finally – finally – sheer elation.

Kyate joyfully grabbed Meno around the shoulders with one arm while waving the paper in front of Meno's face with the other. It was the first time in weeks that Meno had actually seen Kyate smiling, let alone laughing.

"She lives! She lives! She's alive, Meno!" Kyate kept shouting it, over and over.

"Shhhhh .... Kyate, keep it quiet! Nobody's supposed to know that but *YOU*!"

"We've got to go! Niporo *DOES* have her! Let's go today and ...." Suddenly Kyate broke off in mid-sentence and his eyes grew dark. "... My god!" He sucked in his words. "If it wasn't Zeidra, then who was it?"

"What are you talking about, Kyate?"

"Someone died up there. If it wasn't Princess Zeidra, then who was it?"

Both men stared at one another in silence.

"I hadn't thought of that, Kyate." Meno scratched his head and gazed up at the pyramid.

"Meno, where's Shanta? Have you seen the maiden, Shanta?" Kyate grabbed Meno by the shoulders and looked into his eyes, hoping to find some hope there.

"I haven't seen her since .... "He lowered his eyes. "Since Jason was killed." Those words stuck in his throat. "Everyone assumed she went back to join her family."

"I shouldn't have left her alone like that!" Kyate rebuked himself. "I should have secured protection for her before I left! Meno, I wasn't thinking clearly ... you know ... with Jason and Zeidra ... and those damned

Drothuarians! What have I done?!" Kyate dropped his arms to his sides despondently and began pacing back and forth.

Meno grabbed Kyate roughly by his upper arms and shook him. "Stop this, Kyate! We're not going to waste any more time lamenting! Sure ... you've used some pretty bad judgment these last few weeks, but we've already put it to rest. Maybe if you concentrate on getting your Benjai back, you can also recover your sanity! Marry the girl, or whatever it takes to clear your perception! This world doesn't need a blind guide!! Damn! You're pathetic!" Meno scolded.

"You're right Meno ... Sorry." Kyate agreed compliantly. The twinkle in Kyate's eyes was returning, and his face took on a determined look. "Let's go get her, old friend! We'll go to my room and make a plan. I've got an idea, come to think of it."

"Look here, Meno," Kyate said, pointing to two adjoining sectors on the star map, which was spread out across the table, "this was their location when the transmission was received." He slid his finger across the map diagonally and tapped his finger on another spot. "This is obviously the course that Niporo has chosen. Now on the other hand," he traced a line straight across the paper, "if we take the shortest grid ... this way, then we can get to Urampa a full two weeks sooner!"

"No, no, no, Kyate. Look at this!" Meno was pointing to a small intersection almost midway from Earth to Urampa on the grid line Kyate was referring to. "You are a sick man, Kyate! Either that, or you have more courage than sense! This," he pounded his finger on the spot, "this is an asteroid field ... remnants of Pathio. Remember the explosion? You surely know how congested that area is! Oh god ... you do remember what an asteroid field is ... don't you?"

"Come on, Meno ... we've been through fields before. It'll save us time and supplies. It'll give us the jump. We can be all set up, have it all in place ... It's perfect!!!"

"That's not good enough reasoning for me to put my ass on that line!"

"OK, try this... *NO* Drothuarians!"

There was a long thoughtful silence.

"Now that you mention it ... I agree! That's definitely a perfect plan, Kyate," Meno declared, slapping Kyate hard on the back. "I'll get the ships ready and line up the crew." Meno turned on his heel and left Kyate's quarters muttering obscenities under his breath. The truth was, Meno would much rather take his chances in an asteroid belt, than go head to head with the Drothuarians any day!

The low hum of the propulsion systems droned on for hours until the sound faded into oblivion; simply due to the ceaseless monotony of the tone. The two Drothuarian ships glided placidly along the magnetic grid system that Kyate had chosen for their passage. Kyate and Meno were flying the lead; while four of the veteran Deis warriors navigated the other craft. The objective of this mission had been kept classified because it wasn't deemed prudent, at this time, to inform the majority that the Benjai Princess was, in fact, still alive; although a Drothuarian captive. The Galactic Council had been briefed on the clandestine operation under way, and that Deis warriors were piloting Drothuarian craft; yet the purpose and destination was not disclosed. What was issued to the Council was information that would identify these, from other Drothuarian ships. A secret code, transposed on the Drothuarian insignia was only detectable through special optical filters, which were ordered to be used upon encountering any enemy ship.

"Do you see him?!" Meno shouted to Kyate.

"No, but you forget, I've got the advantage!" Kyate laughed, standing at the bridge in the surveillance dome. "He's about two o'clock on your right, there ... about 900 yards out."

"Let's surprise 'em!" Meno quickly checked the output.

"OK. Put the soft barriers up."

Meno threw the switches and the bumpers went up. "Here we go ... slow and steady... You're the one with the X-ray eyes, so tell me which way. Better yet, Kyate, you take the controls."

Kyate jumped down off the bridge and positioned himself at the console. The ship inched forward, both disks seemingly invisible to the other.

"Get ready," Kyate warned.

Meno braced himself.

Boom! Their vessel lurched into the side of the other ship. The microwave shields on both ships went down and both became plainly visible.

"So you want to play TAG, do you?" The voice boomed over the audio receiver. It was Beau, the Captain of the other vessel. The soft barriers immediately went up on Beau's craft.

"Ha! Take over Meno, you're going to navigate! Let's get out of here ... give 'em a run for their money! Show us how good you are!" Kyate chuckled.

Meno quickly took the controls and the ship dropped suddenly, straight down several hundred feet in a split second. Then he skillfully maneuvered the craft onto its side and rolled out to the left. Beau was in pursuit; accurately second guessing Meno's every move. The two Drothuarian ships dived and rolled, pivoting and weaving, rocketing instantly upward and then plummeting straight down as they streaked out across the cosmos, playing the game of space tag, which was actually an exercise in maneuverability; which could one day save their ships.

Beau quickly caught up and ... *THUD*! Kyate didn't particularly like being the loser and he didn't waste any time remedying that situation.

"Move over, Meno! I guess I'll have to teach these guys a lesson!" He shoved Meno playfully aside and seized the controls with a vengeance.

Off they went again. Kyate was on Beau's tail in an instant. *WHOMP*!

"Was that you, Kyate?" The voice came over the audio.

"Yep, now come and get me, sucker!"

Kyate's disk streaked away instantly. He climbed so swiftly, that for a moment, Beau lost sight of him. The craft was almost out of range when Beau finally got a fix on him. He shot out across the void and was closing in fast.

Suddenly something hit the barriers on Kyate's ship; it lurched hard to the right.

"That's not fair!" cried Meno. "They're not supposed to have the microwave shields up!"

"They don't!" Kyate yelled back in alarm. "Something else hit us!" He stopped the ship and climbed up on the bridge to take a look.

"What's going on out there?" Beau's voice came over the audio. He was just now coming into view, and Kyate saw him. At the same time, a small asteroid streaked by on the right.

"Get the hard shields up!" Kyate shouted, taking a quick survey of the area ahead. "We're entering the field! Engage the laser cannons ... we may be able to blast our way through!" He jumped down into the control room.

Meno scrambled with the dials and levers. The scanners were on and the shields were up. "Beau ..." Meno called over the audio, "are you guys set?"

"We're set ... do you want us on you tail or on your flank?"

"Better stay on our tail for a while," Kyate called. "I'll try and guide us through. If it gets too rough ... then come up here and we'll start blasting. You better ..." He was interrupted as the ship was hit again, harder this time.

Kyate lost his balance and was thrown against the wall. "Get in the harnesses guys! This is getting rough, fast!"

Kyate jumped into the control chair and fastened himself in. Meno was already harnessed and calculating positions on the scanner in front on him.

"There's a small one – fast on your right!" Meno shouted.

Kyate rolled left and dived. Beau followed Kyate's maneuvers to the letter.

"Straight ahead – this one's big!"

Kyate zagged to the side of it as it shot by the craft. It looked to be the size of a large building.

"Here comes a group!" Meno yelled. "Kyate, check the screen, you'll have to figure this move!"

Kyate quickly switched on the screen to his left, in order to check the scan. The barrage was intensifying. He engaged the laser canons and linked them to the scan. The cannons automatically locked onto the group of asteroids that were bearing down on the Deis position. Kyate linked up to the computers aboard Beau's ship and set their defenses accordingly, via the remote connection.

"Bring her up here, Beau!" Kyate commanded.

The sleek shiny craft glided up alongside

Kyate's, and the two ships advanced into the storm.

Huge flashes of white light were visible in the black distance as the lasers ripped into the asteroids. Shattered debris rained thunderously against the exteriors of the ships as they slipped through the destruction. Every now and then a larger chunk of pulverized asteroid smashed into Kyate's vessel, jarring the structure so violently that the entire craft vibrated and shuddered in the aftermath.

Kyate adroitly picked his way through the field. When the scanner indicated denser concentrations, the ships would simultaneously move from one grid to the next. Soon, the boulders were superseded by mountainous chunks of rock, being hurled furiously through space, as if thrown by some unseen giant adversary; bent on the absolute annihilation of the Deis vessels. The Deis ships were taking some deadly blows as the flying debris became a rain of terror so intense that the laser cannons were turned off. Now the asteroids would need to be faced head on, due to their immense size and sheer numbers. Smashing them with the lasers had only created another hazard, as the region became impenetrable with the fragments of the shattered space-rubble.

"Beau ..." Kyate called the other ship, "I'm

releasing the link-up ... you're better off on your own, now. This stuff is getting too heavy! Are you up to it? If we both get through this ... I'll see you on the other side."

"No problem, Kyate!" Beau's voice was full of confidence.

"Take care, my friend." Kyate then disengaged the link. Beau was back in control of his own vessel.

The two ships sped off separately now; diving and climbing, rolling and turning; dodging the onslaught of planet sized boulders. They were playing a precarious game of chance with this pernicious aspect of nature.

Too occupied to converse, now, Kyate and Meno defiantly confronted the challenge. The tension engulfed the occupants of the vessel, now on a collision course with destiny. Hours passed with no relief. The assault was incessant and the ship began to tack out of control.

"Meno!" Kyate yelled. "Check the right thrust activator! We've got a serious problem here! ... must have received a severe one ... can hardly get 'er ...." Kyate looked to the screen and saw it coming.

An asteroid slammed into the craft, sending it careening across the grid section directly into the path of a gigantic slab of iron bearing down on them at incredible speed. It was too late. The two had only time enough to brace themselves.

On impact the disk was broken apart at the seams. Pieces of twisted metal were left stationary; floating there in space where they had been deposited by the collision. The larger portion of the craft, while broken, remained intact, but it was catapulted across the void at a velocity that was incalculable.

Kyate and Meno struggled against the G's, unable to move a muscle under the force. The pressure was becoming intolerable and the oxygen was being sucked out of the cabin. Both men silently prayed.

The speed began to decrease. Slowly, too slowly, the disk decelerated, finally coming to a standstill – suspended in the blackness. All was quiet.

Nearly unconscious by now, Kyate was able to grab the emergency oxygenator from under the console. He turned it on and took several deep breaths, then hastily unfastened his harnessing and staggered over to Meno who looked to be dead. Kyate knew instinctively that the life force was there, but he had to hurry. Clamping the mask over Meno's pale face, Kyate administered the air, quickly taking breaths for himself when he needed it. After several seconds with no response from his friend, he began pushing hard on the older man's chest while increasing the oxygen intake.

Meno moaned and tried to open his eyes. The color was returning to his skin. Kyate inhaled some of the oxygen and then returned it to Meno.

"Told you ... bad.. Idea." Meno gasped under the mask.

"Don't talk," Kyate said quickly, trying to keep the air in his lungs. He looked around the cabin surveying the damage. He took the mask from his friend and filled his lungs to their entire capacity, then gave the mask and the container to Meno. Kyate rushed over to a hatch on the floor at the other end of the cabin. Struggling to open it he ran out of air. He returned to Meno and grabbed the oxygen, again refilling his lungs. This time he concentrated on his ability to gain super-strength. He bent over the hatch and grabbing it tightly in both hands, he literally ripped it off the hinges and tossed it aside. Again he had to return for air. The pressure was critical and he knew his haste was imperative. He rushed back to the open hatch.

Kyate disappeared down the opening. Meno worried that he may have run out of air, as the seconds passed. Meno was amazed to hear a faint humming noise beneath him. Feeling stronger now, Meno unfastened the harness and stumbled across the cabin to peer into the bay. To his surprise, amazement, and gratitude, he could see Kyate sitting inside a mini-rover. It was a small craft, about half the size of the control cabin he was standing in. He climbed down into the chamber and entered the rover. The pressure was up and the oxygen was on, and it appeared from all indications that it hadn't been damaged.

"God has heard our prayers!" Meno exclaimed, closing the portal and sitting down next to Kyate.

"He has indeed," Kyate said, smiling at Meno. "We only have one problem now, my friend... Could be you need to pray some more. The outer door of this bay is twisted. I don't know if we can get this little guy launched." Kyate looked over at Meno who had wasted no time commencing with the prayers. The master gave Meno a playful shove, interrupting his meditation. "Come on ... Let's see what the both of us can do."

Carrying the portable breather with them they examined the outer door. The twisted metal around the left edge seemed to be the only obstacle. They worked feverishly, prying the material away from the edges with bars of a steel-like metal they found strewn around the floor. Periodically, it was necessary to return to the rover, because the pressure was higher on the inside of their bodies than it was on the outside, and the pain of the swelling from within couldn't be tolerated for long periods of time. It was a long, tedious chore.

Suddenly the cargo door began to open, and the remaining air in the craft rushed past the men toward the opening, carrying with it all sorts of debris. Everything that wasn't bolted down was being sucked toward the vacuum outside the ship. Kyate and Meno desperately fought their way toward the rover. It was like a wind tunnel, and it took every bit of energy and strength they could muster to advance. They clung to the walls of the bay while being bombarded with flying rubble. They inched their way further across the room.

Without warning, Meno lost his hold and began to slip back toward the abyss. He cried out. Kyate turned just in time to see Meno's fingers gripping the dock, his body outside the ship.

The pressure for both of them was severe at this point, and Kyate wondered if he could save Meno. Would he have the time to do so, even if Meno were able to hold fast?

"Hold on!" Kyate screamed. He wasted no time strapping the oxygen mask to his face. He struggled with a piece of steel cable that was coiled under his feet. Quickly, he anchored it to a steel beam close by, which had been exposed by the torn metal.

Unfastening his belt, he wrapped it around the cable and refastened it to his midsection. He twisted the other end of the line back onto the beam. Kyate slid along the cable toward Meno as fast as he could safely manage. Upon reaching Meno, he rapidly snatched the man's wrist and wrestled him back, up onto the bay. Kyate filled his lungs and then strapped the oxygen mask on Meno. The pressure was deadly and time had almost run out for both men.

Against all odds, Kyate slowly dragged Meno back up the haul, fighting not only the vacuum, but the intense pain of the inner pressure. He thought he may burst before ever reaching the rover. He wondered if Meno was alive. In that one moment, when he had looked down at his friend to apply the mask, Kyate hadn't been able to make out Meno's features; the blood was so thick and small particles of debris had imbedded into his face.

Kyate grabbed hold of the rover in one desperate lunge. He clung doggedly to Meno as he hoisted himself up to the opened portal. Kyate's pain and his exhaustion seemed to dissipate instantly as he mustered his remaining strength and crawled inside, grappling to haul Meno in after him.

Kyate removed the cable and tossed it outside. He closed the hatch and collapsed on the floor beside his old friend, gasping for air and thankful for every breath he could take. He lay there on his stomach, waiting for his inner pressure to equalize. Looking sideways, he could see Meno's labored breathing; he was alive! Kyate flung a heavy arm up and over Meno's chest – He wanted to hug this big burly man – he was so glad to know he wasn't dead! The two laid there recuperating for a long time.

Kyate was aware of the sound of whining metal, and he felt a shift beneath him. He realized at once, that if they were to get out of this dilemma alive, he would have to launch now, or they may become forever entombed in this piece of wreckage. He got up, surprised that he could even move. Positioning himself at the console, he did a quick test of all systems. Everything checked out. He breathed a sigh of relief and then he breathed a prayer. IGNITION .... THRUST... PROPEL .... He shoved the throttle forward and the mini-rover shot out of the bay and into the cosmos.

"*FREE*!" Kyate yelled. "Meno, we're out! We're out of that hell-hole!"

Meno didn't answer.

Kyate turned to look down at his friend, who was lying on the floor beside the control chair. Although he was still breathing, Kyate knew he needed immediate attention. He set the auto-controls, unfastened his restraints, and knelt down beside Meno. Running his large bronze hands over the length of Meno's aura, about four inches from his body, the master ascertained the state of the life force within. He placed his right hand on Meno's crown and his left hand on the man's solar plexus, breathing a powerful healing current into and throughout Meno's weak body. Kyate checked the life force again. It had improved somewhat. Again Kyate administered the healing energy. Once more he examined the aura. This time, all had returned to normal energy levels.

Meno groaned, becoming cognizant of his pain – the awful pain. He was trapped in the mask, unable to speak, unable to see; he could barely breathe. He felt as if his face had been cast in plaster – a living sculpture of the face of terror, memorializing the ordeal of his near death experience.

The master inspected Meno's face. The mask of thick dried blood was obscuring the man's features, making it difficult for Kyate to determine the extent of his injuries. Since the blood was dried, Kyate felt sure that the wounds had only been superficial, yet he needed to clean the area in order to be sure.

Kyate looked around the rover, hoping to find some water, or any solution that would do the job. There was nothing; although he wasn't surprised, since this was a rover, it wouldn't be logical to stock it. He rubbed his hands roughly through his hair and glanced back at Meno, still lying helpless on the floor. This would definitely be another problem. – no food, no drink, no supplies of any kind.

'Well, first things first,' he thought to himself.

He opened the trap to the propulsion system and quickly located the hydraulic pumps. Opening a valve, he drained some of the synthetic oil into his cupped hand. Kyate rubbed the lubricant gently over Meno's face. An agonizing scream escaped from the bloody confinement. Meno's body quaked with the suffering.

"Take it easy, old friend. I'll do what I can for your pain, but this must be done." Kyate spoke softly as he began sending the tranquilizing energy into Meno's temples. He blocked the pain receptacles and increased Meno's release of endorphins.

Meno slowly raised his hand and signaled to Kyate by placing his index finger against the end of his thumb in the sign of an "O".

"Good," Kyate replied, and he caught Meno's hand giving it a firm squeeze.

Kyate waited a few minutes for the blood to soften. Tearing off a piece of his shirt, he used it to carefully wipe his friends injured face, removing the crust that had now become saturated with the oil. Kyate returned again for more oil. After repeating the process three times, the disgusting blood-caked shroud was eliminated.

Meno wrinkled up his nose and opened his mouth a little. His skin was once again pliant; it moved. But still, he couldn't open his eyes. He remained silent.

"Meno ... this isn't pretty. Hang in there, fella ... "

Kyate extracted several splinters of various materials that had been imbedded deep in Meno's skin. The gaping punctures needed protection against infection. Kyate had no choice at this point.

"Listen, my friend," Kyate said, placing a firm hand on Meno's shoulder, "you have some very deep puncture wounds here. If I could get you to a medical facility they would be cleaned and sealed, and you would be irradiated to prevent infection. But under the circumstances, I need to attend to this problem in a very primitive way. I wish it could be otherwise! Meno, forgive me ... but this I must do. Whatever happens, Meno ... and this is critical – *DO NOT MOVE A MUSCLE*!!" Then Kyate lightened the mood a little. "If you wince, I may miss my target and slice off your nose!" he chuckled.

Now, having a pretty clear indication of what Kyate was about to do, Meno grimaced. "Hey," he said weakly, "do you think while you're at it you could remove the crow's feet and some of those age lines?"

Kyate laughed and slapped Meno hard on the stomach, knocking the air out of him.

"That's a fine bedside manner!" Meno chided.

Kyate withdrew his laser sword and adjusted the intensity setting to the lowest degree. He proceeded to meticulously cauterize each wound, searing the flesh from deep in the puncture, burning out the impurities and then sealing the wound with the heat. The sweet smell of the burning flesh nauseated Kyate as he performed this procedure. Meno made animal noises in his throat, but he didn't move.

"There now ... I'll bet you don't even scar." Kyate rubbed his chin thoughtfully. "You know, I would make a very good surgeon."

"What about my eyes, Doc?" There was a tinge of apprehension in Meno's voice. He still was unable to free his eyelids.

"Let's have a look." Kyate bent close to see what the problem could be. Placing one hand above and one hand below Meno's right eye, Kyate forced the upper and lower lids apart. Recoiling in trepidation, Kyate tried hard to conceal his dismay.

"What'da ya think?" Meno asked nonchalantly.

Kyate forced open the eyelids on the other eye.

"Muscle damage ..." he muttered almost inaudibly.

"Hummmm," Meno murmured in a low knowing tone. He sensed something was wrong, but he didn't force an explanation.

"Meno, try to sleep, your healing will be accelerated in the process." Kyate's tone was cold and a little harsh, but Meno understood and remained silent.

Kyate stood up slowly and walked over to the rear view port, distancing himself from his old friend. He scratched at his chest while he surveyed the great expansive cosmos stretched out before him. Rubbing his stomach slowly, back and forth with his open palm; he wondered what he could do, or how he would tell Meno the truth about his eyes. The powerful force of the vacuum had sucked his eyeballs right out of their sockets! No wonder the man had been in such excruciating pain.

CHAPTER 16 – Out Of Control

Zeidra opened one sleepy eye and peeked out from under the satin comforter. She could see Niporo on the other side of the room, positioned in front of a vanity. Standing there in only his tight fitting trousers, he was leaning forward toward the mirror, shaving. She squirmed up onto one elbow to get a better look.

His smooth, thick skin had a golden luster. The expanse of his wide, muscular back and strong, square shoulders caused something to stir in her lower stomach. Her eyes traveled down to the indentation near the end of his spine; it disappeared beneath his belt. His muscles at his buttocks were tightly rounded and solid looking, straining against his snug fitting pants. She could even see the contour of his thighs. She felt the heat rising; churning uneasily, up into her gut. Her breasts felt like they were swelling. The carnal tantalization confounded her.

Zeidra remembered last night. She felt the flush sting her cheeks. Maybe a dream, she thought. Then she remembered Kyate. She dropped back down onto the pillows and pulled one across her chest hugging it tightly, hiding her face in it. The knots in her stomach began to move down. She felt a strange subtle cadence proceeding, deep in her pelvis. The knots were tightening as the rhythm escalated into a vulgar, torrid throbbing.

The princess wriggled restlessly under the blanket, trying to curtail the disturbance, now a ruthless pounding in her depths. She willed the sensations to stop, but the pulsating intensified.

Kyate had recklessly awakened Zeidra's imprisoned sexuality, and had unintentionally left a painful, yearning void in her psyche, by not consummating the experience as he should have. He had reprimanded himself for his selfish, impulsive behavior; and he'd been aware, although after the fact, of the probable consequences. What Kyate feared had indeed transpired. Zeidra's carnal drive was not only initiated, it was insatiable.

Niporo was watching Zeidra in the mirror as she lay there on the bed behind him. He could only imagine what was going on in her sweet little mind as she thrashed around nervously beneath the covers, embracing the large fluffy pillow for some solace. He watched for a long time. His curiosity was heightened by the soft moaning that he recognized from last evening. He wasn't sure he could keep the oath that he'd made to himself. He didn't know if he could stand not taking her the next time she offered herself to him so blatantly. He turned around and looked at Zeidra. He was sure now; he knew what was going on in her head. He could barely see her face as she clutched the softness of the pillow around her.

Niporo walked over to the bed and sat down on the side next to Zeidra. He could see the tears slipping, one by one, from the outer corners of her eyes, which were squeezed tightly closed. He gently pulled the pillow away from her.

She looked up at him sadly, her lower lip quivering like a little girl lost. Without saying a word, Niporo reached down and scooped Zeidra up into his arms. He held her warmly against his bare chest and stroked her hair back away from her face. She melted in against him. She moved her warmth onto him. She encircled him with her arms. He felt her tears on his flesh, burning a trail over his chest and down his midsection. Like a white-hot river, her tears flowed down his body, burning his skin – but incinerating his soul. Now he knew – he understood hell. He knew full well that she wanted it – needed it.

But he also knew that she didn't want *HIM* – She wanted *Kyate*. He would be damned if he did give it to her, and damned if he didn't. And then there was the promise he'd made to himself, just last night. *'What a hopeless situation!'* His body was tense all over, and demanding relief. He knew full well that Zeidra was battling her own demons. They burned there in a silent hell; they suffered in the quiet conflagration.

Niporo thought of Llana who was still sleeping in the lounge. He knew he could relieve himself with lovely, voluptuous Llana. *'After all, hadn't he left her purring like a happy kitten in the early morning hours? ... But what about Zeidra? If he had read the signs right ... what about her frustration? NO!! ... This was no time to be noble ... why worry about anyone else at a time like this?"*

"Zeidra, I'd love to stay and chat, but I've got to take care of something." He grinned that big broad handsome grin of his and winked at her. He released the princess and padded across the room in his bare feet. He was gone. He needed to find Llana.

Llana turned around from the console surprised to find Niporo standing directly behind her.

"What the hell are you doing!?" Niporo demanded. His eyes were ablaze with rage and disbelief. "I can't believe you would betray me like this!"

"Niporo ... I ... I was ..."

"You were trying to configure the communication system? Well did you figure it out?"

Niporo slapped her hard, knocking her off the chair where she'd been sitting. She tried to scream, but he was on her too quickly. Clamping one of those iron hands tightly over her mouth to keep her quiet, he dragged her, kicking and struggling, over to the cargo bay and threw her down the open hatch. He jumped down, and instantly he was on her again. Niporo quickly opened the door to the launch bay and pulled Llana inside. It was sound proof in there, and Niporo didn't have to worry about Zeidra hearing them.

"I thought I could trust you, bitch!" he shouted. His face was almost blue with anger. His nostrils flared and his eyes were glazed.

Llana cowered into a corner. She feared for her life, and she could think of no plausible explanation for what she was doing, since Niporo had seen her trying to send a message. She was silent. Bruised and bleeding, she was trembling so violently her teeth were rattling.

Then, without warning, he half ran; half staggered to the launch bay door. Once on the other side, he closed it and locked it securely, leaving Llana inside; confused and frightened. He put his hand on the lever, and pulled it down. On the other side of the thick metal wall, the big doors at the end of the bay slid open. There was a howling sound, like the wind gusting through a deep canyon. Niporo waited a few minutes, and then he pushed the lever back up. The doors closed.

Niporo climbed the ladder of the cargo bay and stumbled into the lounge. He dropped heavily into the big overstuffed chair and released a huge shuddering sigh.

Just then, something caught his attention outside the window. He leaned closer to peer out. He cringed when he saw Llana's lifeless body, suspended there by the window, bloated beyond recognition, her skin ballooning as he watched. Her face was clearly visible, although her features were stretched and contorted by the expansion. It was due to the pressure difference.

To his horror, the body exploded, throwing tiny pieces of tissue and droplets of blood against the window. A thick cloud of bloody debris floated just outside.

Niporo screamed in terror.

He jumped from the chair and ran to the

control room. He engaged the propulsion system and threw the engines into full thrust, and the ship streaked out across the void.

Zeidra was awakened from her nap by his scream, not really sure if she might have dreamed it. She called out to Niporo as she climbed down off the bed.

Niporo hastily programmed the autopilot, and then hurried into the lounge to close the window covering, fastening it down securely. He ran for the shower room and ducked inside.

Turning on the water, he stepped into the shower and stood there motionless, trying to regain his composure, trying to stop the nightmare. He felt sick. He vomited. He retched. He slid down the length of the wet tile and onto the shower floor. He sat there in the vomit, his face buried in his hands, his arms resting on his knees. Terrorized, he groveled there under the cascading water. That's when he realized that there actually were limits to how vile he could be.

CHAPTER 17 – Eye To Eye

Getting a fix on his location, Kyate plotted a course which would take them to the rendezvous point where he had agreed to meet Beau and the men, on the other side of the asteroid field. God! How he hoped Beau had made it through!

Meno was in a deep, hypnotically induced sleep. Kyate had made sure that his friend wouldn't wake up until he had calculated all the alternatives.

One of the officers aboard Beau's craft was a surgeon, although Kyate wasn't sure it would be of any help without the technical equipment that would surely be needed. With that in mind, Kyate programmed the little remote "probe" to return to the approximate location of the wrecked Drothuarian ship and retrieve the eyeballs if they could be located.

He ran the optical scanner across one of his own eyes, watching the picture appear on the console before him. Magically the picture turned on the screen, as if on a carrousel, becoming three dimensional in the process.

Punching a few keys to change the color and dimension, Kyate loaded the pictograph into the probe's memory banks. Then he keyed in some coordinates, trying to remember the exact location of the wreck. He completed the programming by giving the probe the numbers of the grid section, which was to be its final destination; the rendezvous point with Beau.

Placing the little probe into the firing chute, he closed the cap and pushed the firing button. The mini-craft sailed out effortlessly, heading in the direction of the wreckage, just as it had been instructed to do. Kyate was grasping at straws, but he had to hold onto some hope. He sighed solemnly, as he looked over at Meno. The pathetic man looked so peaceful; he was completely oblivious! Kyate struggled in his mind, searching for a kinder means to impart the truth, rather than disclosing it bluntly. He would have to wake Meno up eventually. *'How would he tell him?'*

Kyate sat down wearily in the chair at the command console and ran his hands back over his forehead, through his hair. He stretched lazily, enjoying the feel of his muscles expanding. He reached down and reclined the seat, realizing that he needed some rest himself. There was nothing he could do about the hunger and thirst, but he could, however, sleep. Kyate closed his eyes and relaxed. Maybe he would come up with a solution once his mind had some time to recuperate.

On the far side of the grid, a crippled Drothuarian ship limped across the emptiness, to the section set aside for the meeting.

"Well, this is it men," Beau said, his voice revealing his exhaustion. He was surprised that they'd made it this far. He had no idea how they would go on.

"Any word from Kyate?" Lexy, the navigator, asked as he climbed into the bridge area.

"Nothing," Beau replied, checking the communications log, to be sure he hadn't missed anything that wasn't an audio transmission, "Nope. I sure hope they're OK. Damned field's treacherous! I can't believe we got through!" Beau cursed.

"By the skin of our teeth, you mean," Lexy interjected, picking up fallen manuals and instruments that had been thrown about the cabin during the asteroid bombardment. "This may be the first time in my entire life ..." he paused to think for a minute, "... that I've actually known *real* fear! Yeah ... the first time. Pretty strange, now that I think of it ... guess I was too stupid to be afraid." He placed some books on the shelving. "Fine line between courage and stupidity ... seems to me. Sure is good to be alive!" he laughed, looking over at the others.

"Lexy, boy! Are you becoming philosophical?" Jerome teased. "That's what I love about life ... and you're just finding out! You just don't appreciate her until you realized you haven't romanced her enough and before you know it ... she's gone! Same way with a woman, too."

Jerome was the chief surgeon for the main Deis fleet. He was older than he looked, and he looked to be about thirty. He was a tall thin man, with a ruddy, healthy complexion and huge, expressive green eyes. He had thick, curly red hair and he wore a mustache that was several shades darker.

He volunteered for this mission because he had spent the greater part of the last fifteen years working side by side with Kyate, whom he respected and trusted with his life. He felt obligated to help Kyate anytime he felt he could be of service; as Kyate had save his neck on countless occasions.

Besides being a strong and courageous Deis Warrior, he was a doctor and a surgeon, holding specialty degrees in twelve areas. His compatriots chided him, often calling him "the twelfth degree red doc". Although he was a genius in his own right, he had an extraordinary sense of humor. It was a true talent and much appreciated by his shipmates.

"Hey! Lexy," Zak, the second navigator was motioning to Lexy to come over to the radarscope, "... take a look. I don't think it's big enough to be a ship, but it's some sort of craft .... I wonder ..."

"Well as fast as it's approaching, it'll be here shortly ... whatever it is," Lexy said, doing fast calculations on the screen. "I just hope to god its friendly!"

By that time, Jerome and Beau were there studying the "blip" on the scope.

"OK..," Beau said, "Let's just assume it's unfriendly. Get the shields up, and lock the rays on that critter. We sure as hell aren't able to run!" Turning to Jerome, who was busy checking systems, he asked, "Can we use the microwave shields?"

"Doesn't look like it, Beau." Jerome paused thoughtfully. "But!... maybe if we all close our eyes when it comes into range, it won't see us!"

Beau looked up at Jerome, with an expression of pure astonishment. Lexy and Zak bust into uproarious laughter, watching Jerome and Beau who remained straight faced. Finally Beau rolled out of his chair and onto the floor. Clutching his ribs, he laughed 'til he ached. Jerome just smiled and walked out of the cabin.

Now that the tension had been diminished, the men continued with their preparations. The unidentified craft was entering their sector and they were as ready as they could be, considering the amount of damaged the ship had sustained.

It came into view and everyone held their breath. They waited silently.

"My god! It's coming right for us!" Lexy shouted. "It must know we're sitting here!" He looked over at Jerome, who was sitting there, in his harnesses with his eyes closed. It struck him so funny that he exploded into hysterics. Then, he realized how inappropriate his giggling was, at a time like this; he guessed how absurd his behavior must appear, and he laughed even harder.

Beau and Zak looked on in amazement, thinking perhaps Lexy was having a "break down". Nobody else noticed Jerome sitting there quietly, his eyes still closed.

Suddenly, all the alarms were going off, and the men braced themselves. A very, very small, shiny silver craft sailed into view and shot straight toward the immobile Drothuarian ship. It stopped just short of impact and hovered. It was tiny; no larger than the screen on the console. Its triangular shape was smooth, and no entrances were apparent. There were two long robotic arms extended from one point on the surface, along with a few flashing colored lights, and an antenna of some kind. It looked menacing, floating there beside the vulnerable ship.

"It's a remote probe!" Lexy gasped.

"Can you see any identification on it?" Beau asked, unbuckling the harness to see for himself.

"Not from this angle," Lexy answered.

"Jerome, can you run an analysis on it? Is it close enough?"

"Already have, Beau. It's coming off the printer now."

Beau walked over to the printer and snatched the paper, and read aloud, "It's Drothuarian, used primarily to collect sample material and retrieve items from outside a craft. Launch and retrieval is executed from inside model LR2435 ...," he stopped reading and looked up, "What model is this? Did anyone get the model number?"

"That's us!" said Jerome. "Both the vessels are LR2435's ... ours and Kyate's."

Beau continued, "Launch and retrieval chute is located on rear right wall of control cabin ..." again he looked up, surveying the rear of the cabin.

"This must be it!" shouted Zak, pointing to a small portal just to his left.

Beau walked across the cabin and ran his

hand around the hatch on the wall. "It says here, that the probe can be programmed to go just about anywhere and do just about anything ... and listen to this... The probe can be retrieved by opening the hatch and turning the retrieval control ... Well we could have figured that one!" Beau laughed, and then stopped short. "Hey! A probe retrieval is *not* launch dependent."

"That means we can bring 'er in!" Lexy was already opening the hatch and examining the interior, looking for the control. Turning it to "retrieve", the crew watched the probe intently as it hovered outside their ship.

The colored lights on the surface of the probe began to change their flashing pattern and the antenna started rotating around, seeking a directional signal. Slowly, it floated closer to the ship and circled until it was flush with the chute. Silently it slipped in and an exterior hatch closed behind it.

"We've got it. What'll we do now?" Lexy looked a little apprehensive.

"I'm not sure," Beau said thoughtfully, "depends on what it's carrying or if it's .... Maybe it's empty ..."

"Well open the trap and get it out, somebody!" Jerome called from the console. "Maybe someone sent out for lunch and the probe got lost ... I could sure use a juicy steak right now!" he chuckled. "Come on girls!"

"Open the hatch, Lexy!" Beau ordered.

Zak, who was standing beside Lexy, stepped back out of the way... Way back out of the way. Lexy gingerly opened the hatch and reached in. He pulled the probe out very slowly and carried it over to the console and set it down in front of Jerome. Jerome examined the surface for some indication of how to extract the payload, if in deed there was any.

"Beau, will you read me the instructions for opening this thing?"

Beau ran his finger down the page and then stopped to read the instructions, "You press the yellow key, while holding down the blue key."

Immediately a hydraulic type of opening began to rise at the top of the probe. It resembled an elevator, lifting the contents from the inside out. Jerome peered into the container.

"Well ... Jerome ... what have we got?" Beau asked, approaching the console.

"Lunch," answered Jerome, still looking at the box.

"*HOLY SHIT!*" cried Beau, as he got his first look at the contents. The eyeballs stared up at him vacantly.

"It's just something about those eyes ... don't you think, Beau?" Jerome said wistfully.

"Close that thing up, Jerome!" Beau

yelled, grabbing his stomach and beginning to gag.

"Believe me, I'd love to ... if you'd be so kind to... to read me the instructions. This is one situation that you and I definitely see eye to eye on!"

Jerome was on the other side of the cabin, waving the paper at Zak with one hand, while holding his abdomen with the other; he was still gagging and retching.

Zak didn't ask what was in the container, he was sure that he didn't want to know, after watching Beau heaving his guts out. He just took the paper and proceeded to read. "Hold down green button and press red."

The container slid fluidly back into the interior of the probe.

"Come on guys!" Lexy, who had been standing several yards away from the console, looked first to Jerome and then to Beau, who seemed to be feeling a little better, now; at least his face wasn't as green as it had been. "What was that all about?"

Jerome was still examining the exterior of the probe. Beau had found a stool to sit down on, right outside the shower room. Zak just stood silently, questioning Lexy with his eyes; he shrugged his shoulders, extending both hands, palms up.

Lexy frowned at Zak, directing the same gesture back at him, in answer to his mute interrogation.

Jerome finally stood up and faced the two. "Seems that whoever sent us the probe, may be a little short sighted .... There's a pair of eyeballs in there." He nodded toward the probe. He walked across the cabin, slapping Zak hard on the back as he passed by him, "Take note ... never lose sight of your probe!" Sitting down at the information CPU, he requested a data search on "eyes", "eyeballs", "optics", "optical". The computer flashed and buzzed and soon the data was appearing on the monitor. Jerome was able to read an entire screen of material in seconds. He quickly refreshed his education on the subject; his brain soaking up the information like a dry sponge in a puddle.

"What do you make of it, Jerome?" Beau asked.

"Well, there should be some way to link it up to our system and get a memory dump of its instructions. If we can figure out where it came from and why it stopped at this exact spot ... then I'd say we could probably figure out the rest ...," He got up from the information center and returned to the probe. He picked it up and holding it over his head, he surveyed the bottom of the metal encasement. "Ah.. Hah!" he announced, sitting it back down on the console.

Rummaging through a compartment

under the CPU, he drug out some long cables, attaching one end to a port on the command unit and the other end to the aperture on the underside of the probe. Sitting down in front of the command console he set some options and then keyed in the word "CONNECT". He held his breath and waited. To his delight and surprised, the lights on the probe began to flash in alternating patterns. The screen was now waiting for instructions. Jerome typed the word "DUMP". The printer immediately spit out a page of information, but the data was listed in machine language and glyphs, and would need to be deciphered to be understood.

"Feed this through the scanner," he said, handing the paper to Beau, who was standing over his shoulder, watching the screen.

Beau leaned to his left and put the paper into the feeder tray on the scanner. The machine automatically drew it inside.

Jerome was busy giving the control unit instructions. When he had finished he looked up at Beau and said, "You know … I don't know … if I really want to know … but there's no way of knowing …!" He was cut short by the wad of paper that Beau quickly shoved into his open mouth.

Beau was nodding his head slowly, "My sentiments, exactly."

They waited.

Data began tracking across the screen in front of them. Jerome studied it silently, while Beau read each line out loud. Jerome looked up at Beau in disgust and Beau was quiet from that point on. The pair realized that the only worthwhile information was the three sets of coordinates: *Origination, Target Destination, and Final Destination.* The rest of the information was system check numbers; logging-data, for temperature, speed, distance, and time; and computer generated garbage. All in all, not much to go on, in solving this mystery.

Beau spread a map out on the table and marked an "X" on each of the three sets of coordinates. Then he drew a straight line connecting the points. All four men stood over the map, trying to make some sense of the tracing. Nothing seemed obvious.

"The only thing I can say, is that this thing was instructed to stop at this exact point," Beau said; his frustration audible.

"Wait a minute! Think about this ...," Lexy placed his finger on the intersection of the grid lines where they were waiting now for Kyate, "this is us ... AND the probe's destination, right? ... Well I'd guess it was Kyate that sent the probe. He's the only one that would know these exact coordinates ... I mean ... nobody else is here 'cept us."

"Not yet, anyway!" Jerome interjected.

"Yeah, but what would Kyate be doing in this location?" Zak slammed a thick finger onto the origination point.

Jerome scratched at the back of his head, his eyebrows were drawn into a tight frown, and he kept looking at the map; like it would give up some secret if he stared hard enough.

"OK …. Just suppose for a minute that it did originate from Kyate. Why would he send us *EYEBALLS*? ….. A joke? … Pretty sick if you ask me …" Beau said rubbing his forehead thoughtfully with both hands.

"No way!" said Zak. "Kyate doesn't joke about anything … you know better than that."

The alert system began flashing, and the alarms started to blare.

Lexy rushed to his post. "Incoming craft!" he yelled. "I'm getting a signal now… there's a video communication coming in!.. *IT'S KYATE!*"

Everyone yelled and applauded. Their own crossing had been so horrendous that they had all been certain that Kyate had endured a bad time of it himself. The crew cheered jubilantly.

Beau bolted across the cabin, and he read the message aloud, "HELLO FROM KYATE… TROUBLE IN THE FIELD … SHIP DESTROYED … CHECK LOWER LAUNCH BAY… IF YOU HAVE A ROVER … TETHER IT AND OPEN THE LAUNCH DOORS… WILL

ENTER   THERE ... ...   MENO SERIOUSLY INJURED."

"My god!" Jerome sucked the words in. "They're Meno's ... My god, those must be Meno's eyes!"

"Well let's hustle! Don't just sit there ... Lexy! Zak! See if there's a rover in the lower hold! If it's there, get a line on it and we'll tow it! Make sure it's on a winch that works ... check it out before you let it go!" Beau shouted Kyate's orders.

Lexy and Zak ran to the opening to the bay and disappeared below.

Jerome was leaning over the table, his hands spread out on the map. "Beau, I think I can do it!" he said in a low determined voice. "I checked 'em out pretty good and I didn't see much decomposition ... the probe is built to preserve, too. Depending on the damage to the nerves and musculature ... I betcha I can!!" He turned his head up and to the side, giving Beau a defiant nod.

"Have you got the equipment on board?"

"I never travel without my mini-lab and my robotic surgery booth! What kind of a self-respecting surgeon would do otherwise? It's in the cargo bay ... Give me a hand and we'll set it up down there. It's a good idea to get on with it as soon as possible ... before those nerves and muscles start the healing ... could complicate things."

"Good god, Jerome ... why Meno! I hope to hell you can pull it off ... but then we're just assuming those eyes are his ... what if they're not?"

"What if all of a sudden this damned crippled ship takes off like an eagle?! Come on, Beau, think logically! Who's the hell eyes do you think we've got here? You think Kyate just saw them floating around in space and decided to bring them along for kicks?! Besides, Kyate said Meno *is* injured ... he needs our help either way. Ya ready?"

"Let's go, pal!" Beau said, slapping Jerome on the back.

All was ready by the time Kyate's craft entered the grid section where the Deis men were waiting. The sleek shiny rover glided into the bay without incident. The heavy doors closed tightly, once the small ship was secured in its track.

The inner door opened and the men rushed in to greet Kyate, embracing him and jostling him affectionately. The crew's happiness was overshadowed, however, by their awareness of Meno's injury. He was a good friend to all of them; they'd all been together for years.

Kyate was surprised to learn that the

probe had preceded him, but he didn't take the time to explain the details of the accident.

"He's still asleep ... he doesn't know, yet. I was just hoping that there would be a chance to retrieve ... them ... and maybe, just maybe ..." Kyate's voice sounded tired; sad.

"Well, Kyate ... due to your unfounded hope and your usual quick thinking, I have a feeling we can save Meno's sight!" Jerome announced confidently.

Kyate raised his eyebrows in surprise and expectation. "Jerome, if you believe you can do it ... So I too, shall believe!" He gave Jerome a firm swat on the shoulder and smiled broadly.

"We've got to get him into my surgery booth ... quickly!" Jerome called out, motioning for the men to help. "How is it that he sleeps so soundly?" he asked, looking inside the rover, at Meno, and then looking back at Kyate inquisitively.

"He's in trance."

"I thought it was something like that. How long before he awakens?"

"When I decide to awaken him."

"You know, Kyate, you'd make a great anesthesiologist ... how'd you like to work for me, for a change?" He spoke while busily helping to slide Meno out of the rover and onto a stretcher. "Over here, men! Just put him here on the table and slide him up so his

head's inside the enclosure .... That's good ....
Just a little more ..... OK! That'll do it. Now
you all just go pray!" Jerome clapped his
hands and then pretended to shoo the men
out of the cargo bay.

"I can help you," Kyate said to Jerome,
hesitant to leave his good friend Meno.

"Kyate, I know you need to get some food
into you."

"You're more perceptive than I thought!"
Kyate said, looking surprised.

"Well not really ... It's just that ... I can
hear your stomach growling, Kyate," he
admitted. "You go on with the others. Trust
me ... I'll do everything I possibly can to
restore Meno's eyes!"

CHAPTER 18 – Too Late

Zeidra could hear the shower running, and decided to take this opportunity to talk to Llana, as she hadn't seen her since their brief conversation late yesterday afternoon, in the lounge.

The princess quietly slipped through the hatch and down into the cargo bay.

"Llana .... Llana! She whispered.

There was no reply.

She looked around, in between, over, and under the vast number of boxes and crates. She didn't see a sign of the woman. She began to wonder if she had actually seen her; talked to her; or if maybe she had been hallucinating, or dreaming.

"Am I insane?" she asked aloud. "My god! I must be, I'm talking to myself! Or am I answering myself? ... No ... maybe Llana's found another hiding place, in the upper level." She brought her hand quickly up to her mouth to stop the blabbering.

"Zeidra! Is that you down there?" It was Niporo.

Zeidra rushed over to look up through the hatch at Niporo. "I was looking for some clothes," she lied.

"I brought you some clothes. They're up here. Come on up out of there, now!" he sounded angry.

She climbed the ladder slowly, and when she neared the hatch, Niporo grabbed her wrist and yanked her up roughly.

He was standing there with only a towel wrapped around his dripping body, and he didn't say another word. Still holding on to Zeidra's wrist, he led her back to the sleeping quarters and over to the corner where he picked up the bag he had brought from her royal chambers. Then he dragged her back through the craft to the shower room, shoved the bag into her arms, and pushed her through the shower room door, closing it behind her.

"Aren't we in a foul mood this morning!" she screamed back at Niporo, through the door.

"Get cleaned up! We'll talk after you're dressed!" he shouted.

Zeidra was glad to see the shower. She eagerly shed her gown and stepped into the enclosure. She turned on the cascade of water. It was as refreshing as a morning walk in her gardens.

She was instantly reminded of the ordeal

her constituents must be facing back on Earth. If what Niporo had told her was true, her heart ached with compassion for the people of Ulonica, as well as the entire planet Earth. If the Drothuarians had taken over, it was no telling what was happening there. And then she was reminded of Kyate ... that early morning meeting ... their first conversation ... the fascination... the excitement ...

"Stop this!" she ordered herself, out loud. *'No.. No ... I'm talking to myself again!'* she thought ... silently this time.

Her thoughts continued in controlled silence. *'I'm glad I'm dead... I'm sick to death of the responsibility! It would be lovely to have a life. To be a person and not a princess! To allow myself to love and be loved ... to see Kyate on his own terms... NO! I can't think about him ... he defiled me! But, then, I don't remember it that way. I don't remember him forcing himself on me at all! I thought I ... Oh my god! ... I remember wanting him.'*

Zeidra turned her face straight up into the running water. Her tears were invisible in the flood. She tried to still her thoughts; those torturing thoughts. She'd tried so hard not to think at all, these last few hours. Too much confusion ... *'where was Niporo taking her? Was it true that everyone thought she was dead? Had the Drothuarians defeated Ulonica? Had Earth fallen under Drothuarian rule? And Kyate ... was he alive? Did he, too, think she was dead? Would she ever see those fascinating eyes again? Would she ever know exactly what had transpired, that late night in her chambers with him?'* She dared not wonder ... *'who seduced who?!'*

She stepped from the shower, completely refreshed. She rummaged through the bag to see what Niporo had brought along for her to wear. She pulled out a long, purple silk tunic, and a flowing, white satin skirt, and put them on.

Zeidra's long curly hair was in a mass of knots and tangles, and she couldn't find a comb in the bag, so she gathered her hair on top of her head, and tied it in place with a ribbon from her skirt. She was thankful that in his haste, Niporo *HAD* remembered her sandals. She smoothed the tunic down with her hands and fluffed the curls around her delicate face. Now that she was "cleaned up", was she really ready to face Niporo?

Warily, she opened the door and peeked out into the lounge. Niporo was sitting on the sofa, fully dressed, now. He was holding a glass of wine in both hands, staring down into the glass, blankly.

"It's a little early for wine, don't you think?" she asked, testing the waters.

Niporo looked up briefly without speaking; then he looked back down into the goblet.

"Niporo ... are you angry with me?" Zeidra walked across the lounge and sat down across from him, in the big overstuffed chair.

"No. Go over there and get yourself something to eat."

"I'm not very hungry, right now," she said. "What's bothering you? Niporo if I did something ..." She leaned forward to touch his hand but he moved away from her reach.

"If you don't want to eat, nobody's going to force you," he said, getting up from the sofa. He didn't even look down at her. He simply walked out of the lounge and into the control room, where he began a series of system checks and course configurations.

Zeidra sat there for a few minutes, feeling as if he'd thrown ice water on her. She decided not to let it pass. The princess jumped to her feet and followed him into the control room, defiantly.

"Why are you acting this way?" she demanded. "If we're stuck on this ship together, you could at least be nice to me!" She sounded like a spoiled little girl.

Niporo ignored her.

"I command you to tell me where you're taking me!" She said it in a louder voice. "If I'm to be miserable ... stuck here with you, I'd like to know for how long! How long will it be until I have some civilized company?!"

Busy with the computer readouts, Niporo

didn't want to be badgered. He refused to buy into the altercation, hoping she would tire of it, and leave him alone.

"You could at least have the decency to tell me what I did to make you sulk like this!"

No response.

"I wish Kyate were here!" she whined, turning to leave the control room.

"What did you say?!" Niporo yelled, swiveling around just in time to see her disappear into the lounge.

He lunged from the chair, and catching up with her, grabbed her roughly by the arm. "Who do you wish were here?" he snarled through clenched teeth.

"Niporo, please don't treat me this way .... I thought we were friends ... If you're angry with me, then tell me why ..."

"I wasn't angry with you!" Niporo shouted, "but I sure as hell am now!"

He shoved her away from him and turned back toward the command console.

"Niporo! What did I do?" she cried.

He stopped dead in his tracks and looked back at her incredulously. "Zeidra!" he said in a low, controlled voice, turning to face her, "I've had a bad morning and it didn't have a damned thing to do with *YOU*!" He took a step toward her. "Then you start your damned badgering, when I just wanted to be left alone!" Again he moved toward her. "And then you have the audacity to throw that sonofabitchin' Kyate's name, right in my face!" He was right in front of her now, breathing down on her, as he spoke; his voice was seething with rage. "After I've done everything in my power to keep from doing to you what *HE* did! After I've used up all the restraint I have! After I've done my best to be honest with you about my feelings!" He grabbed her around her waist and jerked her into his arms, crushing her painfully against him. "So you wish Kyate was here, do you?" His face was only inches away from hers. "Tell you what!" he snarled down at her, "before this trip is over, you'll wish you'd never mentioned that name to me! .... You want to play mind games with me, do you? Thought you'd try making me jealous, to get my attention, didn't you? ... Well you got my attention!"

Zeidra's eyes were wide with fear as she stood there trembling in Niporo's grasp. She knew better than to say a word. She tried to free herself from his hold, he was hurting her; mashing her against that hard, muscular body of his.

Suddenly, his mouth was on hers. His kiss was surprisingly gentle compared with the brutal way he'd been handling her. It was a tender yet demanding kiss. It was insisting that she reciprocate. He eased his grip on her body and began moving his hands along the contours of her back and sides, all the while his lips kept pressuring her for the response he desired.

When his arousal was obvious, he pulled her hips into him, pressing her against it. She succumbed to his prompting, giving up her body to his, willingly; giving her mouth to him sensuously. She moved against him, within his embrace. Her body was taking over again, just as it had before; just as he had commanded it to. Her breathing became heavy, and her temperature was rising, as he held her there, as the passion intensified.

Just when she was at that point, where passion melts away all logic and reason, he released her. Looking down into her pleading eyes, he smiled that big broad handsome smile of his. "Why don't you give Kyate a call!" he said coldly; then walked away.

Zeidra stood there in frustrated humiliation. She felt the angry tears stinging her cheeks. Niporo was no fool. He could read her like a book, after all that was his job! He'd said himself, that he understood her special kind of logic. She hated herself for playing on his adversarial attitude toward Kyate. Niporo had known exactly what she was up to ... But Zeidra wasn't prepared for the consequences.

Days went by, and Niporo conspicuously kept his distance from Zeidra, during the daytime. He only spoke to her when it was necessary, and he spent most of the time in his control cabin.

At night, he demanded that she share the big bed with him, but he never touched her with his hands; he would however, move his body against hers now and then, while he pretended to be asleep. He also made it a point to flaunt his nudity while in the sleeping quarters; observing her reactions, all the while; he knew she was watching him, but he feigned apathy.

Sometimes, in the night, when he would move up against her, he could feel her heart beating, hard, throughout her body. He gained satisfaction from her heavy sighs. He enjoyed how she fidgeted nervously beneath the covers. Niporo made sure to keep Zeidra in a constant state of sexual tension; without saying a word, without her conscious awareness of his determination, he played the game like a pro, and it was beginning to take its toll on Zeidra's emotions. She was unable to sleep, and she had no appetite. She was clearly unhappy and obviously lonely, but *she* also tried to play the game; she didn't speak, unless spoken to, and she fought hard, not to reveal her despondency; although it was a futile attempt, since Niporo had that uncanny Drothuarian perception.

It had been nearly two weeks, and Niporo decided it was time to test his strategy. He knew the princess better than she understood herself. For years he had meticulously kept logs of her habits, her routines, and especially her fertile periods. That made it possible for him to ascertain exactly where he stood in his sinister endeavor. He had carefully calculated Zeidra's cycle, counting the days from her last menses; and this was the day of reckoning.

He had been watching Zeidra from the command console, in the control cabin. Zeidra had been drinking a glass or two of wine each night, to help her sleep, but tonight she poured her wine from the bottle, to which Niporo had added *a little something special*. As was her usual evening ritual, she took her wine glass and headed for the shower. He noticed that she was walking a little more deliberately; slower than usual, and she seemed just a bit off balance.

His timing had to be perfect, in order to pull this one off. He quickly undressed and wrapped a towel around his waist. He waited outside the shower door, to make his entrance before Zeidra could turn on the water. He gave her just enough time to disrobe, and then he burst through the door, innocently.

"Oh!" he acted surprised, "I didn't realize you were in here ... I didn't hear any water ... I'm sorry." He stood there inventorying Zeidra's flawless curves, as she dove for her robe, to hide behind. "No.. no! Honey, don't hide it... I approve of what I see!"

"Get out of here, Niporo!" Zeidra demanded, although her eyes were telling him that she was glad just to hear him say something nice. She clutched the robe tight under her chin.

"Come on Princess," he spoke softly, reaching for her slowly, and catching her behind her neck with one of his massive hands, "We're not going to stay mad forever, are we?" He was pulling her slowly toward him, studying her expression as he drew her nearer. "I'm really sorry we quarreled ... Honey, you know I love you ... and I really want to make love to you .... I need to make love to you."

"Let me go!" Zeidra cried, trying to pull away. But Niporo saw something else in her eyes; something that had turned to excitement when he told her he'd actually make love to her. She was trembling.

"NO! Never!" she screamed at him, reaching up to pull his hand free. Her robe fell to the floor. She tried to convince him to let her go, but what he felt, emanating from her body was pure erotic heat. He could feel it and he could smell it. Now he would taste it.

Niporo caught Zeidra around the waist with his other arm and pulled her up against his body. She struggled violently this time and he could hardly hold her. Quickly he covered her mouth with his kiss, knowing that the struggling would end within seconds. Niporo held her tightly and kissed her gently at first and then deeply.

Suddenly, Zeidra's passions were unleashed in a flood of uncontrollable lust that surged through her entire body. She locked her arms around Niporo's neck and offered herself up to him, in answer to his determination.

Niporo scooped Zeidra up into his arms and carried her into the lounge, laying her down on the sofa. He stood over her, watching her body as it spoke to him. Every movement disclosed a secret. He was fascinated by its language. He was in awe of its ability to convey so much emotion ... so much raw passion ... so much uninhibited sexuality.

Niporo dropped his towel and climbed onto Zeidra's writhing nakedness. Slowly, gently he spread her legs wide, and lowered his body between them. She uttered a low, animal sounding groan.

"Zeidra, will you marry me?" he whispered

into her neck.

She arched her back and shoved her hips up hard against his. Her hands were clawing at his back. The aphrodisiac, he had added to her wine, seemed to be working perfectly.

"Are you going to marry me? ... I want you to promise me, now!" Niporo gasped hoarsely, trying to restrain his need, until she promised.

"Oh god!" she screamed, "do it, Niporo, do it now .... Please!!"

He began to probe against her softness, moving up between her thighs and entering the heat. She moaned loudly now, and bit into his shoulder with her teeth.

"You've got to marry me .... Zeidra! Tell me now! Promise me you'll marry me!" He panted between thrusts.

He'd gone as far as he could. If he moved up into her any further, it would be too late for negotiating. He covered her face with kisses and then moved to her ear, breathing his question against it, over and over again between kisses.

He would see to it that there would be *NO* accusations of rape. He would make sure that Zeidra understood that she alone was in control; that *THIS* choice was *HERS* alone. He would remain blameless.

"Please .... Please, Niporo!" she choked, "I can't take this... please do it now!"

"Will you marry me?" He bit her hard on

the neck and moved just a little further into her.

She struggled under his weight, trying to force his entry.

He slowly withdrew, and she sucked in her breath, only to let out a cry when he began to move into her again.

"Mary me, Zeidra! Tell me! Promise me!" He began his withdrawal once more.

"Yes! I promise! I will! ... I'll marry you!" she screamed.

"And you'll bear my child?" he gasped, barely able to contain his excitement, and laboring to restrain himself from ramming his ardor through in his triumph.

"Yes!" she screamed, "I'll do it! I'll marry you and have your child! Please, Niporo ... Anything ... anything ... just do it ... I can't stand ...."

Niporo covered her mouth with his; arresting her supplication. He kissed her more passionately than he'd ever kissed her before. He could feel that fire raging between them, as her lips burned within his.

Niporo kissed her until she was in a frenzy. Her body was a willing captive, imprisoned under his massive weight. He was taking all of her and she was reeling with the multitudes of erotic sensations.

As Niporo skillfully moved against her pelvis, the pulsing sensation, deep in her core began to move downward, as if to meet his throbbing with her own. She was writhing and moaning and scratching, but he took his time, he didn't want to hurt her.

He was at a point where he could hardly stand it any longer; his need was too great, his desire was too strong. He thrust forward, moving against the obstacle more forcefully. Zeidra cried out. Niporo covered her mouth with his, and kissed her passionately; muffling her cries. He withdrew slightly, then pushed again. This time Zeidra screamed. Niporo reached down and moved Zeidra's feet up on either side of him so that her knees were bent, and her legs were further apart. He knew he had to finish it, before her passion diminished, or the pain of the consummation would be too severe.

He withdrew again and began kissing her and caressing her, moving his body on her, in a hypnotic, seductive rhythm; patiently returning her to a state of uncontrollable desire. Forgetting her pain, she began undulating beneath his movements, begging him to come into her.

Without warning, in the throes of *HER* passion, he thrust his body forward, driving up into her, ripping through her like a white hot blade. His conquest was absolute! She screamed in agony, the pain was overwhelming, and she tried to escape, but

Niporo knew, *THAT* couldn't happen; not now. He was compelled to continue the initiation, until Zeidra found the pleasure in it, lest the princess would be reluctant to make love again. He laid very still on her, waiting for the pain to subside. She cried, and her sobbing shook both their bodies. Her tears were futile, because Niporo had no intention of releasing her; not now.

She thought of Kyate. She knew Niporo had lied. She focused all of her attention on her memory of Kyate.

"Kyate ..." she breathed his name like a prayer.

Slowly, gently, Niporo began to move on her again; entering and withdrawing repeatedly. She cried and struggled at first, but Niporo held her tightly, stopping time and again, to renew her desire for him, and eventually she was lost in his loving. She surrendered it all, allowing him to bore deeper into her, wanting more of him inside her. The pain was completely obscured, by the provocative delirium of having him, knowing him, absorbing him.

Her body was melting around him, and the throbbing, incessant, rhythm, deep inside her, was maddening. Niporo understood, and he persisted in his erotic ritual. Although silently begging for more of him, Niporo denied her. She was on fire with pure lust, consuming all that he would give of himself. Zeidra's moaning became louder, but it wasn't from pain. She was writhing wildly under Niporo's body, but she wasn't trying to escape. Suddenly, her back arched up off the bed, raising Niporo's heavy body with her upward thrust, her teeth sunk deeply into his flesh, and her fingers clawed into his back. This was his moment.

Niporo pressed himself down on her, flattening her body on the sofa. Reaching around behind him with both arms, drawing her thighs up to his waist, he plunged into her eagerly, giving her all she'd been begging for, and more.

Zeidra cried out loudly. She screamed. The pain was excruciating.

"KYATE!!! KYATE!!!" She sobbed between screams.

As she screamed over and over again, initially in agony; the pain soon changed to ecstasy, as she made believe it was Kyate making love to her instead of Niporo. The world was exploding, and the sensual euphoria was devouring their senses, as they reveled in the paroxysm of their synchronous, climactic gratification.

The conception was assured.

The pledge had been consummated.

The universe stood still.

"Kyate ..." Zeidra whispered weakly.

CHAPTER 19 – Urampa

Kyate tossed and turned in his bunk. The visions were distressing. His spirit was agonizing over the scene before his psyche. Thrashing about, trying to break through the veil, to stop them; it was too late.

"Nooooo! Zeidra! Noooo!!!" he screamed, coming straight up off the bed as he returned to consciousness.

"Kyate, what is it?!" It was Beau standing there beside him. He had one hand on Kyate's shoulder, trying to steady him.

"I'm too late, Beau!" Kyate breathed hoarsely. "Niporo has taken his prize! I should have known he would waste little time.. I *DID* know! I'm just as much to blame as the Drothuarian! God forgive me ...!" Kyate sat there shaking his head and running his hands roughly through his hair.

"Were you there?"

"Yes! But I could do nothing ... the veil was too solid ... I couldn't break through! She didn't hear me!" He put his face down into his hands, and let out an animal sounding gut-wrenching groan.

"Are you sure it happened? I mean did he .....?"

Kyate lunged from the bunk, shoving Beau roughly aside, and began striking out at anything within his reach; knocking things from the counters and tables, he threw a chair against the wall. His rage was ferocious, and he lashed out at everything in his path, leaving a trail of destruction, as he crossed the room.

"What's going on in here!?" Jerome yelled, rushing into the room.

Kyate stopped short, and turned to look at Jerome.

"Kyate's gone a little insane, that's all," Beau said quietly to Jerome.

"Hey, Kyate! Pull yourself together! I need you!." Jerome motioned for Kyate to come over to him. "It's time to remove the bandages from Meno's eyes. .... I don't know what's going on with you, but seems to me, you're wasting that magnificent energy on anger, when I could use it in a more constructive manner ..... Like ... to accelerate the healing on Meno's optical nerves ..... If you'd just agree to come with me ....."

The two men stood there dumbfounded ... there were actually tears in the great Master's eyes; he was quiet now, standing at the far end of the room. Whether the tears originated from anger or grief, neither could know for sure, but Jerome and Beau were certain of one thing ... This mission was more personal to Kyate than they had been led to believe.

Kyate glared at the men, his eyes piercing them through narrow slits, a silent warning not to question his motivation; he knew their thoughts. Then relaxing, the master shook his body, loosening the tense muscles; literally shaking off his anger. He took a deep cleansing breath and his facial features softened. The glaze left his eyes.

"Let's go, Jerome," Kyate said in his deep quiet voice.

"Meno's been asking for you ... You're good medicine for him ... in more than a few ways!" Jerome spoke as they walked toward the cargo bay, where the temporary clinic had been set up. "If you could give him just one more *ZAP* of that curious vibration you use, then I think he'll be able to see.– Could use a jolt myself!!" He was teasing, but instantly Kyate laid his hand on Jerome's back, sending a current through his entire body and knocking him to the floor. Dazedly, Jerome picked himself up, first frowning and then laughing. "Damn! Kyate ... I was only kidding!"

"Oh really?" Kyate laughed. "Well I thought you were serious, and it's the least I could do ... "

"The *LEAST*?!" Jerome exclaimed. "If that was the *LEAST*, dear Kyate ... then please keep your hands to yourself from now on ... at least where I'm concerned!"

They entered the clinic and Jerome helped Meno to sit up on the side of the cot.

"Meno, Kyate's here," he said, unfastening the binding that concealed Meno's eyes. "We're going to have a look ... see if the healing's complete. The muscles and nerves should be fully operative by now." He continued unwrapping the bandaging. "Kyate's going to do one more of those *PURPLE RAY* things ... then we'll open 'em up."

The dressing was off. Meno's eyelids remained closed, while Kyate laid his hands over his friend's eyes. Within seconds, Jerome could see the faint violet glow radiating around Meno's head and shoulders. This phenomenon never ceased to amaze the doctor, who secretly wished he possessed those healing attributes himself. Kyate completed the procedure, and then stepped back.

"Whooo! Talk about HOT!! I felt that go clear through my skull!" Meno bellowed.

"Shut up and take your medicine like a *BIG BOY*!" Jerome said patting Meno on the cheek.

Jerome applied some lubricant to each of Meno's eyes and then they waited.

"OK, Meno, as soon as the sealant is dissolved, I'll tell you ... then you can open your eyes." Jerome held up his crossed fingers that only Kyate could see. It was a fifty-fifty chance that the nerve reattachment would be functional.

Three men were silent; each praying for a positive outcome.

"Looks good, Meno," Jerome said, examining the progress, "Now very slowly ... try to open them." He held his breath.

The muscles at the corners of Meno's eyes quivered slightly, but nothing happened.

"It's OK Meno," Jerome reassured him, "the muscles are weak from lack of use, besides the injury ... just keep trying ..."

Meno tried again. This time his eyelids opened very slowly; about half way.

"OH!" he cried, closing them immediately, "the light hurts!"

"Damn! I should have thought of that!" Jerome cursed. He looked over at Kyate and nodded ... being light sensitive was a good sign. Jerome turned the bright light away from Meno's face and dimmed the overhead lamps. "Sorry Big Guy! Now try again."

This time Meno opened his eyes all the way. He blinked several times, and then squinted. Kyate and Jerome could hardly bear the anticipation.

"Is that you, Kyate?" Meno asked, turning

his head in Kyate's direction; leaning forward and squinting.

"YEA!" Jerome shouted. "That's great, Meno! That's all I needed to hear!" he cried excitedly. "You probably won't see clearly for a while, but it'll come ... I know your sight will return!" He was hugging Meno and crying.

"Strange bedside manner for a Twelfth Degree Red Doc, I'd say!" Kyate said quietly, but the pleased look on his face reflected his own satisfaction.

"It's time to change our identities," Kyate said, "since we don't know who we might run into on Urampa ... You never know how many Drothuarians were working on Earth and may have returned. Here's what we'll do ...." Kyate divulged his plan to the crew, in detail, appointing each man his specific role in the scheme.

They were to pose as Drothuarian commerce executives, returning to Urampa to escape the turmoil taking place on Earth. Kyate would reprogram the minds of top government officials. Jerome would be in charge of breaking into the National Computer Data Bases, updating all files to reflect the identities of the crew, and opening bank accounts online. Meno's job was to monitor all landings and have everything in place by the time Niporo arrived; he would pose as a wealthy merchant and offer Niporo and Zeidra lodging. Beau, Lexy, and Zak would locate a suitable estate, rent it, renovate it, and install surveillance equipment throughout the interior and the grounds; they would then be in charge of security.

"Kyate, it sounds like you're planning on spending months there. It doesn't seem that complicated to me, just to apprehend Niporo and return the Princess to Ulonica! Is there something here that I've misunderstood?" Beau asked hesitantly, knowing the Master Kyate didn't appreciate having to justify any of his decisions once he'd set a course of action.

"I'll be honest with you," Kyate began, "I have a private motivation. There was ... a ... misunderstanding ... I made a grievous error in judgment, which I care not to disclose in detail, however ... It's a matter of honor! I must take the time on Urampa, to win ... regain the Princess Zeidra's respect and trust, before I return her to Earth. I also have a personal score to settle with Niporo!" Kyate's eyes grew dark; murderous. They all recognized that iron cold look, and knew that Niporo was already a dead man.

"The main Drothuarian headquarters," Kyate continued, pointing to a point on the star map, "is only three days distant from Urampa ... They're set up on the satellite

Keyto." He paused and rubbed at his chin, then looked up at his crew. "I believe there's a chance we can disable the entire Drothuarian communication network from Urampa, and then go into the complex on Keyto and blow em out of the universe! Maybe redeem ourselves ... *MYSELF*!"

Beau stepped forward. "Kyate, I think I understand this personal vendetta toward Niporo .... As far as teaching those damned Drothuarians a lesson they won't soon forget, I'd like nothing more! And speaking for the crew ... Your honor is our honor, and whatever it takes ... as long as it takes ... to attain your goals .... We're behind you one hundred per cent. Count on it!" Beau looked around at the men. They all nodded, affirming support for their Master and leader, Kyate.

"Now," Kyate said, smiling broadly, "comes the fun part. Just visualize ... in your mind ... the way you'd like to appear, if you were a Drothuarian. Remember ... their features are usually large and their coloring is darker than ours. The better you are at visualization, the better I'll be at providing your designated disguise. OK, now close your eyes, men .... And brace yourself!"

There seemed to be a whirlwind in the cabin as the molecular structure of each crewmember's body began to rearrange itself. Static electricity was quickening the air, and a crackling sound was skipping around indiscriminately.

"It's completed," Kyate stated. His voice was different; harsher, more resonant.

When the men opened their eyes they were astounded. The cabin was filled with strangers; the unfamiliar faces contemplating each other in disbelief and confusion. No one knew who was who, and the voices had changed, along with the faces and the stature.

"Beau! Where the hell are YOU?" a squeaky voice asked from the left side of the room. The man was short and thin and he had the demeanor of a professor.

"Good God! Jerome ... that has to be you! Nobody in their right mind would choose to look like a NERD!" the husky voice chuckled. He was standing right beside Jerome, who turned to look at him in amazement.

"Beau?"

"Yep, it's me!" He was a giant of a man, nearly six foot seven. His black curly hair hung to his shoulders and the handsome features on his face were perfectly chiseled. He had a long straight nose, full lips, a cleft in his prominent chin, and a very strongly defined jaw.

"What an ego!" cried a fairly normal sounding voice, directly across from Jerome and Beau. It was Meno, looking thirty years younger and much like he had appeared at that age, with the exception of his darker complexion and increased height. He saw the men looking at him quizzically. "OK, guys ... I'm Meno, for god's sake! I didn't change myself that much ... thought sure you'd recognize me!"

"Guess who!" It was a boy, sitting at the communication console. He didn't look to be much over thirteen, and beside him was a huge black dog.

The dog wagged his tail furiously, and to everyone's amazement, spoke, "Just call me Zak!" He laughed in his normal voice, "and this ... is my good friend Lexy!"

The crew roared with laughter.

"What a creative endeavor ...."

"Kyate?" Meno stared dubiously at the older man leaning on his cane. He was wearing a long black cloak, and his graying hair was pulled back and tied, at the back of his head. He looked to be about fifty-five or sixty, but even at that age, his distinguished masculine features made him extremely attractive. His height was the same, but his build was stockier; squarer. He retained the same expressive eyes, but his voice was the deep resonant one that the men had heard before they opened their eyes.

"You definitely look like the nobleman!"

Beau said, shaking his head in amazement. "I realize we can keep our names, but you definitely will have to change yours ... and it may be a good idea to change Meno's. What shall we call you, good sirs?" Beau bowed to the men in jest.

"You can call me MILO, that's an easy transition from Meno, don't you think?"

"In private, I prefer my own name, but when others are around, just call me Xanthar," Kyate said, rubbing at his chin thoughtfully.

The supplies and cargo from Beau's crippled ship had been divided and loaded onto the two small Rovers. The remaining energy source in the propulsion drive unit was divided between the two vessels. Meno and Kyate launched first, and then the Rover in tow was winched in, loaded and ejected from the damaged ship, carrying Beau, Jerome, Lexy, and Zak. – DESTINATION ... URAMPA!

"We're coming up on Urampa, men," Beau announced. He switched to the audio transmitter. "Kyate, do you want me to make contact?"

"Go ahead, I'll monitor it," Kyate replied. "Set your orbit here, we'll review the plans before going in."

The two Rovers cut their thrust and settled into orbit around Urampa. Jerome was busy at the control console working out codes to remotely link up with the control station on Urampa. Upon finding the right password, he added the two vessels to the log of expected arrivals, in the air traffic station's computer center.

"All set!" Jerome said, giving Beau the "go ahead" sign.

"Urampa Control ... do you read me?" Beau adjusted the transmitter, trying to find the correct frequency. "Urampa Control ... do you read me?"

"Identify!" a voice boomed back over the receiver.

"Azcon Company ... Drothuarian Commerce ... Origination Earth ...." Beau paused and looked over at Jerome. Jerome nodded his approval. "Request permission to enter your air space. We have two Rovers ... six personnel ... I repeat, we'd like permission to land in approximately four hours."

"Hold on," the voice on the receiver said.

The men waited impatiently, hoping that Jerome had succeeded.

"Permission granted ... use section D-DELTA, tarmac 11-D and 12-D."

The transmission was cut and the men on both ships breathed easier.

The two Rovers descended gracefully through the cloud cover and landed simultaneously on Urampian ground. They unloaded the vessels' cargo onto a rented transport vehicle, and obtained directions where they would find temporary accommodations.

After getting settled in their rooms, the men went down to the lounge for a drink, and to check out their new surroundings. The six of them sat down at a large round table. Kyate was intently gazing at the maid, who was looking over at the men.

"Kyate!" Beau scolded, "don't be flirting with the help, now!"

"Don't be so naive! Can't you see he's working?" Meno punched Beau in the shoulder.

The waitress hurried over to the table, smiling brightly as if she were glad to see the men.

"Beau! Darling! I can't believe it's really you!" the maid squealed, giving Beau a wet kiss, square on the mouth.

"Uh, um ... you know me?" he asked, wiping his mouth with the back of his hand. He was plainly embarrassed, and he scowled menacingly at Kyate, as the maid began writing down orders.

He leaned close to Kyate and said, "You're not supposed to play practical jokes, Kyate ... did you forget who you are ... The Master?!"

"You must be mistaken, Beau ..." Kyate looked serious. "There's no Master among us, and I am certainly not the great and mighty Kyate ... I am Xanthar, the ..." He was interrupted by the maid, Kayta.

"What would you like to drink, Xanthar? I'm so glad to see that your company has made it safely back!?" she said to Kyate, patting him affectionately on the shoulder.

Kyate smiled up at her and winked, "I'll have red wine ... I'm glad to see you looking so well, Kayta ... Beau's never stopped talking about you!"

"Well he sure doesn't seem so glad to see me, Xanthar!" she glanced over at Beau looking disappointed.

"It ... it ... was probably my accident!" Beau struggled with his lie. "Kayta, I've lost parts of my memory, that's it ..."

"Yeah, he's in bad shape," Jerome interrupted, "the only thing familiar to him is his name!"

"Well, I'll just have to jog his memory a little better!" she said, slipping her arms around his neck and easing her body down into his lap.

"Now ... wait a minute, Kayta ..." Beau tried to discourage it, but in mid-sentence, her pretty pouting lips were on his. She kissed him so sweetly, he couldn't help but respond. It was a long, lingering kiss.

Suddenly, the girl was snatched from Beau's lap, and standing there over him was a huge Drothuarian, glaring down on him with homicide in his eyes.

"What the hell do you think you're doing with my woman!?" he bellowed.

"Uh.. Um ... nothing ... I choked, see ... and she was trying to find the.. The bone!" Beau knew he was in trouble and looked over at Kyate, desperately trying to get his attention, but Kyate pretended not to notice.

The man grabbed Beau by his collar and jerked him to his feet. Kyate looked up at the man, then to Beau. Beau's eyes ardently pleaded with Kyate to do something. The man drew back his fist .... Kyate stared directly into the big fellow's eyes.

"Oh no!" the man drew in his breath, and immediately dropped Beau, who landed, surprised and confused, on the floor in front of the "oaf".

Beau saw the wet spot on the front of the man's trousers, scooting backward on the floor to escape the advancing puddle. The man turned on his heel and rushed out of the lounge. Everyone at the table roared with laughter, and Beau climbed back up onto his chair, just glad he was still alive.

"Very funny, Kyate!" Beau growled. "I can't believe you did that! You almost got me killed!"

"It was just a demonstration of how we'll manage to fit in around here," Kyate stated quietly.

"Are you sure you didn't rearrange your brain when we did that transition back on the ship? Joking around is just not you!? I'm a little worried ... Maybe you and Jerome got your wires crossed in the crossing!" Beau said, brushing the dirt off his arm.

"Which me are you addressing, Beau?" Kyate asked, trying to look serious.

"Oh for god's sake, this is hopeless," Beau sighed, throwing up his arms in resignation.

Everyone laughed, including Zak.

"Wait a minute, here!" Kyate said, "Dogs don't laugh, they bark. Kindly remember that when we're in public, will you Zak!?"

"Oh yeah! ... I mean RUFF ... RUFF!"

Kayta returned with their drinks. She sat them down on the table in front of each man according to the order.

"Hold on a second," she said, double checking the tab, "I have an extra whiskey here ... who ordered it?"

"Oh, that's for my dog, ma'am," Lexy answered, trying to keep a straight face.

The bar maid walked around the table and

looked at Zak, who was wagging his tail and looking up the girl's petticoats, showing his large teeth in a doggy smile.

"Would you like a bowl for your whiskey, Pup?" she quipped, scratching him behind one ear.

"Yea, ... and could you scratch a little to the left?" he said, leaning his head to the side.

"OH!" She jumped back in bewilderment. "The dog spoke!"

"I didn't hear anything, did you, Milo?" Jerome asked turning to Meno.

"Nope."

"But I heard him speak!" the bar maid insisted.

"Oh yeah, he can do that," Lexy said, "speak Zak!"

"RUFF, RUFF!"

"I could have sworn ...." The maid wondered away mumbling to herself.

"RUFF ... RUFF, Grrrr! Now give me my damned whiskey!" Zak said, growling and bearing his sharp teeth.

The crew howled hysterically, having more fun than they'd had in months.

Over the next few days, Beau and the boys located an abandoned villa, which they purchased and immediately began renovations on it. Kyate visited local officials, reprogramming their memory banks, causing them all to believe that he was a prominent citizen of Urampa that had been away on business for the past five years. Jerome made sure that the files in all official systems, especially the classified data bases, displayed positive information on each crew member's new identity, along with the company name and status. Meno had managed to obtain the approximate due date for Niporo's arrival, by posing as an old family friend when he paid a visit to the ground control station, inquiring as to the Drothuarian's location. They had about five days to complete their preparations, and they were right on schedule.

CHAPTER 20 – Destruction In The Cosmos

The streak of white hot ice shot across the cosmos, arching through the blackness at incredible speed, leaving a remarkable display of crystalline brilliance trailing behind in the wake of the harbinger of death. The comet's orbit had remained undisturbed for millions of years, but as it bore down on the uninhabited planet Carundai, history was about to be altered.

Carundai was one of the largest planets in the distant star system Heladaise, and was 5,000 times the size of the planet Jupiter in the galaxy Milky Way, in the star system Ziotran. The comet Woranwoad had a diameter of 279 miles, at its head.

On the edge of emptiness, no one witnessed the impact, as Woranwoad plunged through the thin atmosphere of Carundai, and exploded into the planet's crust. Comparable to a massive nuclear detonation, millions upon millions of cubic feet of Carundai's crustal foundation mixed with poisonous gasses entrapped within blocks of broken ice, were thrown back out into space by the force of the violent and volatile collision. This event constituted the genesis of several aggregate projectiles, which continued out across the universe in varying directions and toward countless unsuspecting targets.

One immense block of the conglomerate, measuring 27 miles in diameter, was on a collision course with the planet Earth, in the galaxy Milky Way. At its present speed, the neo-comet would enter the Ziotran star system in a matter of days, and would impact the Earth in only a few weeks, unless it could be detected and eradicated in time. The relatively small size of the projectile would cause it to be virtually unnoticed as it careened toward the Earth.

The preoccupation of the Drothuarian and Alicupion quandary in the galaxy Milky Way was destined to impede the timely counteraction necessary for the preservation of the planet Earth, as the chunk of debris and gas-filled ice, approached its end.

CHAPTER 21 – Retribution

"Get away from me you PIG!" Zeidra spat at Niporo.

"You're technically my wife, and it's been nearly three weeks!"

"I'm not your wife!"

"The promise of a Benjai makes it so!!" Niporo shouted hoarsely, grabbing for Zeidra's arm, but she moved out of his reach before he could catch her.

"I consider that promise annulled, because you tricked me!"

"May I remind you that it wasn't I who turned you into a nymphomaniac!" He sneered sarcastically, "... I actually should thank your Kyate for that!"

Zeidra picked up a heavy metal stein and sent it sailing across the room, hitting Niporo squarely in the forehead. He staggered backwards holding his head.

"You *SHREW!*" he screamed at her, wiping the blood away from his eyes; it trickled down his face from the gaping wound just above his left eyebrow. He started toward her, rage flashing in his dark eyes, and then he stopped. "I promised you that I'd never strike you! You're damned lucky that my word is reliable ... which is more than I can say for yours! .... However ... you did speak the promise and I took you at your word! I have obtained a recording of that pledge ... retrieved it from the magnetic ethers. Would you care to hear yourself ... in your own words, when you committed yourself to me?"

"But you took advantage of me!" she shrieked.

"I'm not sure who was taking advantage of who! When I played it back, you didn't sound like an innocent little victim .... It was pretty damned obvious that you would have done anything! ... said anything! Just to get FUCKED! And what's more, I don't think you gave a shit if it was me ... or anyone else doing the fucking! You were pretty damned pathetic, Zeidra! If anyone was taken advantage of ... if one of us was exploited ... it was me! YOU USED ME ... to service your insatiable carnal appetite!"

"You *BASTARD*!" Zeidra screamed at him, her fists doubled into tight knots; angry tears streaming down her flushed cheeks. "You lied to me! You told me Kyate raped me! You said I wasn't a virgin! You SEDUCED me! ... and then you bribed me with the only option available to me ... to end the affliction that

YOU perpetrated upon my body!!"

"*THAT* affliction ... as you call it, was none of *MY* doing! – Your Master Kyate did that to you! I merely made myself accessible to it ... *YOU* did the rest!! I refuse to take the blame for all of this ... I didn't *RAPE* you! You begged for it and you got it ... and you knew what the price was before I gave it to you! *YOU AGREED ... YOU COMMITTED YOURSELF TO ME*!! There was *NO* deception on *MY* part!!"

"Oh yes there was!!" she stamped her foot in defiance. "You made me believe I wasn't a virgin!! You made me think I had nothing to lose!!"

"A mere technicality, my dear," Niporo said calmly, "and just to set the record straight, Zeidra ... I never told you that you had nothing to lose. As you can now see ... you had much to lose ... as I had much to gain! I knew you had no intention of honoring your word ... you only made the promise to get the relief you needed ... That's why I made sure to secure the recording!" He laughed contemptuously and turned to leave the room.

"I'll see you dead and in hell, Niporo! I'll never be a wife to you! *NEVER*!!!" she choked out the words with such emotion, that Niporo stopped short, and turned around to look at her.

"Oh, Zeidra ... too late! *YOU ARE MY WIFE!* We consummated the agreement ... *IT*

WAS A SACRED UNION BASED UPON YOUR PLEDGE! As far as seeing me in *HELL?* I'm sure you will ... You are *NO ANGEL*, my sweet! And one more thing, my naive little Princess ... I *DID* impregnate you! You are, at this moment, carrying *MY* child!" He turned and left the lounge area, calmly, heading for the control cabin to check the progress of their voyage.

The instruments indicated that the ship was right on course and approaching Urampa which was now visible in the distance. By Niporo's calculations, they would enter Urampian territory in approximately twelve hours.

Zeidra ran to the sleeping quarters and flung herself across the big bed, seething with hatred and remorse. She abhorred admitting that much of what Niporo pointed out, was, in fact, truth. *'And who did she despise the most? Niporo? Kyate? Or did she have only herself to blame? Who else was responsible for her lascivious conduct?'*

"I'm ruined!" she cried into the covers. "My life is destroyed! I can't bear a Drothuarian child! KYATE... KYATE ...!" Her body heaved with the sobbing.

Like someone in trance; in slow motion, she sat up and looked toward the vanity on the other side of the room. She climbed down off the bed and walked slowly over to the sink. She looked into the mirror. What she saw in the reflection was a haggard looking young woman, with a swollen face and puffy eyes; lifeless eyes.

She spotted the straight razor lying on the counter top. Its shiny smooth blade was a tempting solution for her tortured spirit. Hypnotically, she reached for it. It felt cold in her hand. She gazed into the mirror one more time. She didn't recognize the person she had become; she didn't want to identify with the character peering back at her.

The razor slid easily across her wrist, opening a wide gash, stinging the flesh as it cut through the veins. She felt a strange detachment as she scrutinized the layers of tissue, revealed by the incision. And then the blood began seeping into the gaping wound, obscuring the raw edges of the laceration; she wondered what had taken it so long. She watched apathetically as it began to flow freely, over her hand and down into the sink, leaving lovely trails of crimson and pink on the pure white porcelain.

She wondered how difficult it would be to sever the other wrist, as her hand was becoming quite numb. She placed the razor in the palm of her deadened left hand and closed the fingers around the cold steel handle, holding them tightly with her right hand.

"Zeidra!" Niporo dashed across the room, grabbing the razor away from Zeidra's hands. "Good god! What are you doing!" he screamed at her.

Niporo's scream jolted her. Instantly, the realization of what she was doing, struck her like lightening. She looked at her bloody hand and then up into Niporo's terror filled eyes. The world began to spin and the blackness was closing in on her. She collapsed into Niporo's arms, like a tattered and worn rag doll.

Niporo grabbed a towel from the vanity and wrapped it firmly around Zeidra's bleeding wrist. He gathered up her limp body and carried her to the bed.

"So it's come to this ..." he said quietly, as he laid her down against the pillows. He felt a pang of guilt when he saw the blood slowly seeping through the towel. The cut was deeper than he'd thought.

He ran to the vault and pulled out the medical box. Opening it, he hastily withdrew the articles he needed. He returned to the bed and removed the wrapping from Zeidra's arm. The excessive bleeding would have to be stopped. He skillfully applied the tourniquet and watched as the flow slowed. He poured the liquid into the wound and covered it with absorptive material which he bound firmly with adhesive strips. He loosened the tourniquet for a few seconds, and then tightened it again.

The vial was in his left hand and he turned it upside down, piercing the cap with the needle. He watched the drug trickle into the syringe as he pulled the plunger back. He yanked the needle out, and tossed the vial onto the bed. Holding the syringe away from him, he expelled the trapped air until a fountain of liquid shot out toward the ceiling. He rolled Zeidra onto her side and pushed her skirts up out of the way. Pinching the soft white flesh on her hip, between his forefinger and thumb, he administered the drug.

Again he released the tourniquet. This time it was apparent that the profuse bleeding had all but stopped. Niporo sighed in relief, blotting the perspiration from his swollen brow with a corner of the blood soaked towel.

Time was short and the ship was orbiting Urampa, waiting for the "go ahead" to land.

Niporo hurriedly washed the blood from between Zeidra's fingers and applied a clean dressing to her wrist. He dressed her in a long sleeved gown and hoped that the bleeding wouldn't start up again.

"You look like hell, my darling," he said, assessing her appearance; her matted hair and pale complexion, the dark circles under her eyes, "but it's been a rough trip ... I know."

He packed the necessities into the bag, including the vial containing the drug, and the syringe.

Returning to the command cabin, he sat down at the console to check on his landing status. The message was already on the screen, "ALL CLEAR ... PERMISSION GRANTED ... USE SECTION E ... TARMAC E-2 ..."

Niporo manipulated the craft into position and began the descent. After several minutes he was able to see the port and he glided downward toward the designated area, dropping through the clouds in a pendulum like motion, swinging back and forth, the vessel resembled a sleek silver feather descending from a great height.

Niporo cut the propulsion systems on touchdown, relaxing back into his seat to collect his thoughts and recap his plan. When he was sure all of his bases had been covered, he unfastened the harnessing and left the command cabin. He opened the outside hatch and took a deep breath of the cool, fresh air. It felt good to know that he was soon to leave the confines of the ship. He had cabin fever in the literal sense, and couldn't wait to step onto solid ground.

Niporo promptly went to the sleeping

quarters where Zeidra remained in a drugged stupor, there, on the bed. Niporo threw the travel bag over his shoulder to free up his arms, then scooped up the princess and carried her to the hatch.

As he stepped out onto the stair-mount, he saw a mini-transport sprinting across the field, coming toward him.

"Sir!" the man called to Niporo, stopping the vehicle at the foot of the stairs, "I understand you have just arrived from Earth, and I wonder if you have any word of my brother ... his name is Anton, from Ulonica ... have you heard of him?"

"I'm sorry to say I haven't," Niporo answered politely.

"Oh ... oh well, do you have any news of the conflict?"

"Yes, I can tell you all I know, if you'd be kind enough to transport my wife and I to the terminal."

"Sure thing! Come aboard."

"This is a kind gesture, sir. By what name are you called?"

"You can call me Milo."

"Well, I'm certainly glad you were here, Milo. As you can see, my wife is ill ... she's pregnant, and a heavy load to carry that far across the field to the station." Niporo dumped Zeidra's limp body into the seat next to Meno and slung the travel bag off his shoulder and onto the bed of the transport. Zeidra slumped down in the seat, falling against Meno. He braced her with his strong arm and supported her there until Niporo climbed into the cab.

"I'm sorry to hear that she's having a bad time of it," Meno said, knowing he was talking to a dead man, for sure. "Have you arranged for accommodations?"

"Not yet," Niporo replied.

"Well, if you like, you're welcome to stay at our villa. It's just out of town, and a beautiful quiet place. Would probably do your wife good, while she recuperates from the trip." Meno looked over at Niporo's cut and swollen forehead, "What happened to you?"

"Nothing but my own clumsiness," Niporo answered, rubbing his head.

"Must have been a real bad trip for both of you!"

"Yeah, you can say that again ..."

Meno could see that Niporo and Zeidra had both had a tough time during the passage. He suspected that Niporo had drugged the princess, since she seemed oblivious to everything going on around her. Her eyes were glazed and her lips were dry and cracked.

The mini-transport sped out through the gates of the air complex and turned left, heading out of town.

"When's your baby due?" Meno asked.

"My wife has just conceived ... she is about three weeks along."

"She must have gotten pregnant during your trip ..."

"Well, it was pleasurable in the beginning ... a Honey Moon of sorts."

"Isn't that the way it goes?" Meno chuckled, cursing the Drothuarian under his breath. "There it is ... straight ahead of us," Meno was pointing to the grand estate that sat back off the road behind ornate iron gates.

He pulled into the drive and pushed a button on the dash of the transport. The huge gates swung open, and Meno drove into the compound. The gates swung closed behind them as they drove up the long, tree-lined avenue to the main palace.

Niporo marveled at the immaculately tended gardens, a jungle of plants and flowers of every conceivable color and hue. There were cascading waterfalls and fountains at every turn. The air was permeated with the sweet fragrances; and the resounding tones of water splashing down upon the crystal sculptures, saturated the environment with ethereal melodies.

Meno pulled the transport into an elevator which immediately began lifting the transport to the main floor of the building. The big doors slid open and Niporo was bewildered by the ambiance of the extravagance he beheld.

Niporo jumped out of the cab and walked into the main hall, looking around him, awed by the sheer beauty of the architecture and furnishings. Meno came around to Niporo's side of the transport and slid Zeidra into his arms. He carried her into the hall and headed for the enormous marble staircase which descended right down into the middle of the room, seemingly unsupported by anything other than air. Niporo's inattentiveness was conducive to Meno's exit.

As Meno disappeared up the stairs with Zeidra, Beau and Jerome entered the hall, with Lexy and Zak on their heels. They exchanged introductions and proceeded with small talk, keeping Niporo's mind occupied with the conversation. He was totally distracted by the commotion, having disregarded Meno's departure with the princess Zeidra.

Kyate was sitting thoughtfully in the big leather chair, staring out into the gardens through the immense oval window behind his desk. The doors flung open noisily, and Kyate swiveled the chair around to see who was there. His breath caught somewhere between his guts and his throat, as he gazed upon Meno standing just inside the doors that he had just kicked open. He was holding the limp body of the Princess Zeidra in his arms.

Kyate was paralyzed by the spectacle

before him, as Meno proceeded across the room, carrying the princess. He could see her breathing, as Meno approached, but she looked so frail; half dead or half alive, he wasn't sure.

Kyate stood up dazedly and walked over to Meno, who placed the princess in the Master's outstretched arms. Drawing her close to his body, he knew immediately that she was drugged. His relief was tangible as he hugged her tightly to him, burying his face into her neck. He wept openly in Meno's presence, but Meno understood.

Eventually, Kyate carried Zeidra over to the chair and sat down, cradling her there in his lap; as if he were holding a motherless child.

"Kyate," Meno began quietly, "I think there's something you should know."

"I'm already aware of it," he said numbly, running a huge hand across Zeidra's lower abdomen. "I swear to GOD ... I wish I could be the one to have the satisfaction of personally killing that Drothuarian! My spirit will not rest until that Devil is dead. He'll pay dearly for this!" Kyate gently brushed the matted curls away from Zeidra's pale face. "Which room did you prepare for her?" he asked, getting up.

"This way, Kyate."

Kyate followed Meno out of the room and

down the corridor to a huge suite which was conveniently located next door to the Master's chambers. Meno opened the double doors and Kyate carried the princess over to the lavishly draped bed and laid her down.

"Meno, ring for a nurse, will you please?"

Kyate was busy running his sensitive hands over Zeidra's aura, examining her life force. When he had verified that she would recover, he placed one hand on the crown of her head, and the other hand on her diaphragm, and then he breathed the healing energizing essence into her weak body. He bent over to kiss her, but she began to regain consciousness, and he straightened up abruptly.

The nurse knocked softly on the opened door.

"Come in, please," he said to her in a hushed tone.

"Mr. Milo said you needed me."

"Yes, we have guests that just arrived from Earth, they've had a hard time of the passage. As you can see … this woman is ill. She's pregnant, so I've been told." He walked to the closet and opened it. It was filled with women's clothing. "I don't know if any of these things will fit," he lied, "but after she rests, help her to clean up and maybe she'll feel better." Kyate walked to the door. "Keep me updated on her recuperation, will you?" he asked.

"Of course, sir," the nurse agreed.

Kyate left the room and started for the great hall, where Niporo was being entertained by Zak's myriad of tricks. Everyone stopped talking and looked up as Kyate made his way down the staircase.

"Oh, Niporo, Sir," Meno gestured toward Kyate, "This is the Master of the household, you ..."

"You may call me Xanthar," the voice boomed across the hall and echoed through the corridors.

"Thank you for your hospitality, Sir," Niporo bowed to Kyate.

"Your wife is resting comfortably. She's being attended to by our resident nurse ... I hope you don't mind." Kyate was seething as he portrayed the gracious host.

"Is she still asleep?" Niporo asked nervously.

"Quite," Kyate answered.

"I guess I should be with her, if you'll excuse me," Niporo acted agitated, angry with himself for being so easily distracted.

"I should like you to have a drink with me in my study, Niporo," Kyate stated it more as a demand than an invitation, not leaving the anxious Niporo any alternative but to accept. He would keep him as far away from Zeidra as he could, for as long as possible.

"That would be kind of you, Xanthar …. I guess I could use something to drink … help me relax."

Niporo followed Kyate across the great hall and into the lavish study, where Kyate motioned for Niporo to sit. Kyate pushed a button on the arm of the couch where he was sitting and immediately Jerome entered the room.

"Jerome, would you be kind enough to get Niporo and I something cold to drink?"

"No problem, Xanthar," he said, disappearing behind the splendid ebony bar.

Jerome pulled two crystal goblets from the rack that hung suspended above the counter top and set them on the bar. Niporo paid no attention to Jerome as he filled the goblets with a mixture of wine and exotic fruit juices. Looking up from his work, Jerome made sure that Niporo didn't see him empty the small envelope of powder into one of the glasses. He stirred it carefully with a swizzle and placed it on the tray next to the goblet meant for Kyate.

"Here you are, sir," Jerome said, sitting the goblet down on the low table in front of Niporo, "Enjoy your refreshments." He handed Kyate his wine and then he left the room.

"I'll drink to your destiny!" Kyate said as he raised his glass to Niporo.

"And I'll drink to yours." Niporo took a long drink of the wine with the odorless, tasteless powder in it.

Just then, the doors opened and a young woman dressed in white rushed into the room. She bent over Kyate's shoulder and whispered something in his ear. Niporo strained to decipher her words; he couldn't make them out.

"Jerome!" Kyate shouted.

Jerome was there in an instant.

Kyate took Jerome by the elbow and escorted him to the far end of the room. Niporo could see the concern on Kyate's face as they conversed, but was still ignorant of the emergency situation.

Jerome grabbed the nurse by the arm and they left the room in a hurry.

Kyate returned to his couch and gulped his wine, looking coldly at Niporo.

"Niporo, I'm sorry for the interruption, but your wife seems to have taken a turn for the worse. As a matter of fact, she's quite ill."

"Good god!" Niporo shrieked, "I must go to her!"

"No, she's in good hands. Jerome is a very competent doctor." Kyate tried to stay calm. "How long did you say you've been married?" he asked, waiting for Niporo to squirm.

"Not long."

"A year? Two years?"

"We're ... um ... we were only married recently."

"I see. So you didn't waste any time starting a family, or was it planned?"

"I … we definitely planned to have a child as soon as possible."

"Well, I'm sorry you made your wife so sick … I mean the trip!"

"I've got to go to her!"

"No … You'll stay right here."

"Like hell, I'll stay right here!" Niporo started to get up, when the doors opened again.

It was Jerome. Kyate got up and walked to the doors, talking with Jerome for a long time, while Niporo nervously fidgeted in his chair. Finally, Jerome left and Kyate returned to the sofa, but he didn't sit down.

"Tell me, Niporo, why have you drugged your wife?"

"*DRUGGED!* Forgive me, sir, but you must be mistaken!" Niporo exclaimed indignantly. His face was turning red, and the veins on his neck were beginning to bulge.

"Jerome informed me that your wife … what is her name?"

"Um … Uh.. Zana … Her name is Zana. What did he … the doctor say?"

"That your wife, Zana, is having a miscarriage." Kyate watched the blood drain from Niporo's face.

"That's impossible!" he shouted, jumping to his feet.

"Hold on man!" Kyate said, placing an iron hand on Niporo's shoulder. "Sit down here and finish your drink ... there's nothing you can do. It's too late. You simply shouldn't have given her that drug! Not to mention the fact that a great loss of blood put her body into shock, which of course, the drug exacerbated!" He firmly pressed Niporo back down onto the chair and handed him his glass.

Niporo was feeling powerless, at this point, and not appreciating the feeling. He downed the remainder of his drink hastily and sat glowering at Kyate, who was coldly reading the Drothuarian's past few weeks' memories; and Niporo felt it.

"Now, Niporo ... Is there anything in particular you'd like to get off your conscience before you die?" Kyate asked calmly, sitting back down, across from the Drothuarian.

"*DIE!* Are you insane?!"

"Quite to the contrary, Niporo. You see ... *YOU* must be insane, thinking that you could abduct a Benjai Princess and then try to pass her off as a *commoner's* wife." Kyate's eyes were as cold as steel blades, and they cut Niporo to the quick.

"I don't know what you're talking about!" he shouted, trying to get up. But his legs wouldn't cooperate with his will. He fell back into the chair, his eyes wide with fear. "What have you done, you maniac?! The drink! You put something in my drink! Didn't you?!" He was frantic; struggling to get up, but unable to move from his hips down. "Why?! Why would you do that?!" he screamed.

"Ah!" Kyate said, raising his eyebrows, "You *ARE* perceptive, although very stupid." The Master leaned back against the sofa and placed his arms leisurely behind his head.

The silence was an eternity as Niporo grappled to make some sense of what was happening here. Minutes passed. The two men sat silently glaring at one another.

"You sonofabitch!" Niporo spat out the words in a low hoarse whisper. "I know who you are! I recognize the eyes ... Everything's changed, but the eyes are the same ... You bastard! *KYATE!!*"

"Very good, Niporo!" Kyate exclaimed, leaning forward with both hands on his knees. His eyes were burning into Niporo like white-hot daggers. "Now would you care to confess your sins ... before you die?"

"Kyate ... I love her! As God is my witness, I love her more than I've ever loved anyone. I would have never turned her over to the government. If I couldn't have her, I'd be damned if they would. But *YOU!* YOU had to ruin it! You were always on her mind! ...

Always there in the shadows of her subconscious!"

"You're a dead man, Niporo," Kyate said quietly; cruelly.

"What did you put in the drink?" Niporo had resigned himself to his fate, feeling his arms go numb.

"I should have liked to murder you with my bear hands, yet I cannot. Your blood would defile me, so Jerome whipped up a little cocktail that will just creep up on you slowly .... When your lungs and heart become paralyzed, I shall gain my satisfaction from watching you suffer. You took what was mine ... and now I shall have my revenge by seeing you lose what you want most! The Princess Zeidra ... and your life! Niporo, listen while you may... I'm taking them both! Go to your grave, you snake ... tasting your defeat!!!"

Niporo was struggling with his breathing, as the effect of the poison was beginning to move up into his chest. "Kyate ... please ... please? Tell Zeidra ... that ..." he choked and gasped, "that I love her ... and I'm sorry ..." He coughed again and blood trickled down from the side of his mouth, "I'm so sorry!" He gasped and choked. The muscles in his throat contracted. He slumped over in the chair and slid down onto the floor.

As Kyate watched Niporo die, he was surprised that instead of feeling the triumph and satisfaction he anticipated, he was only feeling pity and compassion. It wasn't at all what he expected from his own emotions. This was a man that he truly despised, the man who had taken what Kyate desired most in the entire universe. Niporo had nearly destroyed Zeidra. So why wasn't he feeling the gratification of his revenge? *'Could it be that he was also feeling his own guilt; that he too had contributed to Princess Zeidra's near destruction?*

Kyate got up from the sofa, stepped over Niporo's twitching corpse, and left the study; closing the big doors behind him.

CHAPTER 22 – The Old Coot

"Sir, the lady wishes to see you," the nurse said. "She's on the terrace."

Kyate turned and looked outside through the double glass doors leading from his study. Zeidra was standing on the terrace, looking out over the rear gardens. She was wearing a white lace dress that Kyate had chosen himself. The garment flowed gracefully around her body in the gentle Urampian breeze that seemed to refresh the land every morning about this time. But seeing Princess Zeidra standing there in the sunshine, her golden tresses shimmering in the bright light like an angelic halo, was the most refreshing experience he'd had since arriving on Urampa.

Kyate threw open the doors and walked outside.

"Master Xanthar!" Zeidra turned to greet him.

"Madam."

"I'm so grateful to you ... I wanted to say thank you for allowing me to recover here at your beautiful estate."

"You're feeling well?" Kyate asked, but he could see for himself that her healthy glow had returned. Her eyes were bright, and they twinkled like sunlight dancing on clear blue pools. The delicate pink of her cheeks, that had always made her appear freshly scrubbed, was evident again. Kyate was happier now, than he'd been in months.

"Is there something wrong?" she asked, brushing at her hair, and then her face.

"Of course not, why?"

"The way you were looking ... I thought I had dirt on my nose or ..."

Kyate burst out laughing. "Was I staring, Madam? I'm sincerely sorry, but you ... I can't get over how well you look!" Kyate had always been fascinated by Zeidra's disarming and innocent candor.

"Thank you, I'm glad you weren't looking for my flaws! I was beginning to feel uncomfortable. I feel much better now."

"Would you like to walk with me in the gardens?" Kyate asked.

"I'd love to ... I do love the flowers ..." There was a wistful expression on her face when she said it.

"Are you homesick?" Kyate asked, taking her elbow; guiding her down the steps and onto the garden pathway.

"Master Xanthar, you couldn't know ..." She stopped and looked up at him, studying his eyes. There was something vaguely familiar there, as there was with the firm hand on her arm. "Yes, I am a little homesick," she continued, "but I like it here, too. I haven't much to go home to I fear ..."

They continued walking.

"Well you're welcome to stay here as long as you like," Kyate said, picking some jasmine and handing it to Zeidra.

"I didn't know this grew on Urampa, too!" she exclaimed, putting the sprig up to her nose. She stopped again. This time she stood perfectly still, looking at the jasmine in her hand. A single tear slid down her face, falling onto the delicate flowers she held.

"You're not supposed to cry when a gentleman gives you flowers ... or is it because this gentleman is such an old coot?" Kyate chuckled, trying to lighten her mood. He perceived that she was more homesick than she was willing to admit.. Or was it something else?

"Sir, Xanthar," Zeidra looked up at him sweetly, "what is a coot?"

Kyate was caught off guard and lost his composure completely, laughing until his sides hurt; he fell to the ground and doubled up in hysterics. Zeidra thought he may be having a seizure ... a fit of some kind. She dropped to her knees beside him frantically trying to restrain him. When he realized she was there on the ground with him he quickly pulled himself together and laid there exhausted. Looking up at her confused expression, he tried to think of an explanation for his irrational mirth.

"In answer to your question, young lady ... a coot is someone who laughs uncontrollably while rolling in the dirt," Kyate said, smiling up at her.

"I've never heard of it," she said, looking at him curiously.

"Well, help me up and we'll just try and forget it, if that's all right with you."

"Are you teasing me, Sir?" Zeidra asked. She was pulling hard on his arm, trying to assist him in getting to his feet.

"Young lady, I wouldn't think of it!" Kyate stated indignantly, brushing the dust from his clothes.

"I'm sorry, I just thought I'd ask."

Kyate marveled at her extreme and varied facial expressions.

"Master Xanthar ... you're staring at me again."

Kyate felt his face turn red and he ignored the remark. "Come," he said, taking her arm again, "let me show you my favorite spot."

They walked down the path to a glorious fountain. It was seven tiers high, and made from pure crystal, each tier having its own individual density, which gave each tier a different tone than the others. As the water cascaded over the sides of each one, it actually caused a musical note when it hit the next level of crystal. There was a bench by the fountain, under a trellis of a plant that resembled wisteria, but the fragrance was different; intoxicating and musky.

"I must rest," Kyate said, portraying the older man.

"Let's sit here awhile," Zeidra said, pointing to the bench.

They sat down together and enjoyed the sound of the fountain, and inhaled the sweet aroma of the plant that hung about them in gorgeous clumps of purple.

"What shall I call you, Madam?" Kyate asked. "What name do you prefer?"

Zeidra thought for a minute. "Master Xanthar, I don't wish to sound rude ... and I don't want my statement to be misconstrued as some sort of intrigue, however ... I wish to dispose of my old identity for reasons that are painful and many. So! If you would like to give me a new name ... choose one for me ... I may be inclined to accept it!" She glanced at him sideways and grinned.

"I do admire your honesty, young lady!" Kyate laughed. "In a situation such as this, and a name being such an important embellishment to a person's singular identity, then I shall call you by your true name, and I suggest that you face your past and then plan your future ... running away to nowhere will definitely get you there ... *NOWHERE!* You see, your companion told me the whole story before he died, and I swear to you ... you are safe in my household! Your secret is safe. But you, my dear, are a Benjai ... the only Benjai! It's an incredible responsibility, but nevertheless, it is yours!" Kyate saw the alarm in Zeidra's expression. Perhaps he should have waited to tell her that he knew... He ran his hands through his hair nervously and rubbed his chin, then continued, "What I was asking ... is whether you prefer to be called Princess Zeidra? ... or just Zeidra? ..."

Zeidra's mouth was open, but she was unable to speak. Her eyes were wide in shock and disbelief. Kyate could see beads of perspiration appearing on her forehead. He was afraid she might run. He took hold of her shoulders to steady her and to keep her from bolting.

"Princess Zeidra, are you all right?" Kyate asked in a low quiet voice.

"I'm frightened." It was all she could say, and she was trembling now.

Kyate understood why she would be fearful. After all, she was in Drothuarian territory, and they would like nothing better than to find out that the Benjai was alive and vulnerable for their taking.

"Listen very closely to what I'm about to tell you!" Kyate said shaking her gently, "We ... my men and I, are not Drothuarians! We, too are from Earth ... which is another long story, much like your own. But the important thing to remember, here ... is that you are safe and so is your identity. Do you understand me? More importantly ... do you believe me?"

Zeidra looked up into Kyate's eyes. She felt like her world was slipping out from under her. It was hopeless! Who could she really trust? She began to cry.

Kyate put his arms around her to comfort her and she sobbed into his chest. Suddenly, she was aware of a familiar scent and a strange sensation; an almost forgotten vibration. It was emanating from this man's body. Zeidra stopped crying and looked up into his steel gray eyes. What was she seeing? She couldn't bear to look at them, they seemed so familiar; or were they just a painful reminder?

Kyate was also feeling the same old throbbing; that heavy delicious excitement was moving over him like a slow avalanche. It was the same undeniable chemistry that had nearly been his undoing.

He pushed Zeidra back away from him

and held her at arm's length, afraid of what could happen if he continued to hold her as he had. Pulling himself together emotionally, he cleared his throat. He put his massive hand under Zeidra's chin and forced her to look at him.

"Zeidra, you have to trust me." He peered deeply into her eyes. "I understand confusion," he spoke quietly yet his voice was husky and full of authority, "I understand fear ... . I'm here to protect you ..... You're my charge ..... This is my mission. I would never hurt you and I won't let anyone else hurt you. Do you trust me?"

"Oh my God!" Zeidra cried, "I've heard those exact words before, spoken exactly the same way!" She covered her face with her hands and shook her head furiously. "What kind of a cruel joke is this?! Or am I having a dream?" She looked up at Kyate searching his eyes for some valid explanation.

"Zeidra, hold on here! I certainly didn't mean to upset you like this! What did I say that was so distressing?"

"An old memory ... a bad memory!" she lied and Kyate knew it.

"Would you like to talk about it?"

"No ... Yes... NO! I want to forget it, but you keep reminding me!"

"*I?*" Kyate questioned innocently.

"Yes.. NO ... Well, it's not *you*; it's just

some things about you!"

"What are we discussing here? A person, an event, a place? You've got this old man confused!" Kyate was fishing.

"All three!" she cried, wiping the tears from her eyes with the edging on her skirt.

"Well if you trust me, you can talk to me." Kyate reached over and brushed a curl away from her face.

"His name was Kyate ..." she began, "I don't know if he's dead or alive. I don't know if he knows I'm alive.. That is.. If he's alive. Oh god! It's so confusing!"

"Well what about this man Kyate?" Kyate paused and rubbed his chin thoughtfully, "Are we talking about the Great Master Kyate?"

She was staring at him in amazement.

"What's wrong?" Kyate asked, still rubbing his chin.

"You're doing it!"

"Doing what?"

"You're rubbing your chin."

"So what? I always rub my chin when I'm concentrating."

"Yes, but so does he ... or he did."

"Pure coincidence!" Kyate quipped. "So are we talking about the Master?"

"Yes," she replied in a distant sounding voice.

"Well go on! What about the Master Kyate?"

"I thought ... well, I thought I... I don't know maybe I just ..."

"What did you think, Zeidra?" Kyate was becoming impatient.

"I thought I was in ... well, I don't know, really, because I never was.. But then something happened and I changed. Or he changed me ... but anyway, he's gone and I'm here ... He wouldn't want me the way I am now, so ...."

"Do you have any idea how hard it is to follow this kind of a conversation?" Kyate ran his hands over his forehead and through his hair, pulling at it in frustration.

"You see! That's another thing you're doing that reminds me of him. Xanthar you're driving me crazy. I need to forget Kyate and your no help at all!" she cried, poking a finger into his chest.

"Well, now ... hypothetically ... If this Master Kyate crossed your path again, somehow, in this lifetime ... what would you do? I mean how would you react, Zeidra?"

"I don't know, Xanthar. I should hate him for what he did to me, so I guess I should slap him ... maybe kill him!" her eyes grew dark. "But if he affects me the way he did before, then I don't think I'd have the power to strike him."

"So what does that mean? What would you do then?"

"Xanthar! I don't mean to be disrespectful, but you're not just an old coot, you're a nosy old coot!"

She caught him off guard again by her captivating directness. Kyate roared with laughter, rolling off the bench and onto the ground, just as before, while Zeidra just sat there watching curiously.

"I think you may kill *ME*, if you keep this up!" Kyate chuckled, still lying on the ground at Zeidra's feet.

"I think you should act your age, Sir!"

That's all it took … Kyate began howling and rolling all over again.

After that episode, it was hard for Kyate to maintain a straight face.

It began to rain as they headed back to the palace, and the wind was beginning to blow harder. Kyate took Zeidra's arm and they sprinted down the garden walkway, trying to make it inside before the storm really let go. Zeidra could hardly keep up with Kyate as he literally dragged her along. He seemed to be very fit for a man as old as he looked?

Once inside Kyate's study, they just stood there looking at each other and laughing; standing in puddles, soaking wet.

Kyate was so taken with her charming simplicity, that he was actually pleased with the change in her demeanor. She was so genuine now … her own person. He was secretly wishing he could experience the other side of her … the sensual side of the "changed Zeidra".

Her white lace dress was dripping wet and clinging to her body, leaving little to Kyate's imagination. Zeidra's hair was drenched, and Kyate watched little raindrops running down the length of the ringlets, dropping off onto her face; dropping from her eye lashes, and then falling onto her cheeks where they continued to trickle on down across her breasts; disappearing into the lacy material. Kyate was fascinated as he stood there watching Zeidra shiver, the contour of her breasts was plainly visible and her nipples were conspicuously erect, straining against the thin white fabric on the bodice of her wet dress.

He felt the heat in his loins as his passions were ignited by the sight of her. His arousal was obvious and absolute. His desire had a mind of its own and there was no way in hell he could hide it. His rain drenched trousers betrayed his ambition, flagrantly displaying the magnitude of his sexuality.

The laughing had stopped. Zeidra was startled when she saw the intensity of the man's stimulation. She looked into his eyes and she was immediately trapped. She was standing before him, held motionless by his piercing gaze. She felt as if she were being absorbed into those intense gray eyes. It was a feeling she had no control over. As she surrendered to the silent questioning, she realized that she was being read, interpreted, devoured and energized all in the same moment of time, and suddenly she saw Kyate standing there, not Xanthar! She was re-experiencing a long past event. Everything that was happening now had happened before .... She could feel that strange throbbing in her stomach; and the man standing in front of her was emanating that electrifying erotic energy that was so much a part of Kyate. She couldn't stand it any longer. She turned and bolted from the room.

"You're not Kyate! You're not!" Her cry echoed down the corridors of the villa.

Kyate followed Zeidra down the corridor, across the great hall, and up the magnificent staircase.

"Wait, Zeidra!" he called, but she didn't stop.

By the time he reached her room, her door was closed and locked, and he could hear her sorrowful weeping. He placed both hands against the door and despairingly leaned into it. He knew that he, Xanthar, couldn't

317

comfort the distressed Princess, yet he, as Kyate, was what she yearned for. He was aware that the Princess Zeidra cared for him deeply, although he couldn't fully comprehend *why*, after what he'd done to her virtuous nature. These were the very same contradictory feelings *she* had expressed in their earlier conversation.

Kyate made a fateful decision as he stood inclined there, with his forehead against the huge mahogany door, listening to the Princess crying for him. It was impossible for him to disclose his true identity to her at this time. He and the crew were dependent on their disguises in order to obtain critical information from the local Drothuarian officials. – Drothuarians who were eagerly soliciting funding from Kyate to finance renewed assaults on the Ulonicans of Earth.

"Besides," he said to himself, *"she would accuse me of being deceitful with her if she found out now ... after she'd been living in the same compound with me for the past few weeks. She'd wonder why I hadn't been honest with her from the beginning, about my real identity and my clandestine strategy to annihilate the Drothuarian Government Command at their headquarters on Keyto."*

He hated to admit that he had been buying time with her, in order to ascertain where he stood. – If she could forgive him his transgression, and to discover whether she felt the same attraction for him that he knew she had before. Kyate straightened his posture and placed his hands on his hips; still facing the closed door, he shook his head slowly and sighed deeply. He made the decision then and there. – He would pay Zeidra a visit ... as *HIMSELF*.

The night was black and thick with melancholy. Zeidra stood by the large window in her room, looking out across the gardens at the back of the palace. A warm, gentle breeze caused the sheer curtains to flutter; drifting outward from the window. The rustling of the fabric was the only discernable sound penetrating the stillness, except for the distant resonance of the cascading fountains and waterfalls hidden beyond in the blackness. The blue and purple shadows swayed gracefully in the maze below the window, and Zeidra felt a hypnotic yearning to explore the darkness she beheld.

Leaving her room, she tiptoed down the corridor and descended the staircase, into the hall below. She quietly opened the double glass doors that led to the veranda and stood there on the threshold of a dream-world that lay before her; beckoning her to enter the expansive purple-cloaked labyrinth; to wonder into the spectral panorama of the exotic black phantasm and the dancing silence.

She walked outside and proceeded down the marble steps leading to the garden entrance. She paused, enjoying the warm fragrant air that permeated her senses. She stepped into the fantasy. A sense of unfathomable loneliness engulfed her as she meandered down the garden path. Upon coming to a quiet pool surrounded by night blooming jasmine, Zeidra stopped and strained to see her reflection on the dark water. She could hardly make out her profile as she gazed down at the glassy liquid surface.

Suddenly, she saw two figures instead of one; a taller form standing behind hers. She froze. Her heart pounded so loudly, she thought she could hear it echoing across the water. She was afraid to look behind her. Her eyes were riveted to the murky reflection and the two ghostly figures mirrored there. It was a mute and ominous eternity; standing there paralyzed in time and space; too frightened to turn and confront the specter; too afraid to run, or even move. And then he touched her. A heavy hand came down firmly on her shoulder and she nearly fainted. Reeling dizzily beneath his grasp, Zeidra felt herself being pivoted to face the apparition. She looked up at the intruder, about to scream when she recognized the man steadying her. It was Kyate!

She could see a strange light blazing in his eyes; in sharp contrast to the darkness. His expression was solemn and filled with concern and compassion. He looked deep within her and she knew he was reading her reaction as she leaned into his magnetic aura. Her shock was surpassed only by the joy and relief she felt just seeing him again.

"Zeidra," Kyate whispered, "don't be afraid."

The princess felt a current of energy run through her body, which shook her to her core. His voice was reverberating throughout her being. She could not speak.

"I'm so sorry," he said, "I had no idea what pain my impulsive passions would cause for you ... Can you ever forgive me?" Kyate released his hold on her shoulders.

Still off balance, Zeidra staggered backwards. Kyate quickly caught her around the waist and pulled her back against him. He calmed her. He reassured her.

"I want you to understand what happened," he said, burying his face in her soft lavender-scented hair. "I'm going to reveal the truth to you ... I'm going to let you experience the event from my perspective." He tipped her chin up, so he could see her face.

Silent tears were rolling down her cheeks, as she looked up at Kyate.

"Once you experience the truth, you will know that I ... You will be assured that my... "Kyate's tone was deep and throaty as he struggled for words, "Zeidra ..., know this .... That I've loved you from the beginning ... and I shall love you always! Whether you choose to forgive me is of no consequence where this love is concerned, as I will love you regardless ... and believe me ... it will endure all retribution." He kissed her gently and affectionately, covering her lips with his. She trembled in his arms as her body responded to his kiss. Releasing her mouth before that pulsation could take over, he moved his lips across her face to her ear and breathed his pledge. "I'll never be away from you for long, Zeidra ... So don't worry ... Just know I'll be with you when I'm able. You have my promise." He slid his lips back across Zeidra's cheek to her eager mouth, and brushed light kisses all over her lips. "Even in death ... if that be the case ... I'll be with you ... forever!" He choked on the words.

She melted into his arms and he pulled her hungrily in against his body. Her lips were begging his, as she reciprocated with quick, eager kisses on Kyate's mouth. He began to feel that uncontrollable urge for her; that tantalizing pulsation; his blood was turning into liquid fire. In an instant his kiss was devouring her. Kyate's hands were moving over her body, verifying what he had memorized from his prior exploration. He grabbed her hips and jerked her savagely into him; against his urgency. She let out a little cry of pain. His uncompromising intensity bore into her; bruising her; inflaming her. Kyate's incessant repudiation of his longing and desire had come full circle, and he could deny his need no longer. However, he vowed to postpone the physical gratification of his obsession until he was completely exonerated of his past transgressions and negligence.

With all the resolve he could muster, Kyate forced himself to release his voracious grip on the princess. He reluctantly pulled Zeidra away from him, gently persuading her to let go.

"It's time for you to understand," he whispered.

Zeidra looked up longingly, into his cool gray eyes. Still mute, her expression revealed all that he needed to see; to discern. This satisfaction was his reprieve.

Kyate placed his hands on the sides of Zeidra's skull and concentrated on that fateful evening in Zeidra's chambers. Connecting his consciousness with her awareness, he allowed her access to his memory banks and brought his experience of that night into her experience, providing her full comprehension of the events as they transpired. She became aware of his every thought, every emotional response, every physical sensation. She relived his frustration and his attempted restraint. She felt his pain and then she perceived his pleasure. At last, she was left with his overwhelming guilt which devastated her spirit. She collapsed in his arms, the emotional exhaustion depleting her physical energy. She had fainted.

Kyate gathered her up into his arms and carried her back to her chambers inside the palace. He laid her onto the bed and kissed her gently on her forehead. He removed the golden medallion that he always wore around his neck, and he placed it into her hands, winding the gold chain securely around her fingers. He stood over her for a long while, burning the impression of her into his mind.

"I swear to you, my love," Kyate whispered hoarsely, "if I return victorious ... I shall have all of you ... I will join my body with your body ... ... and my soul with your soul! ... And if I fail ..... I shall deny myself ... your love ... forever!"

CHAPTER 23 – Mission ONE

"It's time," Kyate said, setting the bag filled with electronic equipment onto the desk.

"Do you think it's late enough? I'd hate to find those bastards still awake!" Jerome said, wrapping loops of rope around his elbow and hand. "Lexy should be back any time... He went down to the communications instillation to confirm the guard positions and locate the critical microwave transmitters."

"Where's Beau? We can't wait much longer ... It'll be getting light in a couple of hours!"

"He's in the lab," Jerome answered while struggling with a stubborn knot, "... working on the prints of the Keyto complex... Thinks he can bring the whole thing down with six vacuum charges set from inside... We're talking *IMPLOSION*!"

"That's ingenious!" Kyate said raising his eyebrows. "Attract a little less attention, huh?" He rubbed hard at his chin, visualizing an implosion of that magnitude.

"Well, it was either that ... or use the

neutrinos ... but that would leave the complex intact for the next Drothuarians who come along ... Not very efficient!" Jerome said, throwing the last of the ropes into a pile on the floor.

Just then, Lexy threw open the big doors and entered the room with Zak by his side.

"Well?" Kyate said, "Are we set?"

"Just as we thought! Everything is the same ... They haven't changed positions or locations ... This'll be a piece of cake!" Lexy answered while trying to catch his breath.

"Zak, you understand your job?" Kyate asked pointing a finger at the big black dog.

"Those guys'll be mutton in my paws!" Zak said, smiling his doggy smile and wagging his tail.

Meno and Beau came in from the basement lab. Beau was carrying a bunch of scrolled documents while Meno was burdened with weapons, which he proceeded to distribute to the men.

Beau put the plans into the cabinet and turned to Kyate. "Did you get the bug on Zak?"

"Sorry Beau," Jerome said, "I didn't tell Kyate that part of the plan yet." He took a small device from a box on the desk and held it up for Kyate to see. "*This* ... is going on the inside of Zak's collar. That way, we'll know what's happening on the east side while we're

326

taking care of those microwave units on the west end."

"Sounds good to me," Kyate said.

"Yeah, but that's not all... He'll be able to hear us, too. If we need more time or get into trouble, we can relay instructions to him," Beau added. He was strapping a six-inch mini laser to his thigh.

"Well guys ... I hope your faith in Man's Best Friend is justified!" Zak said, leaning his head to one side as Jerome attached the electronic accessory to his collar.

"No sweat, Zak!" Lexy said, "You're such an adorable mutt ... who could resist such charisma?"

"OK boys!" Kyate said, throwing the bag of equipment up over his shoulder, "Let's go knock out some communication disks!" Kyate motioned for the men to follow him. "Meno, keep an eye on that princess for me!" He looked over at Meno and winked.

"You're the boss," Meno replied solemnly. He was disappointed at having to remain behind, but his sight was still not as clear as it had been, and Kyate needed someone to stay with the princess while they were away. According to their calculations, it would take three days, as the plan was to sabotage the communication stations on Urampa, and then to proceed to Keyto for the final destruction of Drothuarian activity in the region.

Meno watched as the men left the palace, disappearing up the road in the mini-transport, into the darkness. He retired in Kyate's chambers that night, in order to be close to the princess.

The five Deis Warriors parked the transport a hundred yards from the installation and made their way on foot toward the communications disks. The night hung heavy about them like a welcomed cloak.

"Down! Let's belly it from here …. Spread out some… we'll meet at that tree over there by the wall," Kyate whispered.

The men slithered across the ground silently; like single-minded serpents they made their way toward the wall of the complex. One by one they found their way through the blackness to the checkpoint.

"I'll stay here and keep an eye on the number three guard … Beau, you stay on number one… Lexy … number two. As soon as we hear the commotion with Zak … Jerome, you can go for it."

The men waited there on the ground, nearly invisible in the tall grass. The guards' voices could be heard, as they conversed with one another, sounding more distant than they really were, due to the muffling effect of the fog that had drifted across the landscape.

On the other side of the compound, near the front entrance, Zak crept closer to the main gate. He could see the huge microwave disks mounted on the tops of the high towers straight across from the entrance. There were several guards laughing and joking at the post near the front access. He couldn't be sure how many Drothuarians were positioned beyond that point, except for Lexy's report of thirty to forty. He scratched his ear with his hind foot and then snickered quietly at the absurdity of his being a dog.

"Rarf ... grrrrr," he barked and growled, then laughed quietly. "You guys read me? Recognize my growl?"

"Gotcha Zak," Kyate chuckled into the remote transceiver. "What's going on?"

"I got five ... maybe six, here at the gate. Can't see any more from this position, but I'm ready to go in. You guys OK?"

"We're ready when you are."

"OK ... here goes ... over and out!"

"Hey! Did you hear something?" one of the guards whispered, drawing his stun weapon.

"Yeah ... sounded like a wolf ... or a ...."

"Look! It's a dog," the guard said pointing out onto the road where a large black dog was limping toward them, whimpering and holding his right front paw up as he hobbled along.

"Where do you suppose he came from? I haven't seen a dog around here for years! He's hurt. You guys ... look at him ... there's something wrong with his foot!"

As Zak came closer, he hunkered down on his belly and crawled forward, faking pain and fear as he neared the Drothuarians.

Four of the six guards approached Zak, who by then was lying on his side in the middle of the road, whining loudly. He looked up at the towers. From his present vantage point, he saw the guards positioned there, they were straining to see what the disturbance was at the front guard post.

"Nice boy ..." one of the guards said, reaching for Zak's paw.

"Grrrr ... Ruff ... URRRRRR!" Zak growled and snapped at the man's hand.

"You should know better than to frighten an injured animal that way!" another guard scolded the first.

"Well how am I supposed to help him?"

Zak yelped painfully and pawed the dirt with his hind legs, as he lay there stretched out in the gravel. The guards were beside themselves, not sure how to respond to this unusual crisis. The Drothuarians were notorious dog lovers and until recent centuries, the only region of the local universe where dogs could be found, was in the Drothuarian territories.

"Just move slowly ... try to reassure him that you want to help him!" the guard cautioned the Drothuarian who was kneeling close to Zak. Zak continued to growl and snap at the guards, still whimpering intermittently.

"You're doing great, Zak!" Kyate spoke into the remote. "You sure got the attention of these fellows up on the towers! Just keep it up! GOOD DOGGY!" Kyate winked at the others and laughed. "OK Jerome, on your way ... we'll keep you covered!"

It was Jerome's job to find the central processing unit that controlled all satellite transmissions into and out of the facility. If he could find the right access codes, he could program a scrambling sequence into the unit and short circuit anything coming in or going out of the communications center which relayed all Drothuarian information to other source facilities and satellites. If the project was successful, the Deis crew would leave without being noticed and the scrambled information would be undetected for some hours, giving them ample time to implement their assault on Keyto.

Jerome crawled into the main building

without being seen. Zak was creating a scene on the other side of the compound, which distracted the guards on the far side as well. The Deis genius, Jerome, entered into the lower level and eventually found his destination. Working furiously, he scanned the system codes and gained the access he needed. He keyed in the specific commands, cleared the screen, and hurried quietly back to his waiting colleagues.

"No problem, men!" Jerome whispered, bellying up to the others who were lying in the grass by the wall. "I don't think they'll be getting any current events over those dishes for a long, long time!"

"Good work, Jerome!" Kyate slapped him on the back.

"OK, Zak ... can you hear me?" Kyate spoke into the transceiver.

"Grrrr ... RUFF! Gotcha!"

"Keep em busy for about ten more minutes; then make a run for it. We'll meet you back at the transport ... you go wide and make sure you're not seen!"

"ARF ... URRRRR ... OK!"

"Good boy ... here fellah," the guard reached for Zak's paw again.

Zak snarled at the man, showing his glistening white teeth, and then snapped at the man, narrowly missing his fingers. The man recoiled in obvious fear.

"This dog's a mean mother!" he said looking back at the others.

"He's just injured ... they all act like that when they're hurt. Maybe we could stun him just enough to secure him ..."

That's all it took for Zak to envision himself the Drothuarian HOUSE MASCOT! "GRRRRRRR .... Ruff Ruff! No way asshole!" Zak growled as he leaped up out of the dirt, bounding off into the tall weeds at the side of the road; throwing dirt and gravel in the guards face as he'd jumped to his feet.

"I could have sworn that damn dog spoke!" The guard cursed as he wiped the dust from his eyes with his shirttail. "Sounded like asshole!"

"You're crazy!" the other guard called to him. "There's not a canine in the universe that can talk... You're quite a joker, you know that?!" He laughed heartily, helping his friend to his feet.

Zak skirted the field rapidly; doubling back and jumping out of the weeds just as the rest of the crew arrived at the transport.

"Damn! That was close!" Zak panted; his tongue flopping out of his flaccid jowls, as he tried to catch his breath. "Those guys were getting' ready to stun me ... I wasn't about to give em a chance! Let's get out of here!"

"Good idea!" Beau agreed.

The men jumped into the truck and headed for the secluded tarmac on the edge of town where they'd hidden a scout ship that was loaded and ready for the mission to Keyto.

Within minutes, the crew had transferred everything from the transport to the ship. The lift off was silent and no one on Urampa was aware of the departure.

"Kyate, can you please get me out of this dog body?!" Zak said, biting at his hip, and pulling his fur with his teeth.

"Good idea!" Kyate laughed.

He took Zak into the cargo bay and had him close his eyes and visualize himself as he *had* been. They returned momentarily to a cheering crew; sad to lose their pet but happy to have recovered their friend.

CHAPTER 24 – Truth And Consequence

The Urampian sun was filtering into the room through the lace curtains at the window, casting a myriad of shadow designs across the walls and floor of Zeidra's room. She stretched and yawned feeling more rested than she had in what seemed like months.

Instantly, she became aware of something wound around her fingers. She could feel the cool, heavy metal; and when she looked, she was astounded to see the golden medallion swinging from the braided chain in her hand. Zeidra recognized it immediately. It was Kyate's. She hadn't been dreaming ... she had been with him sometime during the night. The memory came flooding into her consciousness; bitter sweet feelings and visions of Kyate's grief and shame; the pain and pleasure of seeing him again; the anguish of unconsummated love. Zeidra sighed deeply, clutching the medallion to her breast and closing her eyes, trying to relive that last encounter; that kiss; the longing.

Someone was knocking at the door.

"Who's there?" Zeidra called.

"It's Nina, your nurse, Ma'am."

"Come in please," Zeidra said, wiggling to sit up against the headboard of the bed, and pulling the covers up over her lap.

Nina entered the room carrying a breakfast tray for Zeidra. "Sir Milo asked me to see to you ... make sure you have what you need. He wanted me to tell you that the others have gone away on business for a few days and Master Xanthar was sorry he didn't have time to speak to you before he left." She set the tray across Zeidra's lap and removed the cover on the plate. "Is there anything I can do for you, Ma'am?"

"Yes .... Umm, Nina ... Are there any other guests staying in the palace ... I mean could there be anyone I haven't met?"

The nurse gave Zeidra a quizzical look.

"It's not important," Zeidra lied, "I just thought I saw someone that I didn't recognize... It was at a distance. Forget it."

"Well there was a gentleman here late last night ..." Nina said, placing her finger on her chin thoughtfully. "I saw him speaking to Mr. Milo in the study ... I've never seen him before and I didn't ask any questions ... you know. I didn't see him arrive and I didn't see him leave. Just caught a glimpse of him standing there when I passed by the door ... it was open ... and I was on my way to turn up the negative ionizer ... I forgot ... I mean, I'm supposed to do that every night before I retire, and I woke up realizing I'd forgotten. It must have been... oh, about two thirty this morning!"

"Did you see what he looked like?"

"Not specifically, Ma'am, he had his back to me ... but I did notice that he was tall and very well built. Had blondish colored hair ... tied back in a little tail. That's about all I can tell you. Where did you see him?"

"I thought I saw him in the garden ... I was just curious to know if you knew him."

"Nope! Sorry Ma'am."

"Well, Nina, thank you for the information." Zeidra waved the girl on, "You may go."

Nina nodded to Zeidra and quietly turned and left the room, leaving Zeidra alone to ponder the meaning of Kyate's presence in Master Xanthar's palace. Xanthar hadn't admitted knowing Kyate personally, although he did act as if he knew of Kyate's reputation. Zeidra tossed her hair back over her shoulders and frowned.

"Something is wrong with this picture ..." she said out loud, "and I'm going to find out what's going on!"

Zeidra finished her breakfast. She rang

for the maid who was soon readying Zeidra's bath. Zeidra opened the large doors to the closet and rummaged through the wardrobe which she thought was remarkable in that everything there was just the right size for her.

"Who's clothes are these?" she asked the maid who was laying Zeidra's brushes and creams onto the marble counter in the bath.

"I don't know, Miss Zeidra ... they've been here ever since I came."

"And how long have you worked here?" Zeidra asked, selecting a lovely purple silk gown trimmed with pink lace.

"Not more than two months," the maid replied, taking the gown from Zeidra's hands and laying it out on the bed beside the silk ruffled petticoat and silver stockings which were already in place.

"Does Master Xanthar have a wife ... or a daughter? A sister? Or ..."

"You're the only female I've seen around here. Your bath's ready, Miss Zeidra."

"Thank you, Janay," Zeidra said, dismissing the maid.

Zeidra pulled her nightgown up over her head and dropped it onto the floor beside the sunken tub. She stepped down into the warm, herbal scented water. The lavender and jasmine oils that were sitting on the ledge beside her, made her more suspicious than before. How could anyone here, know exactly what she liked; what she had always used? In the few weeks she'd been here, she had been served her favorite food, she'd had perfectly fitted clothes to wear, her herbal baths had been scented the way she had liked them in Ulonica, and the bath salts were her favorite. Who would know? This couldn't be mere coincidence. No ... Something mysterious was going on here.

Zeidra relaxed down into the bubbling mineral salts and closed her eyes. Her thoughts were inundated with Kyate's essence; his strong sensitive hands, his cold steel gray eyes with that piercing stare, his expressive sensuous mouth ... She felt a chill run through her body despite the warm water she was reclining in. Her awareness was electrically charged with the arousal awakening in her being. Just thinking of Kyate always evoked that ephemeral shuddering in her spirit; an ice cold flame shooting through her senses, as contradictory as the pleasure and pain she felt in his passion, and the bitter sweet longing in his kiss; the terror and wonder she felt the night in her chambers when he took away her innocence.

"Kyate," she whispered into the steamy air, "where are you?" She sank deeper into the water and let the delicate aromas erase her thoughts. She escaped into the safety of oblivion.

"Milo?" Zeidra peeked into the study where Meno was sitting at a large desk, seemingly lost in his thoughts.

"What?!" he snapped, startled at the intrusion, but looking up to find Zeidra standing there, he immediately softened his tone. "I'm sorry, I didn't mean to bark ... I just wasn't expecting anyone. What can I do for you?" Meno got up and motioned for Zeidra to sit down.

"I should apologize ... I didn't mean to intrude on your thoughts, sir."

"Don't worry about it. Just a little concerned about my friends."

"Oh really? Are they all right?"

"Let us hope they are!" Meno breathed a sigh.

"Has everyone left, but you, Milo?"

"I'm in charge! Is everything OK? If you have any problems ... I'm the man to see!" he managed a laugh.

"I don't mean to be impertinent ... but ... was there a visitor here last night, Milo?" Zeidra asked, sitting down in the big leather chair across from Meno.

"A visitor?" He raised his bushy eyebrows in question.

"Well ... umm... To tell you the truth, I

was curious to know who was here last night ... LATE."

"Just me and the guys ... you know ... Xanthar, Beau, Lexy, Jerome ... Nobody else. What made you think we had a visitor?"

"Oh it's nothing ... I must have dreamed it!" Zeidra sighed, frustrated with Meno's indifference.

"What did you dream, little Princess?" Meno asked compassionately, sensing her discouragement. He leaned forward placing both hands on the desk.

Zeidra fidgeted with the lace on her skirt. She looked out into the garden and felt her cheeks flush.

"I saw an old ... well I thought I saw a friend whom I haven't seen for quite a long time. As a matter of fact, I wasn't sure he was still around ... I mean he comes from a very distant star system and I'd lost track of him." Zeidra squirmed in her chair.

"You lost track of your friend in another star system?" Meno asked.

"No, I met him in Ulonica ... on Earth ... I lost track of him there."

"Well, does your friend have a name?"

"Yes ... but I ... I mean I'd rather not ..."

"Are we talking about someone special?" Meno winked and smiled at Zeidra.

Zeidra immediately perceived something in Meno's eyes that made her certain she was right. She stared at him intently for a few seconds, trying to read the message that he obviously meant for her to see. There was a "knowing" expression on his face and she felt that he wanted to validate her query yet was unable to do so, on a conscious level.

"Milo ... you know who I'm talking about, don't you?"

"Well, you can see ... I wasn't born yesterday."

"Please don't be evasive... Was Kyate here with you last night? Do you two know each other... Is he a friend of Master Xanthar's or are they related? Where is he now ... Kyate I mean?! And ... did he have something to do with my being here? You know ... was this planned?!"

"So many questions!" Meno exclaimed lifting his hands high off the desk and bringing them down hard on the arms of his chair; bracing himself. "Tell you what! If you answer my questions first ... then I'll answer yours! How's that for a deal?" he laughed heartily, looking Zeidra squarely in the eye.

"Depends on the questions?" Zeidra replied, shifting her weight nervously.

"Well, I do know Kyate," Meno raised one eyebrow and waited for Zeidra's response.

"I thought so!" She said. Jumping to her feet, she leaned over the desk, glaring at Meno. "Now, what questions would you have me answer?"

"Why are you so interested in the Master Kyate?" He was blunt.

"Because I saw him last night in the garden, but he didn't tell me what he was doing here... He didn't explain how he knew I was here .... He just .... He just ..." Zeidra threw her hands up and rushed over to the window, looking blankly through the glass, "he just gave me this and left!" She yanked the golden medallion out of her pocket and held it out to her side for Meno to see. "If I hadn't wakened with this in my hand, I would have honestly thought I had dreamed it all ... but I didn't! I'm not sure if I was in trance ... or if I fainted! I'm so confused ..."

Meno swiveled the chair around to look at the medallion. "You're right ... that's Kyate's! I've never known him to be without it." Meno's surprise was all over his face.

"What's going on here?!" Zeidra cried, turning to face Meno.

"It's too complicated for me to attempt an explanation, Princess Zeidra," Meno said, shaking his head, his eyes pleading with her not to press the issue.

"Milo! At least tell me where Kyate is! PLEASE!" she whispered, leaning forward and placing her hands on Meno's arm.

"Zeidra, I can tell you only that they've gone on an extremely dangerous mission ...

It's Kyate's command. If they're successful ... if they can destroy the headquarters, then the Drothuarian threat will be all but ended ... at least for a very, very long time! Other than that ... well ... "

"*OH MY GOD!*" Zeidra cried in alarm. "And if they fail?" She clutched the medallion tightly to her breast as tears began spilling silently over onto her cheeks.

"If they fail ...." Meno covered one of Zeidra's trembling hands with his hand, "they probably won't return." He turned his face away from Zeidra's interrogating gaze and looked out over the gardens.

Zeidra withdrew her hand from Meno's and started out of the study, then stopped and turned back to Meno.

".... And Niporo ... did Kyate kill Niporo? He didn't die from a heart ailment, did he? It was all planned wasn't it? And nobody told me ....?"

"It was planned ... for your safety. And by the way, I'm not Milo ... I'm Meno ... remember me? Kyate changed our identities before we got here so that we wouldn't be recognized by any Drothuarian refugees from Earth. As far as Niporo's death goes ... Kyate is bound by his *LAW* not to shed blood for personal vendettas ... so *NO* ... he didn't kill Niporo, however Niporo's death was neither natural nor was it accidental. And as for you not being told of the plan ... Kyate wanted a chance to redeem himself ... he felt he needed to execute his obligation to the initial mission ... clear his honor, so to speak, before returning you to Ulonica. Until the Drothuarians are unequivocally defeated, he felt that keeping quiet about your being alive was the judicious thing to do. My orders are to protect you until he returns, and if he doesn't return .... I'm not to allow you to go back to your home until your safety is assured. And you see Zeidra, I know the truth .... Kyate gave up his honor because of his feelings for you .... You were, virtually, his singular vice! *GOD! ..... HAS HE SUFFERED FOR IT!!* At any rate, now it's imperative for him to reaffirm his integrity by accomplishing his assignment ... or he may as well be dead! For Kyate ... it's a *DO or DIE* situation no matter how you view it! A man like Kyate can't ... *won't* live in dishonor!"

Zeidra began shaking violently. Her knuckles were white as she clenched her fists in rage. Rage at herself for her unintentional influence on Kyate ... rage at Meno for disclosing the bitter veracity ... rage at Kyate for being such an obstinate and arrogant master of piety.

"How could he be so audacious?! He doesn't need to go to such extremes to prove his honor! Who does he think he is?!" Zeidra stamped her foot and cried loudly.

"He thinks he's a *GOD!*" Meno stated quietly. "At least that's the terminology your people would use to denote who he actually is!"

"*WHAT?!!!*"

"Zeidra, I'm going to tell you something that you must never repeat. You are never to let on to *ANYONE* ... especially Kyate, that you know this truth! Do you understand me?"

Zeidra stood there in bewilderment, half praying that Meno was joking, although she could see by the look on his face that he was deadly serious.

"All right."

"Zeidra, Kyate's origins go directly back to the Críonnachtians. He is older than time, as we understand the concept. He holds the very keys of creation. His powers are more miraculous than anyone has ever comprehended, only because he has never demonstrated his omnipotence to mortals. The only way this man can die ... and I'm talking about death in the literal sense ... is if he is in a state of disgrace when death is encountered."

"*OH MY GOD!* Meno, what does that mean?" Zeidra cried, wringing her hands and backing away from Meno, afraid to hear what he was going to say next.

"It means that until he has redeemed his

sanctification through righteousness, virtue, and valor ... he is just as mortal as you or I. It also means that right now, at this moment ... he's out there as a temporal man ... endeavoring to conquer his mortality and reclaim his divinity by annihilating those damned Drothuarians. God help us all!" Meno shook his head sorrowfully.

Zeidra flung herself into Meno's arms and sobbed into his chest. "Oh Meno, what can we do? I love him so .... But I had no idea he was ... he could be ... Oh I want him safe ... I want him here! Even if it means I'll never know his love, if he's a ... Crionnachtian Prince ... he won't want *ME* ... I'm not worthy! I just want him to live!!!" She pounded her fists into Meno's shoulders.

"Zeidra," Meno said looking down at the princess, "Kyate loves you ... and you *ARE* worthy! You're a Benjai!! It's perfect, don't you see?"

"I'm not worthy! I almost ruined him ... *MAYBE I'VE KILLED HIM!*" she cried hysterically, "Besides, I've disgraced the Benjai! I'm defiled, and I would defile *HIM*!!"

"No Zeidra!" Meno tipped Zeidra's tear streaked face up to his, "you're only mortal, and you're allowed the human weaknesses ... You're not defiled if you're forgiven! Kyate never once blamed you for anything that's happened ... He only blamed himself! All you

have to do is *FORGIVE YOURSELF*!! You do
have that capacity as a Benjai!" Meno grabbed
Zeidra by the shoulders and shook her gently.
"This is just what the Earth has been waiting
for ... didn't you know that? Surely your
mother ..."

"My mother died when I was a baby... A
nurse raised me ... She always said that
someday a Benjai would make a union with a
Críonnachtian ... that it had been written ...
But I'm not the one ... I know .... I'm not the
one!!" Zeidra's body shook with the sobbing
and Meno drew her back into his comforting
embrace, holding her there while she cried.

"You are the one, little princess ... You're
the one. The prophecies are obvious to me
and I'm not even an Earth scholar! Kyate
sensed it the moment he met you ... I knew it
the first time he told me about his strange
attraction to you. I did a little research and it
was all very clear. I'll admit, the two of you
made some serious errors in judgment ... but
nothing good ever comes easy! Even raw gold
has to be put through the fire in order to
purge it of its impurities ... Let's just pray that
Kyate makes it through his final test!" He
hugged Zeidra tightly. "Pull yourself together
and be brave, Zeidra. If Kyate makes it back,
the universe will celebrate your union ... or
should I say reunion! Go to your chambers
and meditate ... I think you will remember

who you really are ... I think you will know your *TRUE NAME*! You and Kyate have known each other many, many lifetimes ... each one signifying a new epoch in the evolution of the spirit on Earth." Meno withdrew Zeidra from his chest where she was happy to hide from the reality of his cognizance.

"You have much to learn about yourself ... *GO NOW!!*" And he gave her a little nudge toward the door.

CHAPTER 25 – The Final Mission

"Look out!! They're coming right for us!" Beau screamed at Jerome who was manning the defensive shields.

"Why would they fire at us?! This is a Drothuarian ship!!" Zak yelled.

"Must be some code we don't know about!" Jerome replied, rushing to implement the defense mechanisms.

"Get us on our side! We'll roll between those two beams! *QUICK!!*" Kyate yelled.

Lexy rapidly manipulated the left lower thrust and the craft rolled onto its right side, narrowly escaping the two red beams being aimed right at them.

Kyate jumped down from the observation dome and keyed the coordinates of the attacking enemy craft into the system. Instantaneously, the laser cannons responded with a blue-red beam of their own, destroying all traces of the Drothuarian gun ship. A thin misty film, suspended on the void, was all that remained of the assailant.

"Have you got the remote probes

programmed, Jerome?" Kyate asked, picking up one of the shiny silver carriers, and checking the interior compartment to see if the detonators were in place.

"All but one," Jerome replied.

"Can we get them in there at the right speed?" Beau asked, turning to Jerome, and looking somewhat skeptical.

"Man ... if these things shoot in there any faster, they'll get there yesterday!" Jerome laughed. "I've got em programmed to get in, position themselves, and detonate in less than twenty seconds," he held one high over his head as he turned around to look at Beau, "Is that fast enough for you?!"

"Are you sure they know where to locate?" Beau still wasn't convinced.

"Well let me put it this way ... unless something serious happens to the optical unit and it can't discern its direction or target ... and as long as the propulsion element is operating at full momentum .... I'm sure! I can't guarantee you a tomorrow, Beau! Good god! I've done what I can do ... the rest is up to destiny!!"

"*OK! OK!!*" Beau waved Jerome off. "I'm just a bit nervous ..."

"Hell! We all are!" Zak shouted from the command console.

"As soon as you're ready, Jerome, let's get those probes into the chutes!" Kyate said, sounding irritable. "I'd like to get this over with before another Drothuarian ship comes along!"

"In they go!" Jerome said, motioning to Lexy and Zak to load the six probes into their firing chutes.

The three crew members loaded the probes and secured the hatches. The tension in the ship was electrifying. Jerome looked down at the hair on his arm; it was standing straight out. "OK, Kyate, whenever you're ready .... I can't stand much more pressure here!"

Kyate put his hand on the launch lever.

"*WAIT!!*" Lexy cried. "Incoming vessel ... four o'clock ... get a lock on it Zak! *FAST!! GET HIM!!*"

Zak took a reading and began keying in the coordinates of the Drothuarian ship. He fired.

"*MISSED!!*" cried Lexy, "*HURRY, MAN! FIRE AGAIN!!*"

Kyate saw the beam coming and there was no time to wait for the hit, he knew it was now or never. He pulled the launch lever. The six remote probes shot out of the launch chutes like silver bullets, hell bent on destruction.

The beam ripped into the ship within a millisecond, throwing the crew members to the floor with a tumultuous jolt. The entire craft glowed blue-red and the surface structure vibrated and shook.

"They only glazed us!" Kyate yelled, struggling to his feet. He staggered to the console and fired the laser cannon, which still had a lock on the enemy craft. It was a hit. The wake of the explosion rocked the Deis ship violently and it was obvious to the crew that the balancing emulators had been badly damaged.

"Kyate! Check the time!" Jerome shouted. He was still sprawled out on the floor of the cabin.

"Eighteen .... Nineteen ... TWENTY!" Kyate climbed up into the observation dome and turned on the telescopic screen. Even at such a distant position a dust cloud could be seen rising above the moon, Keyto.

Jerome pulled himself up and began work at the command console.

"Did we get em?!" Beau yelled up at Kyate.

"We better damn well have blown those sonsabitches out of the universe or we're all dead!!" cried Jerome, running a fast systems check on the Deis craft. "This piece of tin is able to crawl but it ain't never gonna fly again ... If we're lucky and don't run into any more Drothuarians ... we might make it back to Urampa in a week or so ..."

Kyate dropped down from the upper level looking serious.

"Oh shit! Don't tell me we ..." Beau began.

"We got em." Kyate smiled.

"Did we? Are you sure?" Jerome asked, looking up from the console.

"Oh god! I sure hope we did," Zak moaned, wiping at the blood oozing from a deep cut on his chin.

"Well, men," Kyate said, untying the cord which held his hair back in the tail, "We won't know for certain ... not until the surveillance probe returns ... but it looks like all hell just broke loose on Keyto!"

The men all cheered and rallied around Kyate patting him on the back and congratulating him for his quick thinking. If he'd waited a second longer, the probes would have been disabled by the impact of the Drothuarian ray.

"Now all we have to worry about is ..." Kyate ran his hands back over his forehead and through his hair, "why did those Drothuarians fire on us? ... and how do we get back to Urampa. Anybody got a suggestion?" He rubbed thoughtfully at his chin, looking at each man in succession, waiting for some ingenious inspiration to come through one of them.

They all sat down to brainstorm. Time was precious and they were sitting ducks. It was imperative to get out of the area as quickly as possible. No one could think of a solution. Meanwhile, Jerome had set a course back to Urampa and the ship was moving along the grid at a turtle's pace. At least they could move. Hours passed with no acceptable or feasible recommendations being made by any of the crew members, and thankfully no sign of Drothuarian vessels in the area.

"I've got it!" Kyate said jumping to his feet. "Zak, you're artistically inclined aren't you? Get on that graphics system and whip me out a Drothuarian insignia ... big enough to get the attention of any other craft that comes into sight. And .... Maybe if they know we're disabled, they won't attack." He walked over to Lexy. "Lexy, you're going to suit up and install the emblem on the exterior."

"Then what?" Beau asked wearily, looking up from the table where he had his head resting on his folded arms.

"Then, Jerome ... you can start the distress signal!"

"Are you out of your mind, Kyate?! You think we're going to pass ourselves off as Drothuarians?" Jerome exclaimed.

"Exactly! ... Well, to a point." Kyate pulled one of the chairs out and turned it around. Sitting down and straddling it, he continued. "We'll send the call out for help, just in case there are any of those *DEVILS* in the area ... if there are, we'll transfer to their ship ... They won't know right away that we're not Drothuarian ... It'll get us aboard an operative vessel, anyway. At the first chance, we'll overtake them .... And we're back to Urampa!"

"Well since there's no alternative plan on the table ... that sounds pretty good to me," Beau said glibly.

"The probe's coming in," Lexy called from the console.

The small silver craft slid into one of the docks and the exterior hatch slammed shut automatically. Jerome rushed across the cabin to the interior portal and opened it, retrieving the probe hastily. He carried it back to the console and connected it to the computer. After typing in the word "PLAYBACK", he held his breath and said a silent prayer. All the men gathered around the screen to see what the probe had recorded.

"Look at that!" Beau said, leaning closer to the monitor, "You can see the entire facility!"

"Did you notice those streaks of light that just went in ... those were the other probes." Jerome tapped his finger on the right side of the picture.

Suddenly, the picture flashed and the men watched as the buildings, one by one imploded in upon itself and vanished in a cloud of dust.

"We did it!" Kyate said in a low husky voice.

"Why did I ever doubt your genius,

Jerome?!" Beau apologized.

"OK, let's implement the plan!" Kyate gave the command and everyone knew what was expected.

When the insignia was in place and the distress signal was activated, the alarms were set to detect incoming craft, and the men settled in for some sleep. Battered and bruised, they were thankful to be alive and optimistically looking forward to getting back to Urampa, but right now, all they cared about was getting some rest.

Jerome rolled off the bunk and scrambled up into the surveillance dome. The rest of the men were rushing around, half asleep, trying to get to their positions. The flashing alarm lights and blaring buzzers incited a frenzied atmosphere of chaotic movement and distorted sound.

Desperately, Jerome scanned the communication systems for some response to their distress call. Nothing was coming in. Kyate climbed into the dome to get a visual of the approaching craft, praying that it wasn't hostile and planning an attack. Slowly it loomed into view.

"Not good, men!" Kyate called down to the others. "We've got a mother ship on our hands!" Kyate watched as the huge vessel glided ever closer to their position.

"Now what?!" Beau cried from the control center. "How many of those bastards do you think we can handle? A mother ship! Maybe a couple thousand Drothuarians? That shouldn't be much of a problem! We just hit em over the head and take control of that monstrous ship .... Right?!"

"Don't go PANIC on me, Beau!" Kyate ordered calmly. "Jerome, got any suggestions?"

"Yeah! Jump ship!"

"Now why didn't I think of that?" Kyate said rubbing his chin.

"What's going on in that *mad-man* mind of yours now, Kyate?" Jerome leaned close to Kyate, peering into his eyes intently.

"Suit up men!" Kyate yelled, "We're going outside!"

"You're not serious?" Beau moaned.

"They might spot the ship, but they'll never spot a body if it's under their belly!" Kyate said, pulling on his pressure suit. The rest of the crew followed Kyate's lead and began wriggling into their vacuum protection gear. When they had all secured their oxygen tanks and helmets, they gathered around their Master for further instructions.

"We'll crawl into the missile chutes and wait until the Drothuarians board this ship.

While they're looking for the crew, we'll get out through the exterior missile portals and use our thrusters to position ourselves under the belly of that mother ship." Kyate climbed up into the surveillance dome to take another look. "It's almost here ... Now, there is usually an open bay at the back belly end of a mother ship, right? You know, for the scout ships to enter and exit?"

"You're right!" Lexy breathed in his words.

"Yeah!" said Zak, "I see what you're getting at ... we'll just hijack a couple of scout ships and get the hell out! *RIGHT?*"

"OK, Kyate ... so we need a diversion tactic!" Jerome pointed to Zak.

"OH NO!! I'm not going to be a dog again?"

"Gotcha!" cried Jerome.

"Here's the plan," Kyate said thoughtfully, "I'll go in first and take a look, you guys stay out of sight, but keep your eyes on me. If there are any Drothuarians, I'll think of a way to keep them occupied while you guys get a scout ... two if you can! Once I know you're in and ready, I'll do the disabling and you pick me up on your way out! No guarantees, you know .... But we'll just have to pray there are some scout ships in the bay ... and hope for no guards." Kyate took another look up into the dome. "They're here! Let's go! We're just going to have to play most of this by ear!"

Kyate and the crew jumped down into the cargo bay. One by one they climbed into the missile chutes closing the interior hatches behind them. Kyate grabbed a detonator and a small vial of explosive. He tucked them inside his suit then climbed into the chute behind Jerome. They waited for the Drothuarians to board the craft.

Silently, gracefully the huge Drothuarian mother ship glided up alongside the Deis vessel, dwarfing it by contrast. Two robotic arms extended from the third level of the monstrous craft, securing the Deis ship with a metal grip. A wide telescoping tube emerged from the side of the larger vessel, between the metal arms, and protracted to the main entrance of the smaller ship. The Deis crew heard the Drothuarians when they entered the ship through the tube.

One by one the Deis men escaped from the missile hatches and guided their thrusters toward the underbelly of the mother ship. With large magnets attached to the hands and feet of their pressure suits, they walked their way, tediously, to the holding bay for incoming and outgoing scout ships. Five Deis crew members, attached to the underside of the open freight doors of the bay, raised their helmeted heads in unison to survey the inside of the bay.

There they saw five scout ships moored

with metal cables to their individual tracks. No guards were seen in the immediate vicinity near the opening. Kyate climbed up onto the tail gate and moved cautiously into the interior of the mooring area. He drew his laser sword and disappeared around the side of one of the scout ships. Beau, Jerome, Lexy, and Zak waited only a moment and then disengaged their magnets to follow their master into the belly of the enormous vessel.

Kyate crept around behind the three guards that were sitting at a table. They were having drinks and talking loudly. The Deis master backed up against the wall of the bay and quietly extracted the explosive material from his pressure suit vest. Quickly, he inserted the detonator into the vial of liquid explosive and attached the fuse wire to the mechanism, mounted on the wall that activated the freight doors to the holding bay. Just as he was finishing with the device, he dropped the cap to the vial; it bounced and then rolled across the floor, passing in front of the guards; rousing their attention.

Suddenly there were sounds of a scuffle. The men ran for the scout ships. Jerome and Beau jumped inside one of the small craft, while Lexy and Zak released the cables that held it in its tracking. No one could see Kyate. Jerome quickly appraised the start up system of the ship and had it humming and ready for launch within minutes.

Lexy and Zak ran toward the other side, to help Kyate with the disabling. Coming upon Kyate and three Drothuarian guards, the Deis warriors drew their weapons. Two of the guards were restraining Kyate, who had lost his laser sword in the scuffle, while the third guard was aiming his weapon directly at the Master. Lexy pointed to one of the guards for Zak to take out, and without hesitation they blasted away one of the Drothuarians that was holding Kyate, and the one with the phaser, but not soon enough to prevent Kyate from being hit. As the Master went down, Lexy blew the Drothuarian to bits and Zak destroyed the guard that was left. Quickly they grabbed Kyate under his arms, one on one side and one on the other, and carried him to the waiting scout ship which was ready for launch. Dragging him into the cabin, Jerome hit the "LAUNCH" button, and the ship shot out of the bay, while Lexy was still securing the hatch.

"Damn! You could've waited 'til the door was closed!" Lexy cursed at Jerome.

"I'll take the controls, Jerome ... You see to Kyate!" Beau said, looking down at Kyate as he lay there bleeding profusely on the cabin floor.

Jerome bent down, and with Zak's help, eased Kyate's suit off of his bloody body. His flesh was badly torn and burned on his right side, just above his waist, and there was a gaping hole that went right through from front to back. Jerome shook his head, looking up into Beau's horrified gaze, which was full of terror and anticipation.

"I don't think I can save him ...." Jerome spoke almost inaudibly. "It'll take an act of GOD Himself to patch this up!"

"Well for god's sake do something! *ANYTHING!!*" Beau cried loudly.

"I need my equipment! What the hell do you expect me to do when I have nothing to work with but my hands?! I need to repair these vessels in order to stop the bleeding, do you have a fucking needle and thread on you ... you whining sonofabitch?!"

"Wait, Jerome ..." Lexy said. He'd been holding the pressure on Kyate's bleeding injuries. He removed his hand, and peered into the gaping hole. Inserting two fingers into the opening, he felt around quickly. He finally found what he was looking for. He pulled a tiny sliver of bone fragment from Kyate's wound. "A needle!" he said blowing a small hole in the end of the splinter with his mini laser. "And ..." he plucked a few strands of Kyate's long hair and threaded one through the hole in his primitive utensil. "Now you have your needle and thread, Doc! Do your magic ..."

"Thanks Lexy," Jerome said, "I guess I can try ..." He accepted Lexy's offering and began pulling away damaged tissue with his bare hands. "Lexy ... Zak ... you guys can be my retractors and my clamps. Grab that vessel and pinch it off, Lexy. Here ... Zak you keep this one closed off. I'll work on this main bleeder, here."

Suddenly, in the distance, there appeared to be a tremendous explosion. A pressure wave spread out across the void and jostled the ship as it moved through their area. A huge red ball of fire was visible in the blackness far away, in the direction of the mother ship they had left behind them.

"Holy shit!" Beau exclaimed, "What the hell was that?!"

"Did one of you guys plant a detonator back there?" Lexy asked, looking first at Jerome, then at Beau.

They all looked around at each other, questioning with their eyes; each shaking his head "no".

"I'll bet Kyate sent those bastards to hell!" Jerome said, looking down at Kyate's lifeless bloody body, sprawled out on the floor of the cabin before him. "I'll betcha he left those damned Drothuarians his personal calling card ...! Good for you Kyate! You got those sonsabitches! You got em good!" Jerome sponged Kyate's face off with cool water.

"We're gonna put you back together, Kyate ....
So you can celebrate your conquest! Hang in
there, bud ... If you can hear me, Kyate ... just
hang on!"

Kyate didn't respond. His color was pale
gray and he felt cold to the touch. Jerome
could see the life draining out of his master,
even as he prepared to try and save him.

After reattaching the vessels, Jerome
began working on the tissue repair. "He's
lucky ... none of his organs were touched, but
he's lost too much blood!" Jerome cauterized
and closed the wounds as best he could with
the mini laser, then bound Kyate's abdomen
with the elasticized pieces of the pressure suit
which Lexy had cut into strips. "Cut me a six
inch length of that tubing Zak!" Jerome
grunted. "Either of you guys type O positive?"

"I am," Beau volunteered.

"Thank god for that! Get down here ...
you're going to be the blood donor!"

Beau slid out of the control seat and knelt
beside Kyate.

"Now once I get this rigged, I want you to
stay above Kyate and squeeze your fist to
pump your blood down into him ... you got
that?"

Beau nodded.

"OK, now hold real still and try not to

scream," Jerome said as he cut a deep slit across the raised vein on Beau's left arm. He inserted one end of the tubing into the incision and cauterized the tissue around the tube. "Zak, clamp the end of this so we don't lose any blood, while I get Kyate ready!"

Jerome made the same type of incision in Kyate's arm and then quickly transferred the tube from Zak's hand into Kyate's arm. He cauterized the tissue and then looked at Beau. "OK Beau, start pumping and praying." He paused, looking down into Kyate's pale, still face. "Beau, I'm sorry for going off on you like that ... It's just the damned pressure! I've just had too much stress for one day!! We're alright aren't we? I mean we're still friends aren't we, big guy?"

"No big deal, Jerome ... It's OK, don't worry about it ... I understand."

"Jerome!" Beau whispered, "I think Kyate's coming around ... look down here!"

Jerome turned away from the control console to examine Kyate. "Take over Lexy, will you?" Jerome knelt down beside Kyate and checked his vitals.

The bleeding had stopped and his complexion had regained some of its color, although Beau was looking quite pale by now. Kyate's eyes were fluttering a little, and it appeared that he was trying to speak.

"Easy guy ..." Jerome said, placing a firm hand on Kyate's chest to keep him from trying to raise up. "Just hold on a second ... got to unhook you from your blood brother, here." Jerome carefully withdrew the tubing from Beau, while Zak clamped off the tube. After closing Beau's incision, he extracted the line from Kyate's arm and cauterized the opening in his vein. "Done!" he said taking a deep breath and patting Kyate on the shoulder. "How do you feel, Kyate?"

"Like Swiss cheese ..." Kyate spoke faintly.

"What about the pain? Are you able to handle it?" Jerome asked.

"If you give me a piece of ice to hold in my hand, I can defer the pain," Kyate whispered weakly.

"Right ... we have some ice. Zak! Get us some ice, quick!" Jerome placed a cushion under Kyate's head. "You've lost a lot of blood, but Beau gave you a good shot of his ... enough to keep you going for a while, as long as the bleeding doesn't start again. We patched you up the best we could, but when we get back to Urampa we'll do it right ... so just hang in there Kyate ... hold on, guy. I figure about twelve hours and we'll be there. Can you make it?"

"I wouldn't want to ruin your reputation, Jerome!" Kyate forced a little smile, and then lapsed back into unconsciousness.

Jerome shook his head sadly, checking Kyate's thready pulse. "He'll never make it unless we can get back in less than six hours ... He doesn't have twelve!! Beau, can you push that throttle any harder? Go full bore and if we blow ... so what!!"

"You got it!" Beau said, "Hang onto your hats, men! Here we go... I hope this baby'll hold together!"

Beau manipulated the controls on the propulsion system to full acceleration. The ship lurched and shuddered for the first few minutes, but as the speed gradually picked up, the craft settled into a smoother forward thrust.

CHAPTER 26 - Reclamation

"*Oh My God!!*" Meno screamed as he read the communication screen of news coming in from the inner section of the star system Paradies.

"PLANET EARTH IN THE GALAXY MILKY WAY, STAR SYSTEM ZIOTRAN, HAS BEEN DEVASTATED BY THE IMPACT OF A ROGUE COMET. APPROXIMATELY ONE THIRD OF THE PLANET SURFACE WAS SET ABLAZE BY THE RAIN OF BURNING GAS AND EXPLODING AGGREGATE. THE ESTIMATED SIZE OF THE IMPACTING COMET HEAD IS 9 TO 12 MILES IN DIAMETER. SURFACE TEMPERATURE AT THIS POINT HAS NOT BEEN MEASURED. ATMOSPHERE CONTAMINATED WITH POISONOUS GAS AND SOOT. IT IS FEARED THAT MOST INHABITANTS IN THE IMMEDIATE IMPACT AREA HAVE ALREADY PERISHED. MULTIPLE SEISMIC EVENTS HAVE BEEN DETECTED, SOME DISPLACEMENT OF CRUSTAL PLATES. MORE TO BE REPORTED AS EVENTS ARE BEING MONITORED."

"Meno! What is it?!" Zeidra cried, running into the study.

"*OH MY GOD!*" Meno groaned, wringing his hands and pacing the floor. "How do I tell you, Zeidra? How *CAN* I tell you? ... *Oh God!*"

"KYATE!" Zeidra screamed. Her eyes were wide with fear and anticipation.

"No, Zeidra ... it's not Kyate ... it's ... it's your home, Zeidra! It's Earth ... it's been hit by a comet! Read the communication yourself ... My God! What next?!!"

Zeidra rushed to the screen and covered her mouth with her shaking hand as she read the news of the disaster. She was paralyzed with shock and grief. Her mute screams were tied up in the knots in her throat. Zeidra grasp the edges of the desk to support her trembling legs. She was gasping to dislodge her cries of terror.

Meno took the princess by the arm and helped her over to the chair. She sat down limply, still unable to speak. Her mind was short-circuiting with panic and desperation.

"Zeidra, I'm so sorry for you ..." Meno sat down on the edge of the desk in front of the princess. "I don't know what I can say to make this any easier for you ..." Meno fought back the tears welling up in his own eyes. "Since there's no definite information, maybe it won't be as bad as it sounds right now ... The initial reports on any of these kinds of catastrophes are always downplayed over the following few days ... Let's not be fatalistic. Could be our distress is a little premature?"

"I'm so homesick, Meno!" Zeidra sobbed. "And now ... I may never see my beautiful Ulonica again! My people! Oh God!! What has become of my people?! I've got to find out! Meno, isn't there some way to get the facts?" Zeidra broke down and cried uncontrollably.

Meno felt the helplessness overtaking his emotions. He went to the communications console and contacted the local intergalactic information bureau in hopes of garnering further details on the catastrophic event. It was a futile attempt. Meno lowered his head into his hands, and sighed heavily.

Zeidra sat motionless, staring at nothing; catatonic in her despair. The silence was as still and as cold as death.

"Meno!" A voice called from the cargo elevator in the front entrance hall.

Recognizing Beau's voice immediately, Meno jumped to his feet and ran from the study. When he reached the hall, his heart dropped to his gut. Jerome and Lexy were struggling, trying to move off the elevator, carrying Kyate's lifeless, blood soaked body.

Beau steadied Meno, gripping him firmly

on his upper arm; preventing him from charging over to Kyate. Meno looked into Beau's solemn eyes, feeling panic moving up into his throat. Zak appeared from a side corridor with a portable utility table that he'd thrown some blankets over. Jerome and Lexy gently laid Kyate up onto the makeshift gurney. Jerome adjusted the covers over Kyate's limp form and rapidly disappeared down the hall with his patient. Lexy and Zak followed him.

"What happened?" Meno choked, finally finding his voice.

"He caught a Drothuarian ray ... clean through his gut. Awful mess! Lost most of his blood. Jerome says he's in shock. Says he may not make it! He's going to try and put him back together in his medilab... Says we should pray!"

"I need a drink," Meno said numbly.

"Could use one myself!"

They walked down the corridor to the private reception room.

"Guess you haven't heard about Earth."

"What about Earth?"

"It took a comet hit ... yesterday! It looks real bad!" Meno said, pouring the wine into two crystal goblets. He handed one to Beau.

"Damn! How'd it get through? Wasn't anyone paying attention?"

"Who knows?! The news reports are so

sketchy. I can't find out anything except that a third of it is on fire and the air is polluted with smoke mixed with the poison from the ice." Meno downed his drink and refilled his glass. "Want some more?"

"Please!" Beau said shoving his glass over to Meno. "How's the princess handling it? Or does she know?"

"She knows, but she's not taking it well at all! Now with Kyate ... hard to tell what she'll do! She's pretty high strung, you know ... real upset right now!"

"I'll bet," Beau said, tipping his glass and taking a long drink.

Meno reached over and pressed a button on the wall. "I'd better have Zeidra taken care of ... I almost forgot how I left her!"

There was a soft knock at the door.

"Come in!" Meno called.

"You wanted me sir?" Nina asked.

"Yeah ... I left the princess in the study. She's really upset. News from Earth ... you'll hear about it. Just go get her and put her to bed or something! Give her a good stiff drink! She's going to need it!"

"Of course, sir ... I understand," Nina said, turning to leave.

"Wait!" Meno called to her, "One more thing ... if she asks for Master Kyate, tell her there's no news."

"OK," the nurse said, as she left the room,

closing the door behind her.

Meno and Beau collapsed into the chairs, facing each other in silence.

In the medilab, Jerome worked feverishly on Kyate's wounds. Several areas were successfully repaired. He re-sutured the damaged vasculars with micro-sutures and was busy working under the microscope, reattaching nerves. Kyate's blood pressure was beginning to come up since he'd been on the synthetic plasma pump for some time, and his pulse seemed to be a little stronger.

Finishing up, Jerome cleaned the destroyed tissue from the interior of the injury; he saturated the entire area with a potent antibiotic solution and cauterized the severed capillaries. He closed and sutured the musculature and epidermis, using an adhesive solution on the outside edges to prevent scarring. He tossed the last utensil into the stainless steel dish and removed his mask, admiring his work and uttering a tired prayer.

"That's the best I can do," Jerome said, looking over at Zak and Lexy. "All we can do now is wait." He removed his gloves and went to the sink. "You might want to go tell Meno and Beau that there's a fifty-fifty chance, now." Jerome splashed cool water over his face and up onto the back of his neck, shaking it off vigorously, like a water soaked dog.

Jerome walked back over to Kyate and checked the monitors one more time. He pulled a cot up to the side of the table where Kyate was laying, and literally threw his tired body down onto the mattress. He was exhausted, but he wanted to stay close to his master for the next few critical hours. He closed his eyes and sighed.

"Lexy, since Zak's up there with Meno and Beau, would you stay here while I get some shut-eye? Wake me up if you notice anything unusual ... like if the monitor starts to beep, or if Kyate comes to ...?"

"Sure thing, Jerome!" Zak said, pulling a chair closer to the table.

Jerome drifted off easily, his tired mind and body overcome by the stress; both physical and emotional.

The next few hours was a contradictory scenario of hurry up and wait. Waiting for ... a positive change in Kyate's condition ... waiting for some concrete information regarding the situation on Earth ... waiting for any sign of Drothuarian retaliation after the loss of their main headquarters and the destruction of the mother ship.

Life seemed to be on hold; suspended in a stagnant reality.

"Hmm ...." Kyate mused over the extensive reparations to his torso, as he explored his body internally... psychically. "A fine job indeed, men," he acknowledged.

Suddenly caught unaware, he felt his spirit being pulled up and out of his physical body. He felt himself being shot across the cosmos, like a silver bullet streaking across the void at an unfathomable speed. Straight to the very throne of The Creator. He wondered if he had died.

"Kyate," an unknown voice boomed from within a brilliant multi-colored sphere. "You have redeemed your destiny, Son."

Kyate fell prostrate at the base of the throne. Was this a hallucination? He struggled to regain his senses.

"I am well pleased with you," the voice continued, "and your seed shall recompense the Universe. You are blessed and your powers returned in full measure. Go to your Beloved. Be fruitful and multiply. Also, when you learn of Earth's fate... understand that it will be restored. I do so declare it ... DONE!"

With that, Kyate was instantly returned to the palace at Urampa.

"Zeidra ...." Kyate whispered, "I'm coming for you, My Love."

Zeidra sat bolt upright in her bed. It was nearly midnight and her room was pitch black except for a silvery mist, which seemed to be floating in midair at the far corner of the chamber. She watched it hovering there, not sure why she'd been awakened. The entire house was deadly quiet. She felt an uncanny anticipation but couldn't define its origin. The mist seemed to be moving toward her. Her heart was pounding in her ears and she held her breath, as the mist seemed to be taking on a form.

"Kyate?!" she whispered, recognizing the essence of his spirit.

He materialized before her eyes, and she stifled a scream as he came forward.

"Don't be frightened," he spoke quietly, in his normal husky voice.

"Am I dreaming? Is it really you? Kyate, are you really here?" Zeidra was beginning to panic in her confusion.

Kyate reached over and touched Zeidra's cheek. "You're not dreaming ... although I think *I may be...* Nevertheless, I *am* here ... and happy to finally be with you!" He sat down on the side of the bed.

"Kyate, I've been so worried about you. I've missed you so!" Zeidra cried softly reaching out her hands for the Master. "I'm so lost!" she sobbed, as Kyate pulled her into his arms. "My Earth has been devastated by a comet, and I may never see my home again ... and my people ..." Her body shook softly as she wept, there in Kyate's embrace.

"It's not the end of *YOUR* world, Zeidra," he said, moving his lips across her forehead. "Your world is within you. It's not a geological entity ... it's purely spiritual. Don't be sad ... you have much to look forward to." Kyate leaned back so that he could see Zeidra's face. "I've come back for you ... You and I have a preordained agreement to consummate."

"I'm .... I'm not sure I understand ... what are you saying?"

"The EARTH is in need of us, Zeidra. You are the chosen *MOTHER!*"

"*OH MY GOD!*!"

"Indeed!" Kyate said, pulling his princess back into his grasp. He held her there silently, allowing her to assimilate the knowledge that he was mystically bestowing upon her psyche.

"Kyate?" Zeidra said, looking up into his handsome face, "Are you alive?"

"What an absurd question!" he replied, laughing loudly. "Of course I'm alive! Maybe a little bloody and bruised ... a big hole in my side ... and maybe more synthetic blood in my vascular system than real ... but yes,

Zeidra ... I'm very much alive!"

"Oh no!" Zeidra cried, "You mean you've been injured?" She looked him over frantically, trying to find his wounds.

"Zeidra, you do amuse me!" Kyate chuckled. "My corporeal body is downstairs in the medilab ... Jerome did a magnificent job saving it. It will recover, I promise. What you see and feel at this moment is my celestial form."

Zeidra caught her breath, realizing that all of what Meno had said was true. The Master Kyate was in fact, a Críonnachtian Prince ... a *god*. It was clear to her that Kyate had redeemed his spirit and had reinstated the divinity of his destiny. She was frightened by the magnificence of his being, and she began to tremble.

"I'm claiming my reward, Zeidra," Kyate spoke quietly and with authority. "You're what I came here for ... You agreed to it eons ago. You have acquired the knowledge! Now you will assume the responsibility that accompanies the erudition. I will cultivate the garden and plant my seed ... and you will bring forth the harvest, and the Earth will benefit from your labor." Kyate laid Zeidra back, gently, onto the bed. "Don't be afraid," he whispered, "I'm only going to give you my love ..." He was actually glowing, there in the darkness. Kyate's radiance was blinding.

Zeidra closed her eyes, unable to look upon his face.

The Princess relaxed. She surrendered her *all*, to her beloved Kyate. The two became ONE –one body, one mind, one spirit.

Suddenly, the entire universe exploded; taking with it two souls locked in *oneness*. It was the dance of the spirit – two completely merged souls dancing out across the cosmos in an erotic ballet seldom experience by mortals.

Princess Zeidra's prayers had been answered.

About The Author

Ramsey Keller Says:

"I never write "formula" novels... they're just too predictable. Also, I can't abide by any one genre. I just don't fit in a "box".

I consider myself a "storyteller" and as the story plays out in my mind, like a movie, I just write what I'm seeing. - So much for "point of view" !!

I like to combine action, romance, humor... and a little erotic spice if it's an integral part of the story."

Also written by Ramsey Keller:

An Action-Packed Historical Romance

"Absolution"

Young Margaret Waters' innocent life was turned upside down when she met the mysterious Dr. Miles Deihl. He was a dark wild thing; exuding raw sensuality and emanating an inaudible primal groaning.

He was not at all like her childhood beau; the quiet and stable, Nathan Stillman.

A tangle of emotions, with unsuspected twists and turns ensues.

There's a price to be paid for the choices we make.